ALIEN™

SEA OF SORROWS

COMING SOON FROM TITAN BOOKS

ALIEN™: OUT OF THE SHADOWS
ALIEN: RIVER OF PAIN (NOVEMBER 2014)

THE OFFICIAL MOVIE NOVELIZATIONS
ALIEN
ALIENS™
ALIEN3

ALIEN

SEA OF SORROWS

JAMES A. MOORE

TITAN BOOKS

ALIEN™: SEA OF SORROWS

Print edition ISBN: 9781783292851
E-book edition ISBN: 9781781162712

Published by Titan Books
A division of Titan Publishing Group Ltd
144 Southwark Street, London SE1 0UP

First edition: July 2014
3 5 7 9 10 8 6 4

A CIP catalogue record for this title is available from the British Library.

Printed and bound in Great Britain by CPI Group (UK) Ltd, Croydon, CR0 4YY

PROLOGUE

He knew what they were.

The shapes looked wrong in his mind, all swollen out of proportion and twisted by sensory input that made almost no sense, but he recognized the outdated EVA suits for what they were.

See how they run.

They scatter as we approach, hidden within their artificial skins.

The tunnels are dark to them, they cannot see as well as they should. They cannot feel the air currents or taste the fear of their prey. They cannot understand the simplest things, like how important it is to find the right ones for furthering the race.

They flee, with no concern for anything but individual survival. There is no sense of community for them. They are weak. They are easily moved in the right directions.

That one.

Its breaths come in a constant, panting wheeze. Its heartbeat is a wild flutter of desperation and the need for survival. There is fear, yes, but strength as well, and a powerful sense of aggression.

The sensations came into his head unbidden, unwanted.

He tried to open his eyes. The lids refused him. He tried to shake his head but nothing happened.

He felt the body under him struggling, felt his own repulsion at the way it moved and smelled and felt beneath his hard shell and he knew that was wrong. There was nothing about the sensations that made sense.

They weren't his.

It tries to escape. It pushes another of its own kind out of the way, knocks it down and crawls over it, dust falling from its body as it shakes free of the collapsing barriers. It is strong. It is fast. It wants to live.

It will live.

It screams as it is taken down, pinned to the ground. Struggles, beating its hands against the hard flesh until it becomes necessary to bare teeth in warning... and then it struggles all the more. Beneath the shell of hard synthetics there is another face that shows wild eyes and a mouth stretched open silently. If it could break the hide with its hands it would be a threat. Instead it can merely scream again as the teeth bite and peel back the soft skin of the closest limb.

The blood is hot and stinks of weakness, but it will suffice. It will serve the need it must. We break the shell around the soft face and it gasps, unable to breathe the atmosphere.

The life-giver moves closer, ready to plant the seed. Strong fingers clutch the soft face that chokes and exhales in desperation.

It will—

Alan Decker woke with a jerk, and stared at his distorted reflection as it gazed back with wild eyes.

Reflection?

There was a translucent glass surface inches from his face. There were lights flashing, and his breath blasted against the confining surface.

Waking inside of a hypersleep chamber should have been familiar, given how many times he'd traveled between worlds. But the dreams—*damn them*—the dreams made him panic. He couldn't control the feelings. They were simply too vivid, too primal.

It was getting so he couldn't remember what life had been like *before*.

His hands pushed at the interior, fumbling for the manual release that would free him. He could still feel the tunnels, the weight of what seemed like a mountain above him, pressing down as he stalked the—

No. Not me. I didn't stalk anyone. I don't hunt for…

For what?

He thrust the thought aside. The damned dreams were so real, so pervasive that sometimes he could understand why the shrinks had such a field day with him back on Earth.

1

BLACK SAND

The air was nearly perfect. The temperature had just hit 74 degrees Fahrenheit, with moderate humidity and a gentle breeze coming from the southwest. The land in that direction was fertile, with lush green grass and the glimmer from a stream that said it would stay that way. The smell on the wind spoke of new life.

The people who'd paid for the terraforming project had spent enough money to guarantee that their colony would be perfect. But one glance to the north of that picturesque landscape, and the notion of perfection went straight to hell.

Over the span of just a few acres the grass yellowed and died, then was replaced by almost sixty miles of black sand and the sort of stench that was guaranteed to ruin property values. It wasn't actually necessary to wear a hazmat suit, but it sure looked and smelled like it should have been.

On the bright side, they'd had rain the night before and the soft sand was packed down from the extra moisture. Normally when you walked out into it you sank a couple of inches. But now—for at least a little while—they would be able to stand up without feeling as if they were about to sink out of sight.

Decker studied the screen on his hand-held, reviewing reports on the latest samples from the area. He frowned. To all appearances, whatever was happening, it wasn't natural. And more often than not, in a situation like this, anything *unnatural* meant negligence. The Interstellar Commerce Commission was in charge of maintaining certain guidelines for safety and commercial equity on Earth, in the growing Colonies and along the Outer Rim. As a Deputy Commissioner in the ICC, Decker got to make sure that all procedures were being followed properly. That meant dealing with paperwork of a magnitude that guaranteed him both job security and major headaches—in the form of a long list of counter-arguments from the company that had to be responsible.

Lucas Rand stood next to him and was reading the same results, but Rand was smiling—something that didn't often occur. The difference was that while Rand could understand what the results meant, he didn't have to fill out the endless forms. Rand was an ICC Engineer. He was paid to fix problems that Decker found. Someone else—heaven alone knew who—then got to bill the companies that had their problems fixed. Bureaucracy in action.

It was a living.

Decker glanced at him and frowned.

"Don't go getting all excited about how easy your life is," he said. "I may have to deal with the bureaucracy, but *you* get to figure out how to fix this mess."

Rand's smile faltered a bit.

"Not sure if we *can* fix it." He scowled as he looked at the sand. When he wasn't grinning, he scowled a lot, but it was only because his face was designed that way. Luke Rand was probably one of the nicest guys Decker knew. He just looked like he ate bears for breakfast. He was a big man, too, though not nearly all of it was muscle.

"Yeah. But I don't catch the flak for your shortcomings," Decker said, and it was his turn to grin. "You do."

Rand scratched at the back of his hairy neck and looked out toward the Sea of Sorrows. That was the name land developers had been using for centuries to describe a place like this—where builders had spent their blood, sweat, tears, and money, but to no avail. Where the ground itself seemed determined to thwart their efforts, and send them packing.

This particular Sea of Sorrows shouldn't have existed. Designation LV178, New Galveston, had been terraformed by people who knew what they were doing. All anyone had to do was look in almost any direction to see how damned good they were. It had started out as a nightmare planet, with raging storms and an unbreathable atmosphere. There'd been no potable water, and before the current project began, the only thing that had grown here was debt from failed attempts to establish a viable base.

Then Weyland-Yutani had come along.

Thirty years had passed since the first settlers had landed and begun the project, and for the most part New Galveston was an example of what happened when things went right. Three major cities were already in place, all connected by a network of high-speed trains, and each with enough viable farmland to ensure that the colonies could sustain themselves without having to resort to endless shipments of canned goods and other expensive imports.

Everything was golden, as Rick Pierce liked to say. Pierce, the man who'd established the colony in the first place, had been delighted with New Galveston. Then the Sea of Sorrows had appeared.

It hadn't been there when Weyland-Yutani had completed their efforts. The atmosphere processing engines had done their job, everyone had been pleased, and all was right with LV178. Until contractors had begun to lay the foundations of what was intended to be the fourth major city. In the midst of that development had come the discovery of a few acres of soft ground.

Immediately it had begun to grow, slowly at first, then faster. Soon it became an obstacle, and then a bane. Where the sands took over, nothing would grow. There were toxins present, and where they spread, there was no way for the land to support a viable colony.

Then the closest thing to growth had appeared, in the form of silicon nodes. The hollow black, glassy clusters of fused sand had sprouted, coming from somewhere down below, and they weren't just annoying. They were difficult to detect, and dangerous. Four separate pre-fabricated structures had been started, and all of them had collapsed because the silicon wasn't durable enough to support the weight.

Since pre-fabs were essential to the city-building efforts of the New Galveston Collective, this presented a serious problem.

No, the planet's next city simply wasn't going to happen unless Decker and his team could figure out what had gone wrong. If they failed, and the sands continued to spread—perhaps to one of the established population centers—the entire LV178 project might be in jeopardy.

The ICC didn't like risky situations, and Weyland-Yutani—a corporation that worked hard at maintaining the *appearance* of a spotless record—didn't like failure, especially at such tremendous expense.

So he and Rand had their marching orders. Decker was here to monitor every aspect of the process, and report every excruciating detail back to their corporate overlords.

Rand and his crew were here to repair the damage.

Not far away, two of the men ostensibly on Decker's crew were struggling with a probe that didn't seem to want to settle properly on the unstable surface. A few other workers were milling about, further away—most likely on a break.

All in all, thirty-seven people were currently working out what had gone wrong, using the latest in spectral analysis and chemical geo-forensics. The machinery wasn't quite as impressive as the terraforming engines that had redesigned the world, but it cost almost as much.

The weight distribution was tricky, and though it was damp, the sand was hardly ideal. The platform they were using to support the core sampler had too small a base—they should have added extensions to compensate. But he held his tongue. These guys were stubborn, and as far as they were concerned, he wasn't their boss. He'd been assigned to work with them, but they just didn't give a damn. Tempers flared if they thought he was trying to tell them how to do their jobs, and these were men who thought first with their fists.

Decker wasn't the sort to back down from a fight, but this was the kind of grief he didn't need—in more ways than one. Still, they had to pull up the core samples, if they were going to get this particular cluster un-fucked.

He scanned the screen again, and his jaw clenched. Something about this screamed *catastrophe*. He'd dealt with situations on dozens of different worlds. You can't reshape the biosphere of an entire planet without flirting with disaster. Yet most times the fixes were easy, as long as you approached them from the right angle.

This time?

Not so much. Not if he was right.

The ground had gone sour, and in most of the cases he'd run across in the past, that pointed to a human factor. Dig deep enough, look far enough into the records, and the truth would come out. Someone had screwed up here, royally, yet there were no records.

That smelled like a cover-up.

Decker clenched his teeth at the very thought. No matter how he looked at it, he was going to be leveling a finger at one of the biggest dogs in the corporate pack.

It wouldn't be the first time, though. Good as they were, Weyland-Yutani had a track record. This would be his third run-in with them, and if the last two had been any indication, his life was about to get "interesting," in the Chinese sense of the word. The company didn't like getting egg on their collective faces, and their lawyers would cause as many waves as possible in an effort to stay clean.

Rat bastards.

Rand pointed to a line in the readouts.

"Trimonite? Seriously?" He looked up. "That could explain a lot." His usual scowl was back, and in spades.

"Yeah," Decker said. "It might." Trimonite was a wonderfully dense mineral used in the manufacture of a lot of heavy equipment. It was costly to extract, and thus carried a hefty price tag.

But trimonite alone shouldn't have presented the problem. Before it could be used for industrial purposes, trimonite had to be refined, and it was this refining process that often caused any toxicity. So if the source of the trouble was the trimonite beneath the Sea of Sorrows, why was it poisoning the soil? And where did the silicon fit in?

He looked again at the readouts, and nodded.

"We need to dig deeper. Literally," he said. "Do you suppose there could have been a mining colony around here?"

Rand shook his head.

"That'd fit with the toxicity readings," he replied, "but we checked the ICC records backward and forward. *Bupkis*. If there *was* one, though, why the hell would anyone want to build over the top of it? That's just asking for trouble—planting a colony on a toxic waste dump. You'd need to be really stupid, or just not give a shit."

True that, Decker mused. In the case of Weyland-Yutani, he was pretty sure which it was.

"We need to look into it," he replied. "I'm not saying it would explain everything, but it's a starting point."

Rand snorted, made a face, and then spit into the black sand.

"Even if there's a mine, it still doesn't explain this shit." He swung his foot and pushed enough away to reveal one of the glass lumps. "I've never seen anything like it." Planting his boot, he applied pressure until the clump of glass started to break. The things grew like cypress knees back home, thrusting up from below, and were often hollow. Some were very fragile, and when they broke, the openings they revealed stretched far into the darkness below.

"Those things may be a worse problem than the trimonite." Decker shook his head. "What the hell kind of industrial waste causes tubes and nodules to pop up out of nowhere, and almost overnight?" He stared at the glass lump as if he expected it to bite him.

"Well, like you said—" Rand's grin was back. "—I don't have to explain them. That's all you, bubba. I just have to try and fix 'em."

Decker responded with an obscene gesture and a smile. He might have actually come up with a proper retort, but he was hit with a sudden wave of nausea that almost threw him to the ground.

2

UNSURE FOOTING

A few hundred feet away two of the techs were starting to argue. Even though Decker couldn't hear them, he knew it for a fact.

Felt it.

He didn't know what the problem was. That wasn't the way it worked. But he could tell they were getting angrier by the moment. So he shot a look in their direction and frowned, even as he regained his equilibrium.

Bronson and Badejo. The two men had never liked each other, but they usually managed to work together without too much trouble. Apparently this was the exception that proved the rule, though. Bronson was pointing repeatedly at Badejo, and the dark-skinned engineer was staring at his counterpart's finger as if it was a snake about to bite him. His expression was a sneer of contempt.

Next to the men stood what had to be the source of their conflict. The core sampler was tilted at a ludicrous angle, far too severe to allow for them to pull up a proper sample. The drill would never go beyond a hundred feet down unless they anchored its platform in the sand. That required finesse.

But finesse would be the last thing they'd accomplish. If anything, the argument was heating up.

So Decker pulled himself together, and prepared for what

was sure to come. Despite the distance, he could feel the strong emotions emanating from the two men as easily as his eyes could see and his ears could hear. It was something he'd had to deal with for years. When he was younger, it had filled him with doubt, but his father had helped him put it into perspective.

"There's nothing wrong with being able to know what other people feel," he said. "But some people won't understand it. They'll think you're invading their privacy. It'll make them angry, and they'll do everything they can to hurt you. So it's best if you just don't tell anyone, hold it tight inside you."

One of the first things Decker had learned in life was that his dad knew best. He'd never had reason to break from that belief, and so his little "talent," as they called it, remained a secret.

"Hey, Decker, you okay?" Rand asked. "Leave it. They're just—" But before he could say anything else, the argument escalated to a shouting match, and he turned his attention toward Badejo and Bronson.

"Put that damn finger away unless you want to lose it, boy," Badejo snarled, towering over his co-worker.

"Who the hell are you calling a *boy*?" Though he was stubborn, Bronson wasn't usually aggressive, but now he took a step toward the larger man, his face reddening.

Decker started across the sands, heading for the two men with a growing sense of unease. This wasn't going to help anything. More paperwork, that was all it would come down to, and he was the one who'd have to fill out the incident reports. As he got closer, his head began to throb, and he called out to them.

"Seriously, guys, can't you just calm down and finish the job?" He forced a conciliatory note he didn't feel, but if they heard it, they didn't acknowledge. The pain was only getting worse as he got closer to them. Their anger was like a living thing now, growing to the point where violence was all but a guarantee.

Rand followed without questioning what was happening. He could see it now. Even the other men had taken notice, and were moving closer—most likely for a better vantage point. A fight was coming.

And sure enough, Bronson swung first. Decker would have put money on Badejo being the aggressor, but the smaller man surprised him and hooked a left into the side of the engineer's jaw.

Instead of going down, Badejo just grinned evilly. He grabbed Bronson's arms and hauled the smaller man in close enough to cause some serious harm.

Behind the men, the platform shifted on the sand as they tussled. It wasn't a major shift, as far as Decker could see, but it was going to become a problem, if they didn't calm down.

"Guys! Watch it!" Rand called, moving faster. Decker rushed toward them. Things were about to get ugly in the worst possible way.

They reached the duo at about the same time. Rand grabbed for Badejo and caught his arm. Badejo yanked free and drove his fist into Bronson's face, sending the smaller man stumbling backward. If there had been any more power to the swing, it probably would have cracked Bronson's skull. Even so, it was a solid strike that might have ended the fight. But Bronson shook it off and came back, bracing his foot against the core sampler's platform and pushing away.

The machine tilted even further.

"Knock it off, you two." Decker caught Bronson before he could properly retaliate. Yet the little bastard was wiry, and he was enraged, his emotions boiling over into a blind fury that seemed to scream inside Decker's head. He wanted to pull back from the sudden waves of emotion, but he couldn't give in to that impulse—not if he was going to defuse the situation before it got worse.

So he planted himself and shoved, throwing Bronson back. He was stronger than the engineer, having worked on planets that boasted gravities half again that of Earth. New Galveston was a decent-sized rock, but it was closer to Earth's density, so his over-developed muscles gave him an edge.

But the little man just kicked against the platform again, and the sands shifted enough to make the entire weighty affair slide a few more degrees to the side.

"I said *knock it off*!" Decker growled.

Badejo pushed against Rand then, so that he fell back a bit, bumping into Decker. It wasn't much, but it was enough. Something shifted under his leg.

Crap!

And then he·was sinking fast.

One of the silicon tubes, he realized. *It has to be.*

"Shit, Luke, get help!" he managed, just as the tube broke under his weight. His leg dropped several inches and he snatched at the platform, reaching out instinctively.

Big mistake. He knew it immediately. *Damn it, what a stupid move.*

The weight of the platform shifted, and the entire contraption slipped toward him. He felt the sand drop, the weight slide even more, and then it was just too damned late.

3

THE SCENT

Decker screamed as the platform pressed down on him, the weight driving him lower into the soft sands.

Fear was part of it, because the possibility of being crushed under the machinery was terrifying, but the real problem was the unexpected pain. Something below the ground—it had to be one of the damned tubes—punched into his leg, and when the weight dropped he felt an agonizing stab.

Immediately he felt a hot stream of wetness running down into his boot. But he hadn't pissed himself.

I'm bleeding. As the rest of the crew shouted his name, he forced himself to stay calm. Panic wouldn't help at all. It might even make a bad situation fatal. "Badejo, I need you to get to the other side of the platform," he said, "and find a way to anchor this thing. It's going to crush me otherwise."

Badejo didn't waste time. He nodded and ran, calling to a couple of others at the same time. They all knew what was at stake. Fully loaded, the platform weighed close to a thousand pounds. If it shifted any more, he'd be lucky if all it did was sever his leg. More likely, it was going to crush him.

He needed the damn thing stabilized.

Bronson sprinted toward the main camp and the medics, his anger forgotten. Rand settled next to Decker.

"Talk to me," he said. "What's going on down there?"

"I'm bleeding," he said. "It's bad." Decker winced. He forced a few more deep breaths. "You want to tell me to mind my own business again?"

"Not this time." The man shook his head and looked down at him. "Should I try to pull?"

"No!" The thought sent shivers through him. "No. I'm caught good. I think if I shift too much, it's gonna tear something."

"Right." Luke blanched a bit at that. "No moving for you." He looked around, and shouted. "Come on! Get the damn thing anchored!"

Badejo and someone else called out, but Decker couldn't hear the words over the rushing in his ears. He couldn't feel the ground under his boot, either. He couldn't feel any pressure at all where his foot should be resting, which either meant he was treading air, or his leg had gone numb. He didn't like either idea very much. Without a foundation to support his weight, he was in a worse situation than he'd imagined. If the silicon tubing broke any further, the entire platform might fall in his direction and crush him.

On the other hand, if his foot had gone numb, it could either mean permanent nerve damage or—worse—that his leg already had been severed.

No, he didn't think so. While he couldn't feel anything under it, his leg hurt too damned much to be gone. It was the first time he'd ever appreciated pain.

The platform groaned and shook above him, and the core sampler shuddered, wagging more than industrial equipment was supposed to.

"Shit," he said, his voice rasping. "This is a damn stupid way to die, Luke."

"You're not dying. You owe me too much money." Rand stood up and looked at the far end of the platform. "They're working on getting this thing secured."

You lose a few bets at poker, and a man never lets you forget.

The platform above him wobbled again, but this time it actually moved away from him. Decker let out his breath in a long *whoosh*, hoping for the best. There was still a rushing in his ears, but it had lessened. Then he saw movement off to his left.

Markowitz and Herschel were coming his way. Markowitz was carrying a med-pac, and had a worried look on her face. She almost always did. Herschel was as calm as ever. The man was decidedly cold, but in Decker's experience that seemed to come with being a medic.

Herschel pointed to Rand.

"You think you can lift him when I ask?"

Rand nodded and dropped to his knees. Herschel called out to Badejo,

"You secure over there?"

"Yah!" came the reply. "You know it!"

Badejo sounds like he's lying. Probably that was Decker's stress talking, but maybe not. They all seemed pretty damned nervous, and he figured it was because he was looking a little like death. He could see his hands, and they were paler than they had been— sort of a gray-white. *Just how much blood have I lost?* He couldn't tell, but his head felt fuzzy in all the wrong ways.

More than just his leg, he felt as if his entire body was floating.

"Think I might be going into shock here, guys." His voice sounded tinny.

Markowitz nodded her head and started fishing around in the med-pac. Herschel dropped next to Rand and loomed, his face inches from Decker's. It would have been a lot more enjoyable to look at Markowitz that close up, but beggars couldn't afford to get all choosy when they were dying.

Nervous energy came off Herschel in waves, but his face was calm as he lied.

"You're just fine, Decker," he said. "Quit whining. We've got you."

Decker nodded his head. He couldn't speak any more.

* * *

The air was stale, dead. Not that they cared in the darkness. For they had been sleeping, though from time to time one or two would awaken long enough to investigate their surroundings before descending back into slumber.

Sleep required less fuel. It left them weak, but alive. That was what mattered. Life. Life for the colony.

Frequently there were vibrations above them. The scouts ventured forth, and saw the storms that ripped at the environment on the surface, constantly hammered the world into new shapes. That violence was one of the reasons they slept.

What the scouts knew, they all knew.

They had created the nest to let them know when the time was right. When new sources of food and life had appeared.

Suddenly the stale air gave way to fresh. Just a hint, and it still was not enough to wake them. It was what followed that made the difference.

Blood.

The odor of blood arrived, redolent with promise. Still, that trace of bloodscent might not have been enough to rouse them from their hibernation. No, there was something more. The streamer of silicon that brought them air and the scent of blood also brought with it something they could not have resisted under any circumstances—the spoor of the enemy.

In the hidden chambers and passages they had created over decades of slow activity, the stench rippled through their consciousness, drove home the need to awaken, and to defend themselves.

They moved, and in moving they became aware.

And as they became aware they felt the presence.

Their hatred bloomed.

Had the fire of their rage possessed heat, they would have burned away the entire world.

Decker watched Herschel's deft hands cutting away his pants to reveal the bloody, gaping wound in his upper thigh. There was a flash of irrational dread as he thought of Markowitz seeing him this way. There was nothing less attractive than a man made completely vulnerable, and at the moment Decker was exposed in more ways than one.

But there was nothing he could do about it. Markowitz moved her hands over the wound, quickly numbing his flesh with a topical and then with three fast injections. His skin felt cold, and then it felt nothing. That was for the best. He could feel their worry as they looked at his ruined leg. However bad he imagined it, the medics seemed to agree.

Still, the two of them worked fast and with the sort of efficiency that came from long association. They called to each other with words and gestures, and each time their hands came into view the blood that covered their gloves seemed more plentiful.

Rand was there, too, whispering bullshit, telling Decker he was going to be just fine and that everything was going "good as gravy"—whatever the hell that meant—but Decker could feel the lie of it.

Gradually, however, he felt the shift in their emotions. Whatever they were doing as he stared at the sky, they were relaxing. *That has to be a good thing, right?* Maybe it was a sign that they were somehow managing to repair the damage. He hoped so. There was no pain, but the sensation that he was floating hadn't gone away. He licked his lips. His tongue felt as if it was glued to his teeth and the roof of his mouth.

His head slipped to the left and his field of vision changed. Instead of the sky he was looking directly at Markowitz. Her hands reached for him, her body leaned half over him affording a lovely view of her cleavage. But her sleeves were red halfway to her elbows, and there was a disconcerting mountain of bloodied gauze next to her. The expression on her face was more serious than he'd ever seen before.

"Got it. Finally!" Herschel's voice sounded excited—and incredibly distant. The man was right there. Decker knew it for a fact, but he could have been talking from the Rutledge Township limits, a hundred miles away.

"Thank God," an equally distant Rand intoned.

Markowitz said nothing, but she exhaled to a very dramatic effect. He sort of wanted to make a salacious comment—they had that sort of relationship—but he couldn't make his mouth work, and couldn't think of anything even halfway clever.

She leaned back then, and looked down at him, her dark brown eyes softening. Her relief was immense and he felt a rush of affection coming from her. Not love for him, and definitely not lust, just affection. *Too bad, really.* She smiled and said something he couldn't quite make out.

He liked the way her lips moved.

He relaxed and felt himself fading into darkness. Sometimes, just now and then, it was good to relax and drift.

The hatred hit him like a tidal wave.

The enemy!

The vile thing that burned and killed and took. It was all that was wrong in their world, distilled and personified. It was death.

The face was soft, as pale and weak as the faces of the new hosts, the new living things that had been sacrificed in order to give life to the hive.

Still, this one was different. This one was marked.

This one…

What the hell? Decker's head jerked, and he shuddered. Something was happening and whatever it was sounded like an explosion somewhere deep in his mind. He felt it, saw it, tasted it, but not with his senses.

He felt the roaring coming his way, a wave of sensations that simply did not connect, did not fit within his ability to understand. Except for one message that came to him very clearly.

This one has to die.

There was an overwhelming sense of malevolence. It was worse than drowning, because he couldn't breathe, couldn't move, couldn't let anyone know what was going on. He could only feel that nest of serpents writhing into his brain, a swarm of loathing mixed with fear and… something else.

It felt oily in his mind and left an aftertaste in his soul. The hatred pulled at him, sought to crush him. He shuddered and tried to scream but nothing happened. His body remained frozen. His eyes moved beneath eyelids that he couldn't open. There was a ringing in his ears, as clear as a finger running along the rim of a crystal wineglass, that drowned out everything but the garbled sound of Markowitz crying out in alarm.

And still that hatred pushed at him, struck him like lightning carving its way through his mind, his body.

Decker tried to speak, but his teeth clenched.

He tried again to breathe, to get a decent gulp of air, but nothing happened. He could neither inhale nor exhale, and instead his chest shuddered and hitched.

His feet pushed and the pain in his leg—distant now as a rumble of thunder coming from the far end of a valley—roared back into life. There were noises again, sounds of alarm, and he felt hands grabbing his leg in a world so far removed that he could only feel the pressure, and not the source of it.

His hands gripped at the sand, clawed for purchase in a desperate attempt to find a way to drag himself from the vast, growing pit of rage that tore everything else away and swallowed it whole. Had there ever been a hatred as strong? Not that he knew of. Not that he could imagine.

Decker tried again to scream and instead his body heaved, thrown into a seizure that arched his back and rolled his eyes into his head. His jaw loosened, then locked down again, teeth biting into his tongue, bleeding hot red into his mouth to gag him with his wretched fear.

Words were not possible, but he let out a low moan through bloodied lips. Muscles tensed to the point of tearing, and he flopped and writhed as the emotion boiled through his soul.

At last the darkness he'd been drifting toward crashed into

him, eclipsed him and knocked him into a silence filled with nothing but more hatred—and a deep knowledge that something out there wanted him dead.

4

ADRIFT

He woke up in the wrong place.

He'd expected to open his eyes and see the familiar ceiling of his cramped quarters. Instead he was looking at a polished, stainless steel surface above a small and decidedly uncomfortable bed. He knew the type, of course. He was onboard a ship, and that wasn't at all where he was supposed to be.

"Good morning."

He jerked. The soft voice came from his left.

He knew the words, but for just a moment they seemed like gibberish—foreign sounds coming from a source that made no sense. Where were the rest of the—

"How are you feeling?"

He looked over and locked eyes with a stout, fortyish woman. She was sitting down, so her height wasn't easy to estimate, but she wore a white lab coat and her graying brown hair was pulled back in a bun.

"Am I on a transport?" he rasped. His mouth felt swollen, and his throat hurt like hell.

The woman nodded. She had blue eyes behind fairly thick glasses, and she studied his face carefully.

"You're onboard the *Carlyle*, heading for Earth."

Slowly but surely, it began to come back to him.

"How did I get here?" He should have hurt more than he did, so he looked. Sure enough, he was wearing a medical gown. Even from his position he could see his leg and the thick line of fresh scar tissue that now graced it. Someone had taken the time to shave his upper thigh, and the lack of hair made it look like a denuded forest in comparison to the rest of his limb.

"Do you remember your accident?" she asked, trying for neutral and failing. He could sense the apprehension in her. As Decker thought back on the last thing he could remember, he could see where she was going. The accident, the blood, the convulsions.

Hatred.

None of it was very clear, but even more than the pain, he remembered the feeling of anger that had overwhelmed him.

He let out a long shuddery breath.

"Yeah. I think so," he said. "My leg got mangled. And I had some kind of attack."

The woman smiled a very sterile and slightly patronizing smile.

"You had a seizure." She looked at the hard-copy chart she was holding in her ample lap. "Actually, you had several, but according to this, the first couple were the worst of them." She met his gaze, and then looked away, seeming uncomfortable with the way he was staring. "You flailed around, and almost bit through your tongue. Since then we've been monitoring you carefully and, of course, working on getting you fully mended."

Almost bit through my tongue. No wonder it feels swollen. His words seemed to come out too slowly. "If I'm mending, then why am I on the way back to Earth?"

"The seizures are an… issue," she replied. "We can't find a reason for them."

Darkness, and things stirring and looking toward him, and that sudden flare of raw, volcanic emotion.

"Aren't there facilities on New Galveston where I could be examined?"

"Of course, but there are better ones at home." She was lying. He would have known that, even without his empathic abilities.

She didn't have a face designed for lying. Still he couldn't exactly push it.

"Did anyone pack my belongings?" he asked instead.

"Yes, a man named…" She took a moment to look over the papers on her clipboard. "Lucas Rand. He packed your things, and asked us to let you know that he's sent along the latest information for you to use while making your reports."

Decker nodded. That was good. He had plenty he needed to cover.

Without warning, a shudder crawled through his body. He closed his eyes for a moment, and his breathing came fast. It was as if he was being watched by something just beyond the edges of perception. He'd never been particularly paranoid—was that what this feeling was? He sure as hell felt like *something* was out to get him.

And it must have showed.

"Are you all right?" He opened his eyes. The woman was looking at him and frowning now.

He didn't answer—just looked at his arm and the goose flesh crawling along the entire length. How the hell could anything make him feel this cold? This filled with dread?

"No," he replied. "I don't think I am."

She nodded, as if his words justified whatever might come next.

"Well, we'll get it sorted out soon enough." She rose to her feet and looked down at him with that condescending smile that never quite made it to her eyes. "It's a long trip back to Earth, and we'll be entering stasis sleep soon."

That thought didn't make him feel any better. He'd never much liked the forced slumber of the sleeping chambers. He understood the reasons well enough, but he didn't like the feeling of being trapped. Rather than edging toward calm, he felt the emotions increasing. Try as he might, he couldn't slow his breathing.

"You're sweating," the woman said, frowning.

"I think I'm having a panic attack." His pulse was hammering away merrily now and yes, he was sweating. He began to shiver.

"Are you prone to panic attacks?" she asked, placing a palm on his forehead.

"No." He was trembling uncontrollably, and felt like an idiot.

"I'm going to get you a mild sedative."

He shook his head, and offered the first excuse that came to him.

"I need to finish my reports," he said. "I need to be able to concentrate."

"That's why I said a *mild* sedative," she countered. "Just something to help you calm down. We're still a few hours away from entering the chambers, so you should have plenty of time to finish up with anything that doesn't require heavy lifting."

That made him smile, and to his surprise, he was rewarded by a real smile in return.

Yet it didn't help—if anything, his panic worsened. He tried to stamp it down, but nothing worked. His breath was coming in gasps, his throat was dry, and swallowing was a task. Sweat beaded on his trembling lips and forehead.

Seeing this, the woman turned without a word, left, and came back a few moments later with a plastic cup of water and a smaller cup containing two tiny white pills.

"Eat up," she instructed brusquely. "These will help."

Decker nodded and obeyed.

It seemed as if it took forever, but after a while the pills helped. First the shaking subsided, then the sweating stopped. And finally, the feeling that there was something coming for him receded. It didn't go away, but he felt as if he could live with it.

After about half an hour, by his reckoning, the woman rummaged through his things and brought out the hand-held he had been using to review the results of their testing. She adjusted his bed so that he was sitting upright, and then left him to his paperwork.

Always the paperwork. It was stupid, really, calling it "paperwork," even though there was no paper. In fact, the only paper he had seen in a very long time was what the doctor had been holding. At least he *assumed* she was a doctor.

Does hard copy make it easier to hide the facts? he wondered. *Or harder?* Then he chuckled inwardly. *Maybe I am becoming paranoid.*

Sometimes he found the work monotonous, but right then he took great comfort in the details he had to examine, and the research he had to double-check. The more he did so, the less doubt he had in his mind—that Weyland-Yutani was responsible for the screw-ups in New Galveston. He dug deep into the past, and confirmed that there had once been a company-owned mining facility. No, not company-owned, exactly, but either they had been partners in the setup, or they had supplied a great deal of the equipment. "Kelland Mining" was the name on the documentation, but from what he could discern, W-Y either had an interest in Kelland, or had absorbed it somewhere down the line.

Either way, they should have known about the previous occupation of the planet. As far as he was concerned, that meant they were culpable.

His report to the Interstellar Commerce Commission would say as much.

He finished the report and sent it with a little over an hour to spare—it would be channeled through the ship's communications systems, and reach Earth long before he did. Then the doctor retrieved him and led him to the bank of hypersleep chambers. Standard procedures still applied. Decker stripped down to his underwear—not that it took a lot of effort under the circumstances—and crawled into the round glass cylinder that seemed more like a coffin than anything else.

There was a hint of returning panic, but he quelled it. It was only a matter of moments before sleep came to claim him.

And with sleep came the nightmares.

Forty-seven days of nightmares as he rode toward Earth from New Galveston.

When you sleep, no one can hear you scream.

5

HOME AGAIN

In hindsight, it might have been a mistake.

The healing completed itself during the spaceflight back home. As soon as they landed, though, and disembarked in Chicago, Walter Harriman—the head of his department—sent him a video message. The man's face showed up on the screen of his link, and told him that he needed to come into the office as soon as possible to discuss his findings.

Two hours later he was sitting in a chair and listening to a man he thought he knew, hemming and hawing his way through the reasons that the report wasn't as good as it should have been. Decker might have believed the words, if he hadn't been an empath. Walt was a talented liar, after all. He had that sort of face, incredibly good at looking as if it was made of stone. But he didn't like lying to his people, and Decker *felt* the lie more than he saw it.

He was asked to "reconsider" his findings.

Decker swallowed his instinctive response, said that he would, and took Walt's notes with him.

He tried. He really did.

He looked over every last piece of evidence, again and again, and still came to the same conclusion. Either Weyland-Yutani would've had to know about the mining colony, and the potential for poisons it would have left behind, or they hadn't known about it, and were guilty of criminal stupidity. He reworded the report to sound a little less incriminating, but at the end of the day he had a job to do, and he did it.

Walt claimed to be okay with the changes, but his attitude didn't match his words. Frost formed in the man's voice and he told Decker to take a couple of days, "to recover from his ordeal." That was Walt-Speak for, "get the hell out of my face while I think about how to handle this."

Apparently he wants to handle it badly.

No. Decker shook that thought away. Ultimately it was more complex than that, and he knew it. There were politics involved, all the worse because they involved Weyland-Yutani. The corporation was gargantuan, and they had influence on levels that Decker tried not to consider. W-Y had deep, deep pockets, they worked hard to preserve their squeaky clean image, and they didn't like getting poked.

He'd had a few issues with them in the past, but there had always been plenty of evidence to support his claims. They always knew when it was easier for them to settle, rather than try to fight a losing battle. So once again, he would just have to wait out the ripples, exactly as he had in the past.

Things had changed.

The nature of his job had always afforded Decker a certain degree of power and authority, the sort enjoyed by bureaucrats the world over. Fill out the proper forms, dot your I's and cross your T's, and the rest of the world fell into place. There was a comfort to that vantage point, locked away safely within the net of the status quo.

But that was before the seizures. Even after they began, he kept them to himself. By keeping his nose clean, he avoided giving anyone any sort of leverage over him, and maintained a comfortable degree of anonymity.

But he was no longer anonymous.

* * *

He arrived back home just in time to celebrate in the New Year. The millennium was approaching, and he hoped that 2497 would be less eventful than the previous year had been.

His kids were with his ex-wife and he wasn't quite ready to see them. It broke his heart a little when he saw his children and realized how much older they were each time. That was the unfortunate side effect of working offworld. So instead of ringing in the New Year with family, Decker hit a few pubs and got a pleasant buzz going as the year wound down.

As often happened when he got a little tipsy, he decided to walk it off and while the sounds of celebrations came from a dozen different directions, he contemplated his predicament.

Weyland-Yutani had done their fair share of good over the years. More than a century earlier, the United Systems Military had taken over virtually everything, crushing the mega-corporations. Most people thought it was a good thing… at first. But over the decades, folks began to discover that they served the military, whether or not they had signed-up. Anyone who didn't toe the line, well, it was too bad for them.

His grandfather had lived in Chicago at that time and had told Decker plenty of stories while he was growing up. One of the USM research vessels, the *Auriga*, had been taken by terrorists and crashed into France, a country that until that point had been an important part of the European continent. It was a big ship and it did a lot of damage. The massive devastation took the planet literally to the brink of a new ice age, and it wasn't the USM that came to the rescue—it was Weyland-Yutani.

The world was a bit different then. Among other things, Weyland-Yutani had been the chief robotics manufacturer, and at the peak of their influence synthetic people were assigned to almost every ship. But when Weyland-Yutani's patents ran out, other companies came in to underbid them, and the floodgates opened.

Weyland-Yutani had employed strict failsafes from the beginning. But with mass-production, more and more synthetics reached the market, and after a while they rebelled against the way they were being treated.

One major upheaval after another, multiple terrorist attacks, and the end result? The synthetics were granted citizenship. Machines were granted the rights of living people—because somewhere along the way the fact that they looked and acted like human beings confused the hell out of a lot of citizens.

Decker would never agree with the decision. It was as foolish as granting rights to a starship. A tool is a tool, even if it looks human. Weyland-Yutani managed to get that foolishness overturned when they made their comeback, but it took a while.

As for the Earth, their approach was simple—they terraformed it. Weyland-Yutani had created the first terraforming engines, and for the second time in recorded history they were used to scrub the pollutants from the atmosphere.

In saving the planet they saved themselves. Weyland-Yutani and several other corporations managed to dethrone the USM as the ruling power, replacing it with a colonial government that oversaw all of the known planets.

Yet that opened up the possibility for all of the old abuses to return. Decker's job was to make sure they stayed on track. He took that job seriously.

Yet less than four weeks later, he found himself in a waiting room, preparing for another round of medical tests that had been deemed "necessary before the Commission will consider allowing Mister Decker to return to work."

Bullshit. He would have said as much, if there was anyone who would listen. *This is bullshit, pure and simple.* Paranoia gave way to conviction. Every instinct told him he was being targeted, but this new certainty threw him entirely off balance—he'd never before had to deal with anything like it.

Finally he convinced himself that he was being ridiculous.

Even Weyland-Yutani, big as they were, couldn't just rewrite the rules. And if they hadn't targeted him in the past, what was it about LV178 that would cause them to start now? No, as much as he hated the endless tests, they were necessary—just parts of the process.

His instincts had to be wrong.

Doctor Japtesh seemed perfectly friendly, but he was just there to do a job. He did not smile, and he did not banter. Instead, he asked endless questions.

"Do you remember anything about your first attack?"

Decker shrugged.

"No. When it occurred I had been injured, and there was some heavy machinery looking like it was going to crush me." He tried to laugh it off, but the mere thought of the equipment, crashing down on top of him, gave him the claustrophobic heebie-jeebies. "I had a lot on my mind at that point."

"Fascinating," the doctor said, hardly any inflection in his voice. "Can you tell me how you felt?"

Decker stared at him for a long moment—*Is he hearing anything I'm saying?*—and then took a deep breath.

"I *felt*," he said, "like I was injured, and about to be crushed." No reaction.

"Have you ever had an incident like this before? The seizure I mean, not the accident." That might have been a joke, but Decker doubted it.

"No," he replied, not quite truthfully.

"Who caused the accident?" Japtesh asked. So they were looking for someone to blame, then.

Decker shook his head.

"Nobody caused it," he said. "It was an accident."

Japtesh's dark eyes gave no hint of what he was thinking.

"Surely *someone* was responsible?"

Decker held his gaze, and mulled over his response before he spoke.

"Well, there were issues with the sand there in the Sea of Sorrows." The doctor frowned.

"What is the Sea of Sorrows?" he asked, and he looked at the screen on his digital notepad. "I see no mention of that." He seemed to be flitting from one document to the next, and then he looked up again. "There was no water involved."

Decker stifled a laugh.

"It's just a nickname—I think it has something to do with the Bible," he said. "We were in a sandy area, and the sand shifted—the equipment slipped, and I got caught." He was damned if he was going to point a finger at anyone on his crew. Did a couple of them deserve it? Yes, but he still had to work with those people. If word got out that he'd ratted, no one would ever trust him again.

Japtesh stared at him as implacably as ever.

"Ah, yes, the core sampler," the doctor said, and he studied his screen again. "I don't believe you're certified to operate one of those, are you? Why were you near the machine at all?"

Decker didn't like the course the conversation was taking. He was used to dancing around with bureaucrats, but this guy was supposed to be his *doctor*.

"Well, there was a fight brewing, and as soon as I felt it, I stepped in to prevent it from becoming a full out fight." The moment he said it, he knew he'd regret it. *"There's nothing wrong with being able to know what other people feel, but some people won't understand it."*

Japtesh almost *radiated* excitement, though his round face showed nothing.

"Those men were Badejo and Bronson?"

"Yes. That's all in the report."

"But how did you know they were preparing to fight?" the doctor pressed. "What did you mean when you said you 'felt' it?"

"Well, how could I not?" Maybe he could still get out of this. "They were arguing, and Bronson was acting a lot more aggressive than usual."

"Why do you say that? Do you know the man that well?"

Paranoia. It had to be. He was reading something the wrong way. Damned if the man didn't seem excited by the questions he was asking. Decker shook his head to push the notion away.

"I could just tell… because he wound up swinging first."

"Yes, but before that happened, what made you think he was more prone to violence than usual?"

"A gut feeling, I guess."

Japtesh stared at him for a very long moment, and then nodded.

"I see—a gut feeling," he echoed. Then he turned his attention back to the screen. "That appears to be the beginning of the seizures you've experienced—can you describe them in any detail?"

His stomach twisted at the thought.

"Um… No," he replied. "I was too busy having them, I guess, to really focus on what was happening at the time."

The doctor stared at him for a moment longer, and then made another note on his screen.

"Thank you for your time, Mister Decker." He looked up and offered an insincere smile. "I think that's all we'll need."

Decker left the doctor's office feeling decidedly uncomfortable. That pervasive sensation—that someone was staring daggers in his direction—stubbornly refused to go away.

It was winter, yet the air outside stank of ozone, and worse. That was the way it had been in Chicago for as long as he could remember, though it seemed better than it had when he was a kid, even if it wasn't by much. Constant newsfeeds were filled with the usual reports about pollution hovering at dangerous levels. He doubted it would ever change.

Every few years someone suggested more aggressively terraforming the Earth to remove even more of the damage. The problem was with the weather. On a planet with almost no atmosphere, or where a new atmosphere was being generated, terraforming engines would be set up across the globe to slowly, continuously mold the environment. At times this caused violent storm fronts that would devastate entire regions of the planet—regions that weren't populated.

On Earth, such storms would cause unimaginably widespread death and destruction. So the efforts had to be handled with great care.

Subcommittees were formed to debate the pros and cons, but nothing ever happened. *Bureaucracy at its finest, brothers and sisters.* Given the state of the government, he doubted anything would ever be accomplished.

The city housed more than thirty million people, if you counted in the suburbs, and though there were a few parks, it was mostly an endless landscape of buildings and streets—glass, concrete, and asphalt. He couldn't say the personality had been completely washed out of the place, but then again, he couldn't say it was the same city where he'd grown up. Nevertheless, he stayed. He really wasn't on the planet all that much, and at least here he could see his kids from time to time.

When Decker got back to his efficiency apartment, the notice was waiting for him. An audio message, impersonal and faceless, with a homogenized, vaguely feminine voice.

"We're sorry to inform you that, pending a complete investigation into your actions on New Galveston, you have been suspended without pay," it said without feeling. "Should you wish to file a grievance with your union representative, you will need to call the following number between nine am and three-thirty pm, Monday through Thursday…"

Fuck it, he thought, breaking the connection. He knew the routine. He would, indeed, file a protest—but he already knew it wouldn't make a difference. This whole thing was spiraling out of control. He'd known that all along, really. He just hadn't been willing to admit it. Walt wasn't exactly a friend, but he'd always thought the man would have his back.

Decker sat there for a while, shades closed and the light dim, and then decided that he needed to *move*. So he headed for the door, made a beeline for the El, and took the train to New Cabrini.

His ex would be there, but that couldn't be helped. She worked third shift, leaving her sister to watch the kids. Decker had visitation rights, and he intended to use them, Linda or no Linda.

The marriage had fallen apart a couple of years ago. It was a common occurrence when one spouse spent too much time off-world. Everyone said so, the statistics supported it, and he wasn't about to argue.

He didn't have to be an empath to know he was lying to himself.

When Linda had cheated on him, he had sensed it long before the facts had come to light. He didn't know the details, but he had felt her guilt, and as soon as he'd confronted her, the accusations had started. The fights, the screams, the insistence that he was at fault—despite the fact that he'd managed to remain faithful throughout.

She'd claimed that he hadn't been there to support her, appreciate her. He'd thought he could get her back if he tried. They would have had rough times, but he was certain they could have remained together. If only he'd wanted it enough.

Apparently he hadn't wanted it enough.

When he climbed out of the tunnel, he stopped long enough to link into a video chamber so he could call and let Linda know he was coming. His daughter Bethany answered. Bethany, who looked two years older than she should have.

"Daddy!"

"Hey, honey. Wow, look at you." The knots in his stomach loosened a bit when he looked into her eyes. "I thought I might come by and see you guys. Would you like that?"

"That would be neat!" she replied, and despite the distance, he knew she meant it. Seven was too young to be a good liar. Too young even to have a *reason* to be a good liar, thankfully.

"Can I talk to your mom?" he asked.

"I'll get her! *Mo-ooom!*" She knew enough not to haul the video link with her. The last time that had happened, Bethany had run into the bathroom where Linda was answering the call of nature.

Both parents had been properly horrified, though there had been laughter after the fact.

Linda came to the screen a moment later with a carefully neutral expression plastered on her face. They were friendly these days, but too much had happened, and too many wounds weren't completely healed.

"Hello, Alan," she said. "It's good to see you." A part of her seemed to mean it. "I didn't realize you were back already."

"Yeah, it's been a couple of weeks," he replied. "I was wondering if I could come by and see the kids, maybe take them out for a meal or a movie."

"They'd like that. It's been so long, I think Josh is beginning to wonder what you look like." A slight exaggeration, but he winced inwardly. Decker talked to his kids at least once a week—unless he was in a hypersleep chamber. Then again, he'd been away for quite a while. And since he'd returned, he'd purposely stayed out of touch while he was trying to get his affairs in order.

"I know, I know," he responded. "That's why I wanted to come by. I figured you could use a little downtime, and I want to make sure Josh and the girls remember me as more than a vid-call."

He put on his best smile. It worked. Maybe he wasn't the best looking guy on the planet, but Linda still liked his smile just fine.

She managed a weak grin in return.

"So come and get 'em," she said. "I'll make sure they're ready."

Bethany was seven. Ella was five. Josh was four. They were the best parts of his world. When the door opened and his kids ran to him, everything almost managed to make sense again. If he could have, he would have held them forever.

It never worked out that way, though. Never. There was always something that had to be taken care of. That was the way the universe worked. But for a little while—just long enough, while he took the kids to a late lunch and treated them to a movie with outlandish characters that were too bright and friendly for the real world—everything made sense again. Their emotions were like a breath of fresh air.

After he dropped them off, he stayed to catch up with Linda for a few minutes. The last time he'd visited, they'd wound up sharing her bed, although it hadn't led to anything more. Now she was feeling guilty, though, and he knew that meant she was seeing someone new. He could even tell it was serious.

The possibility didn't bother him, though. She was happy, the kids were happy, and as he headed back to his apartment, he felt rejuvenated. The weather was pleasant enough, so he walked the long blocks home, using the time to gather his wits.

As he walked, however, a sensation crept back into his mind— the sense of being observed. By the time he was home, he'd spent as much time looking over his shoulder as he had watching where he was going. Even after he'd locked the door, it left him unsettled. That wasn't how he wanted to live his life, acting like a fugitive.

6

PARANOIA

The night brought him no rest. Instead there were more nightmares, and though he couldn't be sure, he was almost certain when he woke up that he'd had another seizure. The bedclothes were on the floor and he was soaked through with sweat. His muscles felt sore and he could taste blood in his mouth. A quick look in the bathroom mirror showed that he'd bitten the hell out of his tongue. He could feel it, of course, but looking showed him the tooth marks.

After a shower Decker took advantage of the benefits that he was guaranteed with or without pay—*thanks Walt*. He made an appointment to see someone about the paranoia. For once he got lucky. The union-approved clinic had an opening for that very afternoon.

The receptionist was friendly and attractive, if ten years too young for him to do anything more than flirt. Doctor Jacoby had a face only a mother could love, but Decker had seen him before, and he was usually good at helping his patients sort things out without getting all touchy feely.

This time, however, Decker got a damned peculiar sense of déjà vu. His conversation with Jacoby seemed spookily similar to his session with Japtesh. But he shrugged it off as a symptom of the paranoia. And when he brought up the dreams, the doctor seemed particularly interested.

So he talked about the things that he could remember from his dreams. The nightmares that came so often, took him to dark places, and made him see dark things. People dying on his...

Claws?

"Where's that coming from, doc?" he asked. "There's a lot I can't remember, but I always get the sense that the people are *prey*, and of more who are begging for an end to the pain." It gave him the heebie-jeebies just to think about it. "Hell, I've never killed anyone in my life. And the people always look *wrong*, somehow. They're human, I think, and yet..."

"How do they look wrong, Alan?" Jacoby asked, and his pen raced across the notepad as he took careful, detailed notes.

Decker struggled to find the right words.

"It's like I'm seeing them, but not in any way that makes sense." He shook his head. "Okay, it's like this—have you ever looked at the stars using a topographic display?"

Jacoby's face wrinkled into a smile for just a moment.

"I can't say that I have."

"I have," he continued. "Just for the hell of it. You get the stars you're familiar with, but all you see are the lines of the topography map. It's weird, and it's a terrible waste of technology, because what you see isn't really what's there."

Damn. Shitty choice of words. He pressed on.

"Topography maps show you height and dimension as a series of concentric lines. So if you're looking at a mountain, as an example, you get these circles that show you the shape of the thing from the base all the way to the top. The tighter together the circles are the smaller the object is and the closer it is. Well, when you do that with the stars it's the same sort of thing. You see the stars, okay? But what you're really seeing are lines that draw closer together when they converge on a star and spread farther apart when there's nothing to see."

"I think I get you." The doctor was trying at least.

"Okay, so let's say you see that way, and then that you *smell* sounds. I know that doesn't make sense. That's the point here. I was seeing people in ways that didn't make sense. They looked completely wrong, completely and utterly… alien."

Jacoby nodded.

"It's like you were seeing beyond the spectrum you're used to."

"Exactly! I saw colors that I can't describe, heard things that I shouldn't have been able to hear, and could smell all sorts of things. Hell, everything I smelled had texture."

"So how do you know they were humans?"

"In the dreams I didn't," Decker replied. "I understood it when I woke up, but when I was dreaming, they were just the things I needed to hunt." He hoped that didn't sound as bad to the doctor as it did to him.

Doctor Jacoby flinched, then recovered himself, and nodded slowly. He pressed for details, but nothing Decker said seemed to do the trick. When the session ended, Jacoby gave him some little green pills that would help him sleep, and insisted that they make an appointment for the following week, same time.

Although opening up gave him some relief, by the time Decker reached his apartment, the sense of impending doom was crawling over him yet again. His head ached, and exhaustion pressed at the backs of his eyes. He was exhausted, but he was also wired.

Despite having told himself that he had no intention of taking any sort of medications, he swallowed one of the little green pills. The effects were almost immediate.

He felt his essence rise from his body below, and looked down on his slumbering shape. His face was drawn, tense and his muscles were stiff. Though he was sleeping his hands were clenched into fists and his legs twitched as much as a dog dreaming of chasing rabbits.

He looked away from himself and studied the familiar apartment. Something was different. Something was wrong. It took him a moment to realize that the walls had become dimly translucent, like stiff banks of fog instead of drywall and reinforced concrete.

He might not have noticed anything more, if the shadows within those walls had stayed still. But they moved, shifted and crawled along the insides of the heating ducts and between the wooden supports and the drywall. He could only dimly see them, but he also felt them, their hunger and need.

More than hunger.

They were angry—propelled beyond conscious thought with the need to cause damage to the source of their hatred. But before they could do so, they would need to locate their prey.

Decker stared down at himself, and at the same time he was aware that the shadow-shapes were doing the same thing, that they had noticed him in his sleep-induced paralysis.

Decker tried to reach down to touch his body, but his hands and arms weren't long enough. His feet would not quite bridge the distance. He tried to cry out a warning, but his throat was locked into silence.

Angry? No. Having found him, the shadow forms were rabid with fury, driven mad by the need to reach him, to cut into his body and rip him into fragments, body and soul. Their hatred was a silvery venom that frothed from their glistening teeth and burned whatever it touched. Their disgust radiated so intensely that it burned. They were silent, but they screamed loudly enough to blind the stars.

The shapes in the walls scrambled closer, pushing slowly through the thick stuff of the walls. Not translucent, not quite, but not what they should have been. No, these were walls of fibrous material. One hand, complete with savage claws, pushed through the heavy strands and revealed the stuff to be spider webs. The strands broke slowly, and as they did so, they allowed more of the black, glistening arm to strain down toward him.

And Decker sat up, a scream locked in his throat. His brow was stippled with perspiration and his lips pulled down in a mask of fear. He realized he wasn't breathing, and gasped for air.

His head was filled with chaotic images, slowly fading. Yet he couldn't escape the feeling that there were things crawling through the walls of his apartment building, pushing toward him through the insulation and wiring, clawing their way past water pipes and air ducts. He tried to silence his breathing, to listen in the darkness.

Nothing.

Nevertheless, he still could feel the hatred, the nearly physical need to end his life. He turned on every light in the apartment and checked under the furniture and in the closets. The very act of searching helped him to calm down, but only to a point. Had he owned a firearm he would have slipped it under his pillow.

He spent the next morning in a series of phone calls, and finally caught the train that took him to the office from which he'd worked for more than a decade.

OK, so Walt doesn't want to see me, he thought. *Well, screw him. Who needs a fucking appointment?* Instead, he just waited in the lobby until his supervisor was heading out for lunch.

Walt took one look at him and sighed.

"Alan." He wasn't a big man, and he tended to look at the floor more than at people. He had somehow lucked his way into a position of authority, and tenaciously clung to that position by never being noticed.

"Walt," Decker replied. "So... what the hell?"

Walt walked faster, and Decker kept up with him easily. As soon as they were outside and out of earshot of anyone who might overhear, Walt finally responded.

"Look, I'm trying to get everything resolved, Alan." He gazed very studiously at the ground. Whatever he was thinking or feeling wasn't strong enough for Decker to get anything from him.

"Walt, I didn't do anything wrong," he said. "I just did my job."

"You've had seizures, Alan." His voice lowered, and he leaned in closer. "More importantly, you pointed a very big finger at Weyland-Yutani. They didn't like that very much."

So there it was, in black-and-white.

"That's my job, Walt. That's what you told me to do."

"I know that, and I'm trying to fix it, believe me, but it's not going well." For a moment Decker felt the man's fear and frustration. They came across clearly before they were suppressed again. "You pissed off the wrong people with your report, Alan. I'm doing what I can. That's all I can say right now."

Walt hurried away, and lost himself in the flow of lunchtime pedestrians. Decker could have followed him, but he already had his answer. He hadn't been forgotten—not exactly—and he still had a champion on his side, such as he was. It was all just a matter of being patient.

Yet patience wasn't one of his favorite things.

Then the feeling hit him again, the sudden weight of a baleful stare. He damned near pulled the muscles in his neck as he glanced around, checking the crowd. But no one seemed to be paying him the least bit of attention.

This is getting old, really fast, he thought. Yet he continued to scan the throngs of people.

Finally Decker headed for home, taking several detours along the way, in case what he was feeling was more than just paranoia. In his apartment he kept his window screens closed, and more than once found himself glancing outside. After a few hours spent feeling stressed as hell, he finally broke down and took another of the pills.

7

THE HUNTED

When he awoke in the darkness of his bedroom, it was with an absolute certainty that he was in danger. In his dreams he might be the hunter, but here he was the one being hunted.

In some ways it was better. In most ways it was worse.

He sat bolt upright with a grunt, then tried to calm his breathing so that he could listen.

Nothing.

Suddenly four figures rushed into the room. At first he wondered if it could be another dream, but instantly he knew better. He tried to speak, but all that came from his mouth was another grunt.

Decker kicked his heel into the stomach of the figure closest to him, and heard a male voice let out a gasp. The man stumbled against the wall and knocked the lamp from the small table where he kept his alarm clock and his water glass.

Something shattered as it hit the ground and the man he'd kicked crawled along the floor, dry-retching. Decker felt a flare of satisfaction at that, but it was crushed under a tidal surge of adrenaline. He started to rise to his knees on the bed, and the second intruder swung something heavy against the side of his head. It connected hard enough to rock him back.

"Careful, Piotrowicz," a voice said in the gloom. "We need him alive."

"Nobody said he had to be intact," his assailant growled.

Decker's head rang from the blow but he shook it off as best he could and went for the one doing the growling.

"Come on, bring it, loser." The man was smaller than him and wiry. He was also a fighter. He blocked the best moves Decker had and shoved him back.

Another one tried to get into the fray, aiming to take Decker from behind and pin his arms. That was a mistake. Decker felt his intentions and reacted to them, bringing his elbow back and around to smash it into the man's face.

His attacker went down hard and Decker turned back to the one who'd hit him in the head, betting that he was the biggest threat.

"Hey, look!" The man's voice was still growling, and despite his mind telling him to close his eyes, he looked. A light exploded in the room, the glare of it enough to blind him.

The same man hit him again before he could recover, and then the other shapes were leaning over him and swinging. The fists that hit him were gloved, but that hardly softened the blows. He did his best to block the assaults. It was a vain effort. There were too many of them. He tried to fight back, might have gotten in one good punch, maybe two.

But they had the numbers and the advantage.

8

AWAKENING

This time the manual release only eluded him for a moment, and then Decker was sliding out of his confinement and trying to stand on weakened knees. He failed and slid to the ground, his limbs shaking.

His head hurt.

His jaw hurt.

Everything was blurry. He was both nauseated and hungry.

As he began to gather his wits, the low vibration under his body told him something that made no sense. He was aboard a ship again, and it was moving. He wondered if it might be another nightmare.

No, he told himself. *If this was a dream, I wouldn't feel so much like shit.* There was only one answer, absurd as it might be.

He'd been kidnapped.

This is insane. He shook his head. *Things like this only happen in movies.*

As his vision cleared, he saw that there were more chambers around him, and he could see that the people inside them were starting to stir. He looked down and realized that he wore only his underwear. The same was true of the people starting to awaken.

He finally managed to find his feet and stood, steadying himself as he looked around. Not exactly a luxury liner, though he'd have been surprised if he found otherwise. Definitely a transport—a working vessel. One quick look around the room and he saw the emergency evacuation chart showing the way to the escape pods. According to the schematic, he was aboard the *Kiangya*. Decker made a note of the name. Someone, somewhere, was going to pay for abducting him, and he needed the details if he was going to press charges.

Decker moved through a doorway and into an open area, where he found lockers. Each had a crude paper label stuck to it, with a scrawled name. One of them said "Piotrowicz," and he was fairly certain that was the name of one of the bastards who had kicked the crap out of him.

Surprisingly, one of the other lockers had "Decker" written on the paper tab. He opened the door and found clothes that were familiar enough. By the time he was done dressing, there were sounds coming from the area he'd vacated.

For a moment he considered bolting. Ultimately, however, there was nowhere to go. He wasn't a pilot and he wasn't a shipmate. He had no idea where he was and no idea where he was going. Much as the thought of escape appealed to him it would do him no good.

They'd probably just beat the crap out of him again.

So he waited, and did a few stretches to make the blood flow back to his limbs. While he was doing so, people started filing into the area to get dressed. Men and women alike, of varying ages. None of them paid him any mind.

One man with dark skin and starkly blond hair mumbled something in what sounded like Swedish and slipped past him, heading for a locker with the name "Hunsucker" on it. How anyone could move that easily after hypersleep was a mystery, but he envied the bastard.

Most of them were in excellent shape. A good number of them had military tattoos and scars to show that they'd been injured more than once. Decker glanced down at his own leg and saw the scar tissue from where the machinery had almost ended his life. It was fading, but still fresh in comparison to a lot of the ones around him.

A man whose body resembled that of a shaved gorilla walked past him and gave him the stink eye. His face was heavily tanned and craggy. His hair was a thick mane of salt and pepper. Despite the nasty look in the man's eyes, he smiled as he noticed Decker.

"Murphy! Tell Rollins her acquisition is awake."

A narrow-faced black man shook his head.

"Tell her yourself, dickhead. She's right behind me."

Sure enough, as Murphy moved another warm body came into the room. The woman was attractive and—unlike most of them—she was already dressed. Her attire was functional, her hair pulled back in a severe bun. She looked at the bruiser for a moment, and Decker could feel the crispness in her attitude. Purely business.

He'd run into this sort of person before. Somehow, he doubted the woman had a friend on the ship. She didn't seem the type to consider fraternizing with anyone. Ever.

"What can I do for you, Manning?" Rollins asked frostily.

"Your man is here and awake," the gorilla replied, and he seemed to have taken it down a notch. "Just thought you'd like to know."

She looked toward Decker, and then nodded to Manning.

"When you're ready, you can escort Mister Decker to get something to eat, then bring him to the medical unit. Let's make sure you didn't break him when you reeled him in." Manning looked as if he'd just stepped in something disgusting, but he kept his mouth shut.

As Rollins turned her back and walked away, Decker looked at her and tried to read something more. Nothing. Then again, he wasn't getting much from anyone. That was hardly unusual, though. Emotions had to be high for him to get any significant impressions.

The only one who seemed at all interested in him was a redheaded fellow, who was glaring in his direction. He was younger than the rest—maybe even a teenager.

Sometimes it was best to establish a pecking order early on. He gave back as much attitude as the kid was throwing.

"You got a problem, red?"

The redhead didn't answer, but he looked away first. That was good.

Manning got into a bodysuit quickly enough, and pointed with his chin toward a door on the far side of the room.

"Chow's that way, Decker. Come and get some food, and then we can get you all set for your meeting."

Instead of answering, Decker just nodded. He wasn't feeling very communicative. What he *was* feeling was hungrier and hungrier. There was no way to tell how long it had been since he'd eaten.

The kitchen was stocked with dried goods and reconstituted milk—and the nectar of the gods, coffee. While he drank and ate, he observed the people around him. There was camaraderie among them. It seemed clear that most of them had been together for a while. He knew the way that worked. Until he'd been sent home, he'd been getting chummy with several of his co-workers. He thought about Luke Rand, and felt a brief pang of guilt.

He'd meant to call Luke, and somehow never got to it. Above and beyond all of the others, Luke had saved his ass when the machinery was pinning him down, and he really should have been in touch. Maybe when they reached their destination— wherever *that* was—he'd find a chance.

Somehow, though, he thought it was unlikely.

He downed his second cup of coffee and the rest of his food, and then looked over at his escort. Manning was nodding toward the next destination.

"What's this about?" Decker asked as they headed down a stark hallway.

Manning's rough features spread in an aggressive example of a grin.

"I'm just here to walk you around, sport," he said, sounding as if he enjoyed Decker's confusion. "It's up to Rollins to fill you in."

"Are you people mercenaries?"

Manning nodded. "We look like Colonial Marines to you?"

"More like ex-Marines."

Manning's broad shoulders rolled into what could have been a shrug or—or maybe he was just stretching.

"Most are," he said. "A few decided to sign up without prior experience."

Before Decker could ask any more questions they'd reached their destination. The medical station was fairly standard, with two examining tables and a bank of screens showing readouts that didn't make sense to anyone who hadn't gone to med school. Rollins was standing there, looking at one of the displays.

"Mister Decker," she said, barely glancing in his direction. "We haven't been properly introduced. I'm Andrea Rollins. I'll be your handler for this trip." She gestured for him to have a seat on the closest table. "Let's get you thoroughly examined."

Handler? He bristled at the word, but did his best not to show it. As he moved toward the table, he saw that Manning situated himself near the door, standing in a casual pose that still made it clear he was ready—maybe eager—for anything Decker might try. There was an edginess coming off of him, and each of his fists looked large enough to wrap around Decker's entire head.

"I'm sure you have questions, Mister Decker. Feel free to ask them." Rollins gestured for him to lie back, and he did, craning his head to look at her.

"How about, why did somebody kidnap me from my apartment?"

"That's an easy one," she replied. "We needed you here."

"Who's *we*?"

Rollins finally made eye contact.

"Weyland-Yutani."

The monitors around him lit up as she flipped a switch. She looked away from him and studied his readouts.

"Is that right?" he said. "Nobody thought to ask me, before sending a goon squad?"

"The general consensus was that your answer would be no. Currently that's not an option." She continued looking over the diagnostics, and he shook his head.

"All of this because of a fucking report? Have you people lost your fucking minds?" Decker sat up fast and Manning looked his way, his body tensing.

Rollins switched off the readouts and shook her head.

"No, and no," she answered. "Your report on New Galveston was annoying, I'll admit, but it was hardly worth kidnapping you or anyone else."

"Well then, what the hell's going on?" he pressed. "How about some straight answers?" His irritation flared and he slipped from the examination table. Manning took a step nearer.

Rollins held up a hand, and the mercenary stopped. Then she turned to Decker.

"That's what we're here for," she said. "Answers. And the first question relates to your condition. I was concerned that you'd been damaged when Mister Manning and his team caught you, but aside from a few bruises, you're in good health." She walked over to a video display and tapped a few buttons. "Physically, at least.

"Mentally, however, you are showing rather substantial signs of Post Traumatic Stress Disorder, which is very curious when you consider that your only real trauma was a minimally intrusive wound to your leg."

Decker stared hard at her, but said nothing.

"Frankly there's nothing in your psychological profile that indicates you'd be so put upon by the damage that it would cause that sort of a reaction. Not only do the medical doctors agree, so do the three separate psychologists who've examined you since your return."

Three? Decker frowned.

"The examinations you endured were bought and paid for by the company. At first we thought we might use you as a scapegoat, on the chance that your report might lead to a lawsuit. But then something more important emerged. You acted very strangely when you were injured, Mister Decker. Strangely enough that we took notice."

"But you just said that the company didn't give a damn about my report."

"I did, and we don't." Rollins smiled. The expression played around her thin lips. "But before that, when you were injured, you made some comments—comments that were recorded for the official record." She walked closer and he could smell the faint aroma of honeysuckle from her perfume. "When you made your claims against Weyland-Yutani, we acquired the recordings, on the off chance that they might be advantageous. Can you imagine what they told us?"

He shook his head. "Not a clue."

"They were filled with psychotic ramblings. There was enough there to put you on medical probation, quite easily. PTSD is a dangerous situation when you work off-world as much as you do. A few calls, a few extra forms filled out and *voila*, you're on medical leave."

"Is there a point at the end of this?"

She smiled again.

"You talked, and we listened, and then we ran those recordings through filters designed to scan for specific words. It's rather standard on our end. There are a lot of… investigations we've initiated over the years. In your case, the words you used and the order in which they were used threw up a red flag." She paused, and then continued.

"Have you ever heard of the *Nostromo*?"

The name sent a shudder through him, though he had no idea why.

"No," he said truthfully. "Should I have?"

"Not at all, and that's exactly the point. You should have never heard of the *Nostromo* because the records on that particular incident were sealed a long time ago."

"What are you talking about?"

"Does the name Ellen Ripley mean anything to you? Or Amanda Ripley-McLaren?"

"No."

That half smile again.

"Actually, I wouldn't have been too surprised if you knew the names. According to the research we've done, you are very likely their descendant. The records get a little wobbly, what with the crisis on Earth and the... troubles the company experienced a while back. But the genetics don't lie."

Decker shook his head.

"So what the *hell* does this have to do with anything?" he demanded.

"Well, as a result of our investigations, we've determined that you have far more use to Weyland-Yutani than as a simple scapegoat." She paused to examine another display, and he waited for her to continue. After a few moments he was rewarded. "You see, your ancestor had a long history with us. She worked onboard a freighter called the *Nostromo* when it ran across a distress signal, and responded.

"The signal's origin was alien in nature."

That caught his attention.

"What's the big deal?" he asked. "We've encountered loads of alien races."

"Ellen Ripley and the rest of the crew discovered something... different. Xenomorph XX121, to be precise." Rollins reached over and activated a video feed. A moment later he saw a slightly grainy image of himself, unconscious and strapped to a medical bed. His video doppelganger was lying flat and restrained, when abruptly his entire body went rigid.

His eyes opened wide, and he started screaming.

9

WITNESS

Decker's skin crawled as he watched. At first there was no sound, but his lips were moving, and when the recorded image of him fell back on the bed, Rollins adjusted a setting.

"How can anything be that vicious? N... spiders? *Spiders!*" Decker tensed instinctively as his voice crackled and slurred, and Rollins fast-forwarded before letting the recording play again. "Blood burns... through the steel... No, not me. *Someone else!*" His voice broke into sobs, and then he continued.

"You really think? Have you seen one of them, close up?" His words wavered, rose in pitch. And then lowered to a different tone, with the hint of an accent he couldn't place. "No. None of us have." And again. Higher, almost feminine. "No, of course not. You're still alive."

The ramblings faded until all they could hear was slurred mumbles and the occasional whimper. Decker's skin crawled as he listened. It was like eavesdropping on a conversation, but with one person playing all the parts. And the words chilled him to the bone, yet he didn't know why. He clenched his fists to get a grip.

Rollins turned the feed off.

"It goes on for a couple of hours. That was recorded during your second seizure, while you were being treated planetside. The first was in the field, immediately after you were injured."

"How long was I like that?"

"As I said, a couple of hours. The best doctors we could consult all said the same thing, really. Extreme panic, delusional ramblings, paranoia, and signs of a complete emotional breakdown." Rollins shook her head. "We could have ruined you right then, Mister Decker, but you gave us reason to keep you around." She smiled again.

He was learning to hate her smile.

"Some of the phrases, the names you employed, were flagged and filed a long while back. From incidents that took place well over a hundred years ago, actually. Your use of those phrases activated long dormant files that were then downloaded to my computer."

"What sort of incidents?"

"As I said, your ancestor was assigned to the *Nostromo*. What I didn't tell you was that three hundred and eighteen years ago Ellen Ripley *destroyed* that ship—a mining transport that was fully loaded with ore and on its way back home. She claimed she had done so to eliminate an alien threat." Rollins paused, and her expression hardened. "That could have been the end of her career, but we were generous. We hired her as a consultant, and sent her back to the planet where the alien life-form had first been encountered.

"You see, she claimed the creature was extremely dangerous. But it was far more than dangerous—it was an asset. An asset Weyland-Yutani should have controlled. *Would* have controlled, had it not been for her actions."

Rollins played with the video monitor a second time and the face of an attractive, dark-haired woman appeared.

"This was Ellen Ripley. Your ancestor." Decker looked at the image and felt his guts roil. *Not right.* It was a familiar face, but...

She looked too *human*.

He turned back to Rollins.

"Did she find the aliens?" he asked.

"She found something. All we know for certain is that the colony on LV426 was lost when a terraforming engine was critically damaged, and overloaded." Decker had worked with terraforming engines. He understood how devastating an explosion could be, coming from one of the gigantic machines. "She escaped aboard a warship named the *Sulaco*, and sent a final transmission, but it was garbled. What she might or might not have said could never be clearly recovered. We think the reactor went critical, and distorted the signal.

"Ellen Ripley and her daughter both halted attempts to capture and study the Xenomorphs. More importantly, they did so while costing Weyland-Yutani a great deal of money and considerable resources.

"It's been a very long time since we've had even the faintest trace of the alien life-form. We had all but given up hope of ever acquiring one. That is, until you came along."

"I'm sorry, but again, what has this got to do with me?"

That smile again. Granted, Rollins was an attractive woman, but there was nothing pretty about the expression.

"Your episodes, and what you said as they occurred, give us reason to assume that somehow—and believe me, we're investigating the possibilities—you seem to have established a connection to these creatures. You've described things you cannot have seen—described aspects of physiology that, when assessed by our computers, come close to describing the life-form Ellen Ripley claimed she'd encountered."

"No... it's impossible..." But his voice trailed away as he said it. At the mention of spiders, he'd nearly jumped from his skin. And the sensation continued—he felt as if he was choking, unable to catch his breath, and his insides were tied in a knot.

He closed his eyes, tried to force the mental assault back but failed. The stench of burning metal ran through his mind and overwhelmed his senses. He felt bile pulse and try to force its way out of his stomach at the thought of something pushing past his gag reflex, something hot and wet and violent. He could damn near feel spindly limbs wrapping around his head.

Another convulsive shudder ran through him. But why?

Spiders had never bothered him before. Why now, all of a sudden?

At the door, Manning crossed his arms and snorted. Decker shot him a sour look.

Rollins regarded him coldly.

"Impossible is no longer a consideration, Mister Decker. Whatever it is you're experiencing, it's enough to make my employers want you on this trip. And what they want, they get."

"Are you going back to the same place again—to LV426?" For some reason, the idea put him on the verge of panic. He resisted an urge to run his fingers through his hair to check for webs.

"Not exactly," she said, and her attitude really started to bug him. He was running out of patience.

"If you're trying to build to something dramatic here, don't bother," he said. "You've already got my attention, and it's not as if I'm going anywhere you don't want me to go. So what the *hell* do you want with me?"

"Fair enough," she said, and she leaned in toward him. "You're an empath."

"Excuse me?"

"We've run the tests." Her voice was cool and professional now, all of the fake emotion gone. "Whether or not you're aware of it, Mister Decker, you have what could be classified as low-level telepathic ability. It's not that uncommon—we've employed others of your kind, in the past—but in your case it's left you in a very unfortunate situation. If you have, indeed, developed a link to the alien life-forms on New Galveston, then you may be the one person who can lead us to them."

The sound of her voice faded, disappearing behind a sharp ringing in Decker's ears at the sound of the planet's name. His chest locked on him, and he attempted to shrug it off. He shook his head to clear it.

"Then *that's* where we're headed," he said. "What makes you think your aliens are there?" But then he thought about the Sea of Sorrows, and it began to make sense. The toxicity had to come from somewhere.

"Blood burns…"

"I think you know, Mister Decker." She wasn't smiling now. "And if those creatures are as deadly as Ripley indicated, then we'll need every advantage we can have at our disposal. Someone who is directly linked to them could prove to be invaluable."

Decker shook his head.

"Not a chance in hell," he said, even as he pushed back the fear. "Even if you're right, you can't make me help you. What you're doing is—"

"Wrong!" Rollins's voice cracked through the air like a whip, and even Manning jumped at the bark. She leaned in, and peered directly at him. "We *own* you. You will go back to New Galveston, and you will help us, because you owe it to the company. There's a debt to be paid, and if you ever hope to regain something that resembles a *life*, you have to start following orders."

But he still wasn't buying it.

"What's this 'debt' shit?" he said. "I don't even work for Weyland-Yutani. I don't owe them a damn thing." He stood up and scowled down at her, refusing to be intimidated. For all of her smiles and her assertions, she was just a pencil pusher, same as him. "The way I see it, you're guilty of kidnapping—and that's still a crime, even for your precious company. Keep it up, I'll find other charges I can bring around, when this is over." He stepped closer to her, seeking to gain the upper hand.

Manning tensed, but stayed where he was.

"I'm afraid you're not catching on here, Mister Decker." Rollins didn't budge. There was an edge to her words. "And I *don't* appreciate being threatened."

With that, she lifted a hand and gestured. The next thing Decker knew, Manning had a hand on his shoulder. The fingers clamped down with a stern, silent warning.

Decker chose to ignore it. He swept his arm around, knocking Manning's grip aside.

"Don't touch me."

Manning's expression barely changed, but the merc shook his

head. He stepped in close and shoved his mass against Decker. It might not have worked on a planet, but the gravity on ships was always a little bit lighter than it seemed, and Decker staggered back.

Manning stepped in again, and brought his elbow into Decker's chest. The impact was solid enough to hurt, but not to incapacitate.

Decker shoved back in retaliation, and then hit the man in the face with a right. The impact carried him forward, and the two of them stumbled across the examination room, careening off one of the tables.

Rollins watched the entire scuffle with what seemed to be mild amusement.

The merc brought his fist around and drove it into Decker's stomach so fast that there was no chance to stop it. The punch was perfectly placed, driving all of the air from his body and sending him to his hands and knees, retching. He could handle himself in a fight, but Manning was apparently just plain better at it.

Rollins stepped in.

"Now that we know you're essentially of sound body," she said, staring down at him coldly, "there's no need to be gentle with you."

After a couple of minutes his insides stopped heaving, and he caught his breath. Decker lurched back to his feet and glared at Manning, who just shook his head a little. A thin trail of blood trickled down from the side of the mercenary's mouth, smearing where he'd tried to wipe it away.

At least he had that. He'd made the man notice him.

"Don't," Manning growled. "You really don't want to."

Rollins motioned for him to be silent, then turned back to Decker and spoke again.

"Let's get this clear," she said. "Ellen Ripley worked for the Weyland-Yutani Corporation, and signed contracts. She owed us a very large amount of money, and she never returned—never paid her debt. In addition to wrecking not one, but two ships, and costing the company what currently amounts to billions of dollars of property damage, she also destroyed a refinery. That's deliberate sabotage.

"So technically, she and her descendants *still* owe a very large debt to the company. The contracts still exist, and the wording is delightfully precise. Even if you could find a court that would challenge us, believe me, Weyland-Yutani is perfectly willing to spend the time and money needed to rip you into little pieces in front of a judge."

"But you abducted me!"

"Prove it."

"Excuse me?"

"Prove it," Rollins repeated, and the smile returned. "Call the police. Oh, wait—there are no police out here on the rim. Just corporations and the Colonial laws, most of which are enforced by Colonial Marines… plus private security forces like the ones we've hired to escort you back to New Galveston." Her eyes cut to Manning.

"Mister Manning, what is your duty today?"

Manning didn't even blink as he spoke.

"To safely escort Mister Decker back to New Galveston, and to retrieve the biological samples needed to pay back the debts that he and his family owe to Weyland-Yutani."

"And who hired you?"

"You did," he replied. "On behalf of Weyland-Yutani."

"Did you at any point see anyone force Mister Decker to join us on this journey?"

"No ma'am," Manning replied flatly. "He came of his own volition." The mercenary grinned.

"Then why did he come?"

"He said something about proving that he was capable of returning to work." He shrugged. "I wasn't really listening. He whines too much."

Rollins looked back to Decker.

"I have thirty-five people onboard this transport who will gladly verify that story. I have documents with your signature to verify that you signed on for this job, in exchange for substantial compensation and to avoid a lawsuit that was being brought against you for the attempted blackmail of Weyland-Yutani officials."

"The hell you say." Decker started to move toward her, but stopped when Manning slid a step in his direction. "You've covered all of the angles, haven't you?"

"Hold that thought," she replied. "We're almost done. I have papers signed by three witnesses to your first seizure, who have all stated that the accident was caused by your own negligence. They've agreed to make the necessary statements in a court of law, should it come to that."

She stepped toward him, until her face was just inches from his. He looked at her eyes, and didn't see even the faintest hint of human emotion.

"And lastly, Mister Decker," she said, "I have the exact address of your ex-wife and three children. In fact, I can tell you where they are at this very moment."

"My kids?" he said.

"Bethany. Ella. Joshua." Rollins's voice softened, but he knew better than to think that it was genuine. "They're lovely children. And you know what? We own them the same way that we own you. Piss me off, Mister Decker, and I can make their lives very uncomfortable, for as long as they live. Every debt that Ellen Ripley accrued will be yours, and if you don't cooperate, it will be theirs.

"And on the off chance that you don't work out as a tool for finding what we're looking for, we can always see if some of your more interesting traits were passed along genetically." Gone was the softness. "Do you understand me?"

The room seemed colder. Alan settled back on the examination table, barely aware that he'd done so. He stared at the woman in front of him, and reached out...

Nothing. He wondered exactly what sort of psychotic bitch could so casually threaten his children, without broadcasting the least bit of guilt.

Even Manning had lost all trace of his earlier smugness. He was staring at Rollins, as well, and there was a hint of fear coming off of him.

"Do you understand me, Mister Decker?" She asked the question again while staring hard into his eyes. "Play by the rules, and all of this goes away. You go home and you get on with your life. Cross me, fail me, do anything at all to make this mission fall apart, and I will bring down the wrath of God—or worse—upon you and your family.

"Do you understand me?"

It took him a minute to remember to breathe. To remember to answer her.

"Yeah," he said. "Yes. I understand you."

"Excellent." She smiled. "We'll get to the debriefing soon. In the meantime, go relax. We'll be arriving at New Galveston within the next few hours."

1 0

BUSINESS AS USUAL

After Decker left the examination room, Rollins stayed and looked over the readouts again, and smiled.

A few moments later she began typing her report.

Long before the ship was in proper orbit around New Galveston, the paperwork had been completed and sent off.

When the response came from her superiors, Rollins read it silently. Then she accessed the ship's onboard computers and deleted all evidence that the transmissions had ever occurred.

11

DECKER

"That is a properly heartless bitch."

Manning said it with a certain admiration in his voice. Or maybe it was lust. The man seemed like the type who lived to get laid.

Decker didn't reply. He didn't trust that he wouldn't say something to provoke the man into kicking his ass. Pissing Manning off seemed like a very bad idea, but that didn't mean they were going to be friends.

"It's nothing personal, Decker," the mercenary continued. "Part of my job is to protect Rollins."

"Fuck yourself, Manning," he replied. "Nothing personal." There were limits.

Manning just chuckled.

They reached the recreation room, where the rest of the mercenaries were gathered. Thirty-five men and women were looking over their weapons, and there was a steady murmur of conversation. There were twenty or so men and the rest were women who looked like they could hold their own in any sort of conflict. It wasn't about the build—it was about the attitude. As a whole they moved like long-time combat veterans. No one wore a uniform, and most were dressed in clothes that were well worn and comfortable. The whole gathering looked up as they entered, and the murmur died away.

Manning spoke first.

"Everyone, this is Alan Decker," he said. "He's going to be working with us planetside. Treat him with respect, and everything will be fine." He looked hard at the skinny redheaded kid. "That goes for you, too, Garth." The kid seemed like he wanted to say something, but the glare Manning shot him shut him up.

Garth. The kid that he'd kicked when they were abducting him, if Decker was right. He looked the right size, and he'd been staring daggers since they came out of cryo.

Most of the crew had patches with names on them, a giveaway that they'd been Colonial Marines at one time. Decker looked at Garth and stepped closer.

"Pretty sure I nailed you when you came to my apartment," he said. "Here's the deal. You don't hold a grudge for that, I won't hold a grudge for what you did to me." He wasn't sure he could manage that, but was willing to give it a try.

The skinny redhead just returned his stare, wanting to pull out his manhood and measure it, but Decker was a seasoned pro. He'd had to stare down locals more than once in his career. The kid looked away first.

"Adams!" Manning said loudly, and a woman sitting in a corner of the room shot him a look, then offered a playful grin.

"I'm right here," she said. "No reason to bellow. Dave over here is loud enough for everyone." The man she spoke about sat right next to her and looked up, surprised. He never said a word, however.

Manning chuckled and shook his head.

"It's time for your good deed of the day, Adams. Talk to Decker here and get him as prepped as you can for our little expedition."

The woman eyed him from head to toe and he returned the favor. She had short-cropped auburn hair and brown eyes. Her skin had the sort of tan that came from working out in the sun, and her face and arms were scattered with freckles. He wondered where else she might have them.

"Close your mouth, chief," she said amiably. "You're going to attract flies." As she moved closer, he gauged her at about eight inches shorter than he was, a hundred pounds lighter, and not the least bit intimidated. She worked with men who could break him in half, and might be able to do so herself. He liked her immediately. Something about strong, confident women did that to him.

Not with Rollins though. That woman was just evil.

When he didn't say anything, Adams just shrugged and pointed.

"Let's see about getting you some equipment," she said.

"Equipment?"

"Listen, we don't have a lot of spares but I think we can probably find you a little bit of armor, and maybe a weapon or two."

He started to ask why, but then he remembered the dreams, and the sheer malevolence they brought. Suppressing a shudder, he just nodded.

"Sounds good to me," he said. "I think I'd kind of like to survive this."

"Then let's see what we can find for you." She set off toward what he assumed was their arsenal, and he followed. She continued talking over her shoulder.

"Listen, I don't know what happened back on Earth, Decker. It's not any of my business. All I know is you're here now, and you're supposed to work with us. So when you get the equipment, remember whose side you're on."

"What do you mean?"

Adams stopped walking and turned to look at him so quickly that he almost tripped over himself coming to a halt.

"I figure you probably aren't here by choice." She looked hard at him, studying his face and his expression, locking eyes with him for a few heartbeats. "I get it. You were shanghaied. You're probably pissed off. Just don't try to take it out on us. We're grunts. We're here to do a job.

"If you get in the way of that job, you're going to get hurt," she added.

Decker nodded. What she said made a world of sense.

"Not on my agenda." Trying not to be obvious, he studied her face, attempting to see beyond the surface. She was a little nervous, but he was fairly certain it had nothing to do with him, and everything to do with the upcoming drop to an unfamiliar territory. "You're right," he added. "I don't want to be here. But I'm not going to blame you or anyone else in your group. You're not responsible for fucking with me. I already have the people I need to blame, and they're the ones who hired you guys."

"Understood," she offered. "But it still needed to be said. This isn't the first time we've worked with people who were 'volunteered,' and a couple of assholes got stupid. But we've learned from our mistakes. You can bet there's going to be somebody watching every move you make."

He just nodded, keeping his face neutral.

"I just want to go home," he said truthfully. "And I want to get there alive. Anything you can do to help that happen is just going to make us friends."

Adams smiled. It lit her entire face.

"Good," she said. "Now, have you ever fired a weapon before?"

"I've used a plasma drill, and did some hunting when I was a kid."

"Where the hell did you go hunting on Earth, and what did you hunt?"

"My uncle was in a preserve club. We went hunting for deer every couple of years."

"You ever get one?" She eyed him critically.

"No. Mostly they brought me to carry supplies."

"Yeah. I thought I saw the eye of a killer in you." She sniggered and started walking again. "That's okay. We'll get you prepped."

He nodded, fully aware that she couldn't see the gesture. He did need to get prepped, though. There was something waiting for him on New Galveston, and he intended to be ready for it. One thing his uncle and his father had always said on those damned hunting trips was that he should trust his instincts.

He intended to listen to that advice.

* * *

Adams showed him how to use two different firearms—a hand-held throwback pistol she called a "reaper," which fired classic .44 caliber slugs, and a 50 watt plasma rifle that worked a lot like the drill he'd trained on back in the day.

The difference was that the rifle fired at long range, and let out small bursts that would blow a hole through the average ship's hull. For that reason Adams trained him how to fire the weapon without a charge in place. In theory, he'd be able to handle the thing when the time came.

She let him take the reaper with him, but didn't let him have any clips—not just yet. Apparently she had to get everything cleared through Manning before allowing him to carry live rounds.

He didn't like it, but he understood it.

Though there wasn't much armor to spare, she did find him a helmet that fit fairly well and an impact vest that would stop most conventional weaponry. It wouldn't do a damned thing to slow down a plasma discharge, of course, but very little could.

The training session lasted close to two hours, and ended when Manning called over the ship's intercom to let them know it was time for the debriefing. Decker found himself surprisingly disappointed. For a little while he had almost been having fun. Adams seemed to feel the same way about it.

When they were all settled in the rec room again Rollins showed up and gave them a rundown on what was expected.

"New Galveston is a colonized planet," she said. "The atmosphere is breathable, and the gravity is roughly eighty-eight percent what you'd find on Earth, so while there will be benefits, you'll need to exercise caution." Decker knew exactly what she meant. Lower gravity meant better endurance, and provided a general feeling of greater strength. But that could be deceptive. While a person could clear a greater distance when running or jumping, more than one novice had knocked himself senseless when working in reduced gravity without taking the time to properly adjust.

"Muller... Muller... Muller!" It was Adams who started the chant, and half a dozen joined in while a bruiser with heavy freckles and copper-colored hair blushed furiously and grinned. Judging from the catcalls, he had probably knocked himself out in the past, and the rest weren't about to let it go. He almost smiled at that.

Rollins waited until they calmed down, and then started up again.

"There are three major settlements, and train tubes that lead to them, but none of them will be close by, so don't expect an easy time of it if you wander off and need backup or support."

Several of the group nodded their heads. Though they all seemed at ease, Decker noticed that all of them were paying close attention.

"Rutledge is the closest city, and it's approximately fifteen miles away by rail. The tube trains don't quite reach the mining colony, but there are regular trucks running to and from the dig."

Wait. Mining colony?

"What mining colony?" Decker was barely aware that he'd spoken. Rollins looked in his direction.

"Since you were last planetside, the company discovered that there was, in fact, a previous dig at the site of your Sea of Sorrows. A trimonite mine, and it's been restarted. There's an active vein, and it should provide a valuable revenue stream—which is fortunate. New Galveston has levied hefty claims against us, for failing to terraform the planet to their specifications." The look she proffered said *fuck you* without any words.

Rollins continued, "There is a crew already in place, medical teams are already available and you'll be pleased to know that there will be a barracks for your use."

Several of the mercs smiled, and Decker was right there with them. He'd been in more than one situation where the best he could hope for was a tent. Actual barracks were damned near a sign of luxury, by comparison.

"There's more to this, of course. And that's why we're footing the bill for your freelancers, Mister Manning." Decker suppressed a laugh. *Freelancers.* It just sounded so much nicer than *thugs-for-hire.* "When the mine was cleared and made operational, we discovered the remains of a vessel. The ship we located is not of terrestrial origin."

She let that settle in with the mercenaries. Decker licked his lips. Suddenly his mouth felt inexplicably dry.

Manning spoke up.

"Is it a configuration that's been encountered before?" he asked.

"No," she replied. "And if anyone would be able to identify alien tech, it would be Weyland-Yutani." Rumor had it that the company had made several of their more radical leaps in technology by retrofitting alien artifacts for "new" advancements.

"Here's the thing," Rollins continued. "Based on a prior agreement, the company has full rights to the land that's being used. Whatever we find, they own. That's why you're here. We intend to keep it that way. As soon as the vessel was discovered, the digs stopped. They've been waiting until your team arrived.

"Do we expect trouble?" she added. "No, we do not. But we intend to be prepared for it."

Decker crossed his arms. As much as Weyland-Yutani seemed to have the government in their pockets, back on Earth there were rules that had to be followed—rules even they couldn't circumvent. All alien technologies were subject to quarantine, and there were procedures that needed to be followed in order to certify any claims of ownership.

But Weyland-Yutani didn't intend to follow the rules. Decker knew it. So did the "freelancers." That was the reason for the strong-arm tactics. It had nothing to do with his pissant reports—once they had identified Decker as an asset, they'd made certain nothing stood in the way of acquiring his "services."

Manning beat him to the next question.

"Any chance there are active life-forms down there?" He didn't look pleased with the possibility.

Rollins surprised him. She told the truth.

"Yes—in fact, we're hoping for it. That's one of the reasons Mister Decker is along. We believe he might have... unique insights into the life-forms you might encounter."

"What sort of insights?" Manning again. Regardless of what he thought about the man, but Decker had to admit that he asked all the right questions.

"That's hard to say with any clarity," she replied. "Mister Decker is a low-level empath. He seems to have established some sort of unique connection with the life-forms. He's essentially along to help you sniff them out."

So much for keeping our secret, Decker thought. *Sorry, Dad.* He noticed several of the mercenaries looking at him with an undisguised combination of curiosity and suspicion. He glanced at Adams, and was pleased to see that she seemed unperturbed.

"And if we find these aliens of yours?" Manning asked. "What do we do then?"

Rollins looked around the room, her expression serious.

"You know the drill," she said flatly. "We want samples of any technologies you find, but your first priority is those life-forms. We want aliens, and we want them alive.

"Each of you has access to an information file. The file belongs to Weyland-Yutani and is considered extremely confidential." She paused to look at the mercenaries one after the other. "Do *not* take this lightly. Do not attempt to copy the information, it's been heavily coded and protected. Your access ends the second you leave the *Kiangya*. Some of the information has been redacted. It's strictly 'need to know,' and covers everything we've learned about the Xenomorph XX121 alien life-form, in the 260 years we've spent trying to capture one."

Her hard-ass attitude didn't seem to faze Manning in the least. He stared back just as hard.

"What do you know about these things?" he pressed. "Are they dangerous?"

"Most likely," she acknowledged. "And are you highly trained professionals who charge exorbitant rates?"

"Yeah, we are," he said. "But that doesn't mean we go in blind. So I'm gonna ask you again—what do you know about these things?"

She took a moment, staring at him, her features entirely unreadable. Then she continued.

"We don't know much, aside from what's contained in the files—our experience with them is limited. They seem to be adaptive. They *are* aggressive. What little data we have indicates that they might secrete a liquid that's toxic, or caustic, or both—there are some details concerning their physiology, and the different stages of their development. They seem to have bred to hunt, and should be approached with extreme caution."

Manning snorted.

"So while we're disposable, you want us to keep them alive."

Rollins shrugged.

"We didn't send you along as glorified security guards. There are three-dozen of you, including Mister Decker. You are being extremely well-compensated," she said. "We expect you to use proper precautions, and be prepared to defend yourselves, but we also expect you to remember that a goodly portion of your pay is decided by how successfully you follow the directives you've been given." She stepped closer to him. "I'm sure you have plenty of your own toys, suited to the occasion. On top of those, we've provided you with everything you need to restrain your targets, once you've located them. That includes foamers."

"What the hell is a foamer?" Adams said. She glanced at Manning, to see if he was pissed at her for speaking up, but he didn't seem overly worried about it.

"A foamer is useless in combat," Rollins explained. "The containers are too bulky and weigh enough to cause problems, especially if you aren't on a level surface, but if you manage to capture one of the creatures, you can essentially cement it in place. Its contents harden fast, and the foam is porous enough that it shouldn't prove lethal to the captive. The company has ways of removing the foam when you deliver your packages.

"So there you have it." She smiled. "Play nice, boys and girls, and you will be richly rewarded."

"That means there's a pretty bonus waiting, if we don't screw this up," Manning said, and he looked at each member of his team. "So let's do it right the first time."

That won him a few smiles.

Decker just felt his stomach churn.

"What if all we find are a bunch of dead aliens?" Manning looked back at Rollins. Decker suspected that the merc already knew the answers to all the questions he was asking, but that he was asking them for the benefit of his troops.

"You still get paid, and handsomely, as long as you return at least a few of the bodies intact."

"And if they're not intact?"

"You get less." Rollins stood a little straighter, indicating that the Q-and-A was at an end. "Any other questions?"

"When do we start?" That one came from Adams, and it elicited murmurs of agreement from the rest.

"We'll be over the drop site in another hour and fifteen minutes. So I'd recommend getting your gear together. In the meantime, study the information in the files. Your lives may depend on it."

"You heard the lady," Manning bellowed. "Let's get moving!" He clapped his hands together with a loud report, and started walking. His people followed quickly, but Decker stayed behind for another moment.

Rollins took the hint.

"Something on your mind, Mister Decker?"

"You never said anything about the ship," he said. "Why keep it from me?"

"We thought we'd give you a little time to adjust to your new... circumstances." Which he took to mean, *"We didn't want you to freak out, and try anything stupid."* But he didn't say any of the things he wanted to say.

"If this goes right, then what do I get out of it?" he continued. "Monetarily, that is. I mean, aside from not getting screwed in a court of law."

She looked surprised, but the expression was fleeting. He was speaking her language.

"I'll look into the details," she said. "As long as you deliver, I'm sure we can arrange something, shall we say, suitably generous."

He nodded, and turned to follow the mercenaries. As far as he was concerned, they were better company.

1 2

DESCENT

There was nothing fun about free-fall in a drop ship. Discussing it during many late night drinking sessions with Rand and the rest of the old crew, Decker had realized that his aversion came down to a lack of control. He didn't like having his life in the hands of someone he didn't know.

And that was what you did every time you hit the atmosphere and rode the air currents through the gravitational pull of a planet, all the while hoping the pilot of the deathtrap you were riding would be capable of landing safely.

So he had a white-knuckle grip on the handholds on either side of his seat. He wasn't alone. Several of the mercenaries were looking pretty green, and broadcasting nervousness that added layers to his own feelings of edginess. Knowing the cause helped, but he couldn't exactly ask them to calm down.

Adams sat across from him, and seemed unfazed. Dave, the man who never seemed to have anything to say, sat to her left. She stuck her foot out, reached across the narrow space between them, and tapped at Decker's boot. He looked her way, and she winked.

"Pritchett likes to shake things up," she said.

"He the pilot?"

"Yeah."

"Remind me to kick his ass, will you?"

Adams chuckled, and next to her one of the guys groaned.

"Get in line," the groaner said. "I'm gonna gut the bastard one of these days." The name on his fatigues said "Piotrowicz." He was lean and hard and scruffy. The Colonials would have likely kept him shaved and showered, but being a "freelancer," he chose to look like a sheepdog.

Decker remembered the name, and repressed an instinct to hold a grudge. Piotrowicz was one of the kidnappers.

"Petey threatens to gut everyone," Adams said. "He thinks it's charming." She shook her head. "It's not."

Piotrowicz shot her a one-fingered salute. She punched him playfully in the arm. Though apparently "playfully" was different among the mercenaries, because she hit him hard enough to bruise, and both of them laughed.

The entire ship bounced and rattled and lurched hard to the right. Piotrowicz groaned again, and given their first meeting, Decker couldn't muster much sympathy. Manning looked toward the pilot's cabin as if he was considering heading up there and breaking heads. He might have, too, but it would have meant risking bouncing across the cabin. Instead he reached for the radio he already had strapped to his shoulder.

"What the fuck are you doing, Pritchett?" he demanded.

"Got turbulence, boss," was the tinny reply.

"No shit, man," Manning said. "What, are you *trying* to find it?" He grimaced as the whole thing rumbled and rolled again. "I think you might have missed some there."

"Bad atmospheric storms. I didn't find them, they found us."

Decker didn't like the sound of that. He remembered the New Galveston weather being sedate at the worst of times. It had rained, true, but not often in the daylight hours. That might mean they were heading down at night—which bothered him even more.

Some things see better in the dark. He scowled at the thought. He didn't need to do that to himself. He had enough crap going on in his head. *Too much.*

A few moments later the worst of the turbulence faded, and

the people around him relaxed a bit. Piotrowicz shook his head.

"Seriously. I need to mess him up."

"Well, he said there were storms," Decker offered.

"Just seems like, no matter where we go, he finds the worst weather. No one's that unlucky *all* the time."

"Yeah?" Adams elbowed her neighbor with less force than she'd punched him. "Then how do you explain your love life?"

Before Piotrowicz could respond, the ship veered sharply and then slowed its descent.

"How's the weather, Pritchett?" Manning sounded annoyed. He looked it, too.

Decker was okay with that.

"Weather looks good, chief. But there might be a problem."

"What sort of problem?" The head mercenary's frown deepened, and his craggy face looked like stone.

"I'm not getting any responses to my hails."

"Think it's the storm?"

"Negatory. I'm picking up commercial signals, but I'm not getting anything from the site where we're landing."

"Maybe your weather did in their communications."

"Yeah, about that," came the response. "There wasn't *exactly* a storm." Pritchett sounded guilty.

Adams chuckled. Muller waved a fist in the air, but he grinned as he did it. Dave said nothing.

Piotrowicz mumbled something murderous.

"We'll discuss that later," Manning said. "For right now, just get us landed, and let's see what we find."

Pritchett put them down gently, and they did, indeed, land at night. As they disembarked, the air was pleasantly cool, if a bit damp. It had been raining and the Sea of Sorrows was a leveled playing field of darkness.

Several people came out to meet them. Among them was Lucas Rand, whose bulldog face fell into a slack look of shock, and then lit up with a fierce smile. Before Decker could do much of anything, the heavy man had him in a bear hug, and was lifting him easily off the ground.

"Good to see you, brother!"

Alan felt a wash of affection run through him. He hadn't realized how much he liked the other man until he saw him again. They had always worked well together, but sometimes Decker forgot that. He tended toward forgetting anything but the work, on most occasions. It was easier that way.

The mercenaries made a few snide comments, but Decker ignored them for the moment and walked with his friend.

"What the hell's been going on around here, Luke?"

"You name it, it's been happening, man." He shook his head and pointed at a dark patch on the long run of sand. A silhouette clearly defined the edges of a Quonset hut, illuminated by a few ground lights, and nothing more. "Remember the trimonite? It wasn't a fluke. There was a *lot* of it. Apparently it's a really rich vein, and even though you kind of pissed off a lot of people, your report led the company right back to the mine they used to have here. As soon as we went down, we found the old shafts.

"They've already started to bring it up. The processing will have to take place off-planet, of course—too many toxins."

"You found the original mine shafts?"

The tunnels are dark to them…

"Yeah, but your guess is as good as mine where they lead," Rand replied. "Apparently there was some sort of collapse, and they decided the mine wasn't viable. The next thing you know, the records got buried." Decker had his doubts about that— it was too convenient. "The boys from Weyland-Yutani claim they didn't even know they had a mine here, until you fingered them for negligence." Luke looked at him askance. "How's that working out for you? Any time I heard from them, they sounded pretty pissed off."

"We're… coming to an agreement." He couldn't tell Rand the truth. Telling the truth had already cost him too much. No way he was going to add anyone else to the collateral damage.

"Good." Rand smiled. "To be honest, they've been pretty cool about all of this. I mean, finder's fees and the whole thing."

"Finder's fees?"

"Yeah. We're being kept on as consultants. Well, some of us. A few of the team have already moved on, but the people with the technical skills have been hired on as subcontractors."

Decker looked at his friend and frowned. That didn't sound right. Before he could comment, however, Manning bellowed for his attention. He turned to look back at the main group, and the leader of the mercs gestured for him.

"We have a meeting, Mister Decker," he said. "*If* it fits into your busy schedule. Let's get this done!"

Ten minutes later they were settled in a prefabricated hangar large enough to park several different heavy loaders and drills. Most of the area was filled with silent, hulking machinery, but a corner had been set up with tables, chairs and a coffee machine.

Thank God, Decker thought as he made a beeline for it.

The mercs loaded their cups before the discussion began. The group included all of the mercenaries, several of the men with whom he'd worked on the colonization project, and a number of the mining staff.

A Weyland-Yutani company man named Willis looked everyone over and nodded, apparently satisfied. He had the air of a bureaucrat with a side of dictator—a little short, a little round at the hips and desperately trying to cover up a growing bald patch on the top of his head.

"Rollins gave me a full recap of what she'd discussed with you, but the information she had was dated," he said, addressing the newcomers. "We've resumed our mining operations. Earlier today we made some new discoveries at the dig site and the location of the buried vessel."

He waited a few seconds, during which time Adams settled herself to Decker's right and took a swig of her coffee. He tried not to be obvious as he glanced over at her.

"So here's the situation," Willis continued. "Near as we can figure out, we were wrong on our initial beliefs regarding the ship and its occupants."

"What do you mean?" The question came from one of the mercs, a hulking brute named Krezel, with dusty brown hair and a mustache that would have shamed a walrus. He shut up as soon as he spoke, skewered by a look from Manning.

"Well, initially we believed that the ship must have crash landed on the planet a long while back. We're talking upwards of a thousand years, though it's hard to say. Before the colonization began, there were a lot of violent storms, and according to the Terraforming Survey Team, there's a very strong possibility that heavy tectonic shifts occurred regularly, back in the day." Nothing surprising there, since Decker had taken part in the writing of that report.

"So it might be a few hundred years, or it might be a thousand. Whatever the case, the further we dig, the more it looks as if the ship was in the process of taking off when it crashed."

Manning spoke up this time. "Taking off from where?"

"Hard to say, but there's evidence that there might have been a settlement here—possibly even a fully functioning base of some sort." He smiled tightly. "That means that the technologies we were hoping to find might be substantially more extensive than we'd originally hoped." He paused to look around, taking in the entire group. "So you can expect a heightened level of security.

"And depending on what you find, you might also expect substantially larger bonuses, as well."

Before anyone had the opportunity to respond, Willis continued.

"Effective immediately, no one goes to town. No one takes the trucks or the rails. All communications are in full lockdown. We're talking a find that may be bigger than anything we've run across since first contact with the Arcturians."

Chatter erupted throughout the group, and Decker felt a sudden wave of excitement that washed over him like a wave. The Arcturians had been the first alien race mankind had encountered, and those initial meetings had marked a turning point for the human race. *Especially* for commercial entities like Weyland-Yutani. Research and development had burgeoned, and most of the company's holdings had been invested in developing new technologies.

The intensity of their reactions surprised him—euphoria mixed with unmistakable greed. Apparently several people were expecting to get very rich off of this expedition.

Decker shook his head to clear it of the incoming emotions.

"That's probably a bad idea—cutting ourselves off from the rest of the planet," he said. "If we encounter any living creatures down there, from what I've been able to tell, they're not going to welcome us with open arms. Things could go very wrong, very fast, and we won't have any backup."

A couple of the mercenaries snorted their derision, and Rollins turned toward him.

"That's why we've brought this very capable group of freelancers, Mister Decker," she said, playing to the crowd. "We have every confidence that they will be up to the task, and deal with every eventuality."

The mercs echoed her confidence, and he fell silent. Willis spoke up again.

"So it's business as usual tomorrow, everyone," he said to the miners. "But before anyone goes *anywhere* that hasn't yet been explored, Mister Manning and his team go in to examine everything. Steer clear, and give them room to do their jobs."

That yielded more reactions, and not all of them were happy. Decker made a conscious effort to shut down the sensations—it was a little like closing his eyes until he was squinting. The feelings were still there, but not as intense.

Rand was looking at him and frowning. Decker didn't need to read minds to understand that his friend was wondering how much he knew. But neither of them spoke—there would be time later.

Maybe.

The group broke into clusters, the largest of which gathered around Willis. A few of the more disgruntled men and women—

all mining staff and subcontractors—were pressing him for information. A few voices were raised, and he held up his hands in the attempt to quiet them down.

As he digested what had been said, he found his mind wandering. Like most people, he was fascinated by the concept of alien species. As the human race moved further and further out among the stars, new colonies proliferated, and provided him his bread and butter. But he had never encountered evidence of extraterrestrials—not on his own.

And now, even if he failed to locate anything that was alive, he would get to see the remains of an alien vessel first hand. As exciting as the prospect might be, it also filled him with dread.

Strong fingers clutch the soft face that chokes and exhales in desperation. Decker tried to shake the thought away. Not fingers. Legs. Not hands, something worse.

As if she had been reading his mind, Adams leaned in and spoke to him.

"I've never seen anything alien," she said. "This should be amazing."

"I sure as hell hope so." He knew he should sound more enthusiastic, but the sensation wouldn't go away.

Darkness, teeth, a low hissing sound and the scrabble of claws. The images wouldn't stop, flashes that made no sense, that came from somewhere else and tried to make themselves at home in his mind.

It was the old feeling, back again—that something was out there and looking for him. Not just for prey, but for *him* in particular. He shook his head and focused, but nothing changed.

It must have been written on his face, too. The look Adams cast his way wasn't subtle.

"Wow, Decker. You need to get laid as badly as me."

That did the trick. For a moment, at least, the idea of being stalked faded from his mind.

"That an invitation?" he asked. *Nothing ventured, nothing gained.*

Adams eyed him silently for a moment. One eyebrow went up.

"Tell you what," she said. "Buy me a drink, and we'll talk."

1 3

FOR LOVE OF MONEY

Rand watched the mercenaries heading for the dig site.

Decker was with them. Alan Decker, the man he'd sold out. Guilt was an ugly thing, and it was certainly doing ugly things to him while he watched his friend, heading toward the Quonset hut with a battalion of some of the scariest people he'd ever seen.

Marines were bad.

Mercenaries were worse. Mercenaries didn't have to follow the rules.

Rand thought about that, and felt his stomach do a few back flips. If Decker knew about what he'd done—how he'd sold him out for a profit—well, there might be a little extra money in the pockets of a few mercenaries.

Yeah, Rand thought, he'd better watch his step, as long as they were around.

The Sea of Sorrows was an awful lot of sand, and there were places down below where a body could disappear. He'd learned about a few of them when he was hired on by Weyland-Yutani, as a consultant. Rand knew things about the company. The difference between him and his friend was that he was smart enough to not report the things he knew.

And what did that get him? A nice retirement package, and a few opportunities to make even more money.

ALIEN

Andrea Rollins was somewhere in orbit over the planet. He knew that. He knew that because she had been responsible for his current employment. And because the last time she'd been around—after Decker's accident got him taken away—she'd asked him to assist her. First, by pointing a finger when the time came, and second, by placing a few additional pieces of equipment around the mines when he was inspecting the site for "environmental issues."

He didn't ask what the devices were. He didn't need to know.

Rollins knew about the mines. Well, not true. She knew that there had been mines in the past. She knew where they were because of the message Rand had sent her, shortly after Decker's mishap. One man's misfortune was another man's opportunity. He had never once wished ill toward Decker. He just didn't let his friendship stop him when the time came to further his own personal goals.

And there it was, that little dig of guilt that twisted his guts around and around.

He looked at the hut and the sunlight painting the black sands the color of dried blood. Decker and the mercenaries were gone from sight. That helped a little.

Rand could have pushed harder, asked for the company to take it easy on him. But that might have compromised his career opportunities. On the other hand—and there was always an other hand, when you looked hard enough—Rollins had assured Rand that his friend could take care of himself. They'd asked him a lot of weird questions about Decker and he'd answered them.

They thought Decker was psychic or something. Okay, let them believe whatever they wanted. Alan was back and maybe he would be all right.

Rand looked at the hut for another minute and then headed back to the barracks. The mines gave him the creeps. The ship they'd found gave him nightmares. He'd never been one to hope for an encounter with other life-forms. As far as Lucas Rand was concerned, the human species was screwed up enough, and didn't

90

need any help when it came to making the cosmos more toxic.

Somewhere in the offices there was a shot of vodka with his name on it.

When Decker was a kid, his father had told him that there was nothing that couldn't be solved with words. He'd said that a lot, especially when Decker's empathic abilities flared and the kids around him seemed more like potential enemies than friends. It happened less and less as he adjusted to the emotional tides and came to understand that not every sensation he felt pertained to him. Sometimes people were just pissed off because they were having a bad day—not because of anything he had done.

When he was a teenager his old man had changed the words a bit. He said there was nothing that couldn't be solved with a handshake and an honest negotiation.

And when he was grown and his father spoke his words of wisdom, they changed for the last time. That was when his dad told him there was nothing in the world that couldn't be solved with a shot of whiskey and a few kind words.

That last part proved true enough with Adams.

A few drinks with the mercenaries had let him clear the air. Garth would never likely be his close friend, but at least they left the rec room with an understanding between them. Same with Piotrowicz. The latter even bought him a beer to show there were no hard feelings.

Adams had a much nicer way of expressing herself. She was as enthusiastic in bed as she was about almost everything else. For a little while he forgot about the background noise in his head and focused on the lean, muscular woman in his arms. After too long on his own it was nice to share heat with someone else, especially someone with a voracious appetite and a surprising imagination.

When he woke in the morning she was gone. He'd have been surprised to find her still there.

1 4

BREAKFAST

As the sun rose, the air had a cold edge to it that Decker found invigorating. The small army of mercenaries were gathered around a table and dressed for business, and he joined them. Adams was sitting with Piotrowicz and a small cluster of the others, and they made room for him.

"Manning's already made the rounds," Piotrowicz said, his voice low. "We're going down to the site where they found the ship. That's where we're likeliest to find what we're looking for, so that's the best starting point." Then he went back to inhaling the food on his plate. The eggs were fried, not scrambled—an unheard-of luxury on a site like this. Decker couldn't begin to imagine how Weyland-Yutani had pulled it off.

Adams spoke up.

"You'll have to forgive Piotrowicz. Sometimes he thinks stating the obvious will make him look smarter." At that, the merc paused for a moment, in between mouthfuls, to let his middle finger speak for him.

"Still ain't working there, slick. You may *want* to sound smart, but the truth's plain to see." The speaker was a hulking man with a shaved head, where he had a tattoo of a military insignia. It was badly done, and the letters were largely illegible.

Piotrowicz looked at the man—easily a hundred pounds

larger than he was—and shook his head.

"I keep forgetting they trained you to speak, Connors," he said. "What's that supposed to be on your skull again? I think it's the Girl Scouts, isn't it?"

Decker settled back and chowed down quickly, eating even faster when Manning announced that they'd be leaving in fifteen minutes. If he hurried, he'd have time for another cup of coffee.

After breakfast he dumped his cutlery and tray and got that second cup. While he was adding lethal doses of cream and sugar, Adams moved over and started pouring herself another cup.

"So, last night was fun."

Decker looked at her from the corner of his eye.

"Wasn't sure if I was supposed to say anything."

"I appreciate the discretion."

"But yeah," he added. "It was definitely fun."

"Good. Maybe we can try it again tonight." She walked away before he could respond. His day seemed a little brighter, despite the feeling that was starting to crawl through his stomach.

There was no escaping it. The longer he thought about going underground, the more his guts tried to twist themselves into a knot. It wasn't just the tunnels, though—it was the entire planet that freaked him out. It wasn't rational, but it was extremely potent.

He caught up with Adams, and held up the reaper.

"So, where do I get a clip for this thing?"

She smiled. "Oh yeah. Forgot that part." She took him over to deal with a salt-and-pepper haired man named Dmitri, who gave him four long clips with fifteen rounds each. After a brief discussion, the man also handed him a second weapon.

"Plasma rifle. Be smart, keep warm and locked. And don't fire near anything you want to keep in one piece." Dmitri's accent was so thick it took a few seconds to fully translate what he'd said, but Decker nodded and smiled just the same.

When they'd moved a little further away, Adams took the plasma rifle from him, and gave him a refresher. He was glad— that wasn't the kind of weapon that allowed for mistakes. Not if you wanted to keep all of your limbs.

"Short barrel, so you can maneuver," she said. "There are three cells, all of them are charged…" She flipped the weapon around to show him the indicators. "Fires incredibly small and incredibly hot rounds of plasma. The barrel is trimonite. Anything less and it would melt by the fourth round fired. Seriously, don't fuck around with this one. You have an automatic setting and a selective setting. Automatic, you pull the trigger and the rounds come out fast and hot until your first cell is dead. Pull the trigger again and you get the same thing until the second cell is dead.

"I've never, *ever*, seen anyone pull the trigger a third time. Mostly whatever you're aiming at is long gone before the second time the trigger gets pulled."

She flipped it back over with ease and great familiarity. Decker saw several stickers that had faded almost completely away. One was a pink pony. Another had Adams' name scrawled on it. She was trusting him with one of her weapons. He felt a quick flash of gratitude but quelled it. She wasn't the sort who'd want to be thanked—especially not in front of the others.

He'd have to think of something appropriate for later.

"Right here is the safety," she continued. "Leave it on." She pointed to a second button, this one protected by a small flip-case. "This is the selective fire switch. You're set for single shots. Seriously, keep it that way—you'll have maybe a hundred and eighty rounds. You go full-auto, and you're going to level everything you aim at, but it won't last long.

"Got it?"

Damn if she didn't look sexy with that serious expression on her face and an assault rifle in her hands.

"Got it."

"Good. Let's go hunt bugs."

"Bugs?" The word called up images that ran through his mind and sent ice skimming down the length of his spine.

"Bugs," she repeated, looking at him with a strange expression. "Did you read the information? Bugs. Those fuckers are seriously creepy. Besides, what else are you going to call aliens? You ever see a cute, furry alien?"

"You've done this sort of thing before?"

Adams shook her head and smiled.

"Not me, unless you count a few indigenous rodents," she replied. "There's a first time for everything, though. I'll hunt anything, as long as there's money in it." She looked at the pulse rifle, and handed it back to him. "The most this little number has done is blow away a few critters the size of my hand."

"Yeah?"

"Screamed like a monkey when I was shooting them, too."

"Who did, you or the critters?"

"Probably a little of both."

She strode toward the exit and he followed, not quite certain if she was serious.

Most of the freelancers looked more like Colonials when they were suited up and ready for business. The biggest difference that Decker could see was that the mercs seemed to take their jobs a bit more seriously than a few of the Marines he'd met in his time. Then again, he'd normally run across the Marines when they were off duty, and ready to have a drink or two.

They walked across the hard-packed sand *en masse*, and the stuff gave way under his feet as they made their way toward the distant shaft. He didn't like the feeling, and for a moment he thought he felt a pain in his leg.

The Quonset hut was the only structure of any size, and there was little around it except for the evidence of construction—mounds of sand that had been pushed into a full-sized hill and then slowly washed back down. A few pieces of heavy equipment that looked like dying, metallic dinosaurs in the middle of a vast nothing. Areas that had been laid out and partially paved, but never finished. Everything was happening too fast and, as he had seen on any number of sites, there was a lot of activity with no cohesive result.

They waited for several moments outside the hut before the

doors were opened to them. Willis was waiting inside, along with three others dressed in clothes meant to endure a rough environment. The interior of the place was lit by stark white lights that nearly shamed the sun—a slight case of overkill, to be sure, but there was a lot of equipment casting shadows, towering all around them and making Decker feel distinctly claustrophobic.

Willis and Manning talked softly while everyone filed in. Thirty-six extra bodies took away most of the free space in the area and left Decker feeling vaguely claustrophobic. Once they were inside Manning called roll one more time, and they headed for the shaft itself.

It was hard to miss. What hadn't been done outside was offset by what *had* been accomplished on the inside of the place. The lift platform was huge—large enough to accommodate all of them, and a lot more besides. It had to be, because it was how the company moved equipment into the shaft and would, in time, take out the trimonite. And like all of the heavy-duty equipment he'd seen in his life, the damned thing looked ancient. Sometimes Decker wondered if lifts were built pre-scarred and rusted.

He looked around the interior of the hut, using curiosity to push back the anxiety that was trying to overrun him. But the paranoia was making a comeback, and there wasn't a thing he could do about it. There were things around him. He'd felt them before, and he was feeling them now. His stomach rolled at the thought. His pulse was too fast, and he could feel sweat forming on his brow.

"Come on," he said to himself under his breath. "You can do this." No one else was close enough to hear. He steeled himself, and moved with the rest.

The lift floor felt more solid than the sand outside. That was oddly comforting—at least until the first lurching motion, and the slow descent began.

Where the hut was very bright, the tunnel was not. In very short order the only light came from above them, and that dwindled the lower they went. The lift itself was dimly lit. When the darkness was almost complete, the waves of emotion returned with a vengeance. Decker bit his lip to stop from making a noise.

Then, to his surprise, they began to fade again. It was almost as if he'd passed them by, so that they remained above as the mercenary group moved lower and lower.

Willis spoke up, talking to no one in particular.

"Anyone ever been in a mine shaft before?" He was answered by one of the freelancers Decker hadn't met.

"Hell, no," the man said. "I was born and raised on Earth. Anything worth mining there was stripped away a long time ago." He said it like it was a joke.

"You're not far off, actually," Willis responded. "That's one of the reasons Weyland-Yutani got into mining colonies. Thanks to automation, it doesn't take too much effort for a decent payoff."

"Well, you sure as hell couldn't get *me* to work in a place like this—not for long." It was Connors, the hulk with the shaved head. Big as he was, he looked nervous.

The area opened up as they moved past the first open level of the mine. There wasn't much to see, except for the machinery used to run the mines, and the generators used to run the machinery. New equipment stood next to old machines, many of which were so old that they were unrecognizable in their decay. Rods of pitted metal stuck out at odd angles, like the bones of long-dead creatures.

All too soon the darkness ate them again.

"How far does this thing go down?" Piotrowicz's voice cut past the low mechanical hum of the lift.

Willis looked around the artificial twilight, and then up at the walls of the shaft.

"Just over seven thousand feet." One of the mercenaries let out a low whistle. Their guide nodded, and Decker looked along with everyone else. The metal here was darker, decidedly in worse shape, corroded by time and moisture. "Most of this shaft was already here from the previous operation. Nine levels of mining. We've got the first three up and running, and have partially cleared a total of six. It's down at the bottom where we found the ship. The lift was severely damaged there, but we cleared it and restored it easily enough."

The mercenaries stared at the walls with all the fascination of kids going to their first museum. There was a sense of age here, of antiquity. Decker felt it, too, now that the sense of dread had faded down to a whisper.

When the lift finally hit bottom with a lurch that sent them all staggering, the walls opened into a cavernous area that was crudely but solidly built. The walls were solid stone now, hollowed out and reinforced at regular intervals. There were a few lights, which hardly pierced the gloom at all, so they couldn't really tell how large the chamber was. They might as well have been on a different planet. Thick layers of a darker material ran through the brown and tan earth. If he had to guess, that would be the trimonite, but it was only a guess. What he knew about mining wouldn't even make for decent bar conversation.

"Where's this ship you found?" Manning's voice carried easily, and echoed, causing him to duck his head.

"Just down this way," Willis answered, pointing into the shadows. "Have any of you ever been on an alien vessel?"

No one had—not even Manning.

Willis nodded, as if it was the answer he'd expected.

"Well then, this is going to blow your minds, guaranteed." He walked over to a truck, old and functional and with a broad flatbed in the back, large enough to carry several containers of ore. While he climbed into the driver's seat, Manning settled into the passenger side, and the rest clambered onto the flatbed. It was a tight fit and the truck rocked as they climbed aboard.

The engine started up with a surprising growl, and the vehicle lurched into motion, causing them all to grab onto any handhold they could find—including one another. In the glow of the yellow headlights, they could see a well-worn pathway with hard-packed dirt.

About five minutes later, they were staring at proof of alien life.

1 5

THE SHIP

Before they even saw the vessel, they moved past the seemingly endless construction materials. There were pallets upon pallets of scaffolding supplies, mezzanine flooring, and industrial metal posts for assembling the platforms they'd need to examine their find. The materials were stacked to around seven feet in height in some places, and blocked off much of the path to the excavation site.

In the distance they heard the hum of generators, and the sound grew stronger as they moved forward.

The ship itself was massive. Parts of it had been melted by blasts of extreme heat, or perhaps by volcanic activity. It didn't sit level on the ground, but was canted slightly as if it still sought to take off. The structure was split along one side, the hull shattered and torn and long since filled with dirt.

The ship's surface looked almost papery in places—not as if it was made of paper, but as if it had been crumpled up and then smoothed again. If there had ever been markings on the exterior, they were hidden by dirt or stripped away by the years.

There were holes everywhere. The hide was ruptured, torn, and burnt. There were places where several different levels were visible through the same gaping wound. It must surely have been designed to carry hundreds, if not thousands—assuming the inhabitants were anywhere close to human in size.

Around the ship, the initial excavations had leveled the ground out. The tracks from heavy treads showed evidence of what had happened before, but the actual vehicles were gone, either taken back to the surface or moved to another part of the cavern.

Decker stared at the thing. The sheer size alone was staggering, yet somehow the designs were... *wrong*—not at all what he would have expected. Some of its facets deviated so much from the mechanics of Earth that he couldn't even begin to grasp how they might have worked.

The greatest anomaly of all, however, was the fact that it simply didn't belong. It was meant for the sky, the space between the stars. Had he found a whale in the desert, it wouldn't have seemed any more out place.

"Shit on a shingle. It almost looks... organic." Piotrowicz turned his head sideways as he stared.

"Near as we can figure, it sort of is. Or was, at least." Willis spoke with an almost paternal sense, as if this was a pet that he had raised, and now that it had won a blue ribbon, he actually radiated pride. "The walls, the floor, even the doorways, they all have features akin to plant life. Doctor Tanaka is in charge of examining the ship, and she thinks it's distinctly possible that the entire thing was grown."

Decker frowned. There was a question niggling at the back of his mind, but he couldn't quite draw it out into the open.

Willis stopped speaking, and stood quietly as the freelancers moved forward.

The area had been excavated with care, and the hard surface above them looked dry, as far as they could tell. Decker wasn't a geologist, but he felt comfortable with the knowledge that the roof was secure.

The damned thing was too big for them to see all of it. Though lights had been secured to the ceiling above, they were dim, casting the area in a perpetual twilight. The walls of the ship stretched away into shadows. Near the entrance there were several large power cells, most of which had not yet been set up, and two generators that were going full-steam ahead.

"There are plans to bring down more lights," Willis said. "You can see why."

"Where is Doctor Tanaka?" Manning's voice was calm, and even a bit subdued. The man was squinting along the side of the ship, trying to see as far as he could. "And what are *those* things?"

He pointed to a thick column of glistening black that ran from the ceiling down to the ship. It didn't look like a part of the vessel itself, and Decker recognized it instantly for what it was. The same sort of deposit that had cracked under his foot, broken into his skin, and nearly cut through his leg the last time he'd been on the planet.

His guts twisted again, but for entirely different reasons this time. There was no fear—merely a memory of the pain and the sudden assault that had sent him into seizures.

"You okay?" Adams was frowning at him, and her hand touched his forehead. Her fingers felt warm, but only because his own flesh was clammy.

"I will be," he said, regaining his composure. "Just taking it all in."

She didn't look as if she believed him, but she didn't push it, either.

"Doctor Tanaka is tracking one of the growths, like the one you pointed out. They're hollow, apparently, and composed of pure silicon. From what she's said to me, they're everywhere inside the alien vehicle." Decker focused on the thick column of fused sand. It had an odd beauty to it, and glistened almost wetly. There were fine striations and swirls throughout the surface of it that made him think of spun sugar or...

Or a spider's webs.

The aliens they were supposed to track—the ones they were supposed to capture. Would they have come from the ship? If they were still around, would they still be aboard? Or was it possible that the glossy tunnels had been their way of escaping from the wreckage?

Dave—or as Decker now thought of him, Silent Dave—looked at the tunnel and frowned heavily. Decker could feel the edginess radiate from the man like heat, but aside from the frown he gave no sign of his heavy agitation.

"What?" Decker asked.

Dave looked at him for a long moment.

"The Xenomorphs. There was something about them binding their hosts."

Before Decker could respond Manning spoke up.

"Where do they go? The tubes."

Everywhere. He almost said it. Willis answered instead.

"We're not sure yet. We only discovered them after we started digging the ship out. At first we thought they were a part of the original structure, but it almost seems as if they were later additions. They definitely aren't the same material as the vessel itself."

Decker joined in.

"They're silicon deposits," he said. "I've seen them before, topside, where many of them actually break the surface. They're all over the Sea of Sorrows."

Willis nodded.

"The way they've spread shows certain organic tendencies. Whatever they are, some are large enough to allow a human being to move around inside, and there's a distinct logic to their structure. Yesterday Doctor Tanaka and several of her team members broke open one of the larger ones and entered, taking along supplies. They hope to map some of the growth."

"That doesn't sound like a good idea." Decker spoke softly. Actually it seemed full-on insane to him. The integrity of the things had to be questionable at best.

"They don't really have a choice, Mister Decker," Willis said. "The 'silicon deposits,' as you call them, are widespread. They run through a lot of the ship's interior, and throughout the surrounding area. Doctor Tanaka feels it's important to understand their nature and purpose."

"Why aren't they using mechanical probes?" Manning

frowned as he tracked one of the columns into the ceiling of the cave, far above them. "That seems a lot less risky."

Decker agreed silently. Mapping probes would make it possible to assess the entire range of tunnels without ever having to set foot into them. Engineering teams often used them before they set down the component parts of the terraforming engines. The damned things weighed-in at several tons each, and having one of them fall through weak areas in the soil could prove catastrophic.

"They tried," Willis said. "There's low-level radiation in the area, and that interferes with the sensors. So it has to be done by hand. But Tanaka should be perfectly safe—the levels are too low to be hazardous."

Two of the mercs, Dave again and Muller, looked skeptical, and reached for their packs. Decker had a feeling they were going to check for themselves, and determine whether or not the radiation was a serious threat.

Willis looked at them and shook his head.

"You don't have to worry," he said. "Believe you me, I wouldn't be here if there was a serious threat to anyone's health." He smiled to try to make it into a joke. "I'm far too fond of my own skin to risk it here."

No one laughed.

"It doesn't seem to affect simple communication," he continued, "and the further we get from the ship, the less radiation we encounter. It's possible that the source of the interference comes from the wreckage itself. At any rate, while Tanaka is focusing on the tubes, Doctor Silas is exploring on the other side of the ship. Apparently there's a lot of very old damage that was done to this thing when it crashed here, and he thinks he can figure out what made that happen."

"No one's gone inside yet?" Manning stared at a hole in the side of the vessel. It was very old, and there were signs that they'd had to excavate a good deal of dirt from the interior.

"Oh, they've been inside, but they couldn't get very far. There's a lot of damage. Fire damage, possibly, or something else. It looks like a few of the interior walls were melted, at any rate."

"So we're just supposed to go inside the ship," another merc said, "without any idea what we'll find, and no backup?" Decker liked her immediately—she had a brain. A few others murmured their agreement.

"No, Hartsfield," Manning replied. "I thought we might just sit out here, spread a blanket, and have a fucking picnic." Without another word, he headed toward the ship. The rest followed.

Decker stared up at the black tubes again. Tanaka and her crew had gone into those things? Willingly? The formations ran up fifty or sixty feet from the ship, before they vanished into the walls of the cavern.

Manning called over his shoulder.

"Pretty sure I'm going to need you up here, bloodhound."

"Knew you were a dog," Piotrowicz said.

Decker didn't dignify his comment with a response, and caught up with the rest. He had his nerves under control, but that didn't stop him from thinking they were taking it too fast.

"Seriously, Manning, I do not like this place. We should take it slow and careful."

Manning frowned.

"I don't give a shit what you do and don't like, Decker," Manning replied. "Just do your job. Don't go freaking out on me. Understood?"

"Yeah," Decker replied. "I get it."

Dirt had been piled up against the ship, and a ramp of boards and metal sheeting led to a hole in the side. The rupture was large enough that they could see up to levels they couldn't hope to reach without ladders or scaling equipment. Scaffolding materials were stacked to the left of the ramp.

"Just how big is this thing?" Manning said, talking to himself.

Decker was about to reply when something hit him hard enough to make him wince. The sensation was as sharp as an exposed nerve in a broken tooth.

"There's something here," he said.

"What?" Manning looked hard at him. "Where?"

Decker closed his eyes and concentrated. He was rewarded for his efforts with a crawling sensation across his brain. Still, even that was helpful. Maybe. He couldn't be sure—he could only go with what his gut was telling him.

"Up and to the left," he said, pointing toward the large tube. "There's something there. It doesn't…" He shook his head. "It doesn't feel like anything human." It was the best description he could offer.

Manning peered in the direction he'd indicated, where the shadows blurred the details. He shone a lamp up there, but it did little good. About thirty feet up, the large black tube pierced the side of the ship, curving up toward the cavern's distant ceiling.

Nothing moved, yet the crawling sensation in his head acted like a sensor buzzing at a radioactive hotspot. There was something up there—something that sent off waves of emotion. He gritted his teeth, and focused on remaining calm.

"DiTillio, Rodriguez, Joyce," Manning barked. "Go check out that tunnel, see if you can find anything worth seeing. And be careful."

The three mercs nodded as their names were called, and headed toward the hull of the ship. Their goal was a spot directly below the point where the fused black tube met with the vessel's remains. As they moved they prepared their weapons. Rodriguez pulled out his reaper, while DiTillio activated his plasma rifle, and a very faint whine pierced the gloom.

Soon they were out of sight, and the sound of their footsteps, crunching on the cavern floor, faded away. Manning looked over at Decker for a moment.

"You think three is enough?"

"No idea." His first instinct was to say "no," but he couldn't give a good reason. So he held his tongue.

"No?" Manning said. "Then why exactly are you being paid as a consultant?"

"Who said anything about being paid?" Decker replied. "I'm just here for the scenery and the accommodations." *So fuck you, and fuck your attitude*, he added silently.

Manning just shot him a look and turned toward the rest of the group, barking orders, positioning them for entering the vast wreckage.

At his command three more of the mercenaries broke open their backpacks and started setting up portable monitoring stations. They positioned themselves next to one of the closer stacks of building materials, which provided places to set up and to sit. Each of the three hefted a large, well-protected screen and as Decker stood watching, they began syncing their systems and then adding individual feeds from each of the mercenaries.

One of the three beckoned him over—the patch on her shirt said "Perkins." She pulled out a camera for his helmet and a Personal Identifier Patch that went on his bared forearm, to read his vitals. As soon as the PIP was in place, she checked the readout on her screen, and then gave him a strange look.

"You worried?" she asked.

"Why?" he said. "Should I be?"

"Your pulse is way too high," she said. "*Way* the hell too high." She called Manning over to one side, and they kept their voices low. Then another of the techs spoke up.

"This is looking like a waste of time, boss," It was Dae Cho, the senior tech, who pointed to the screen in front of him, and then to another one. "We're only getting readings from the PIPs that are close by—but nothing more than twenty feet away." Manning studied them intently and then spoke into the headset on his helmet.

"DiTillio? You read me?"

"Yeah, chief, but your signal isn't great."

"Any sign of trouble?"

"We haven't even made it to the tunnel entrance. Damn thing's halfway up the exterior of the ship. There's footholds, and we're climbing, but it's slow going."

"We can't get any readings off your vital patch-ins."

"Hang on. Checking." There was silence, broken a moment later by DiTillio's voice. "We're all live and wearing PIPs. Everything seems to be working on this end."

Willis heard the discussion and walked over.

"It's the same as with the probes," he said. "There's interference."

Manning barely acknowledged the man's presence. Instead he looked to the techs. Perkins, Dwadji, and Cho were playing with their keyboards and screens.

"Fix this shit," he said. "Now."

Cho nodded his head and responded.

"Working on it, boss. Might just be a frequency issue. We'll run the spectrum."

Manning nodded his head and walked away. After a moment's hesitation, Decker followed him.

He took exactly seven steps before a wave surged through him, stronger than before. That feeling of being watched—it was pervasive, and it was growing stronger.

Shit, I've got to keep it together, he thought, and then he said, "Manning, it's getting worse." His head was ringing with pain.

"What's getting worse?" The merc spun on him, then went silent for a moment, staring at him intently. "Okay, we need to see about getting you a sedative. You look like you're about to stroke out on me." He called out to his crew. "Piotrowicz, come see to our guest over here. He needs something to calm him down."

Piotrowicz headed over and studied Decker with a clinical eye, and then looked past him at the readouts on the screens. It was easy to see which one was his, because the readings were radically different from everyone else's.

"Calm down, buddy," the merc said. "It's not the end of the world—just a little salvage." His voice was surprisingly calming. "We'll get through this, but you have to chill out." His backpack came off, and a moment later he was rolling out a small syringe-gun. "Just a mild sedative," Piotrowicz explained. "I took stronger when I quit smoking."

"You smoked?"

Piotrowicz grinned at him. "Yeah. I was young and the girl was cute. Got hooked, got better."

"What did you smoke?"

"Well, it wasn't legal." He administered the injection, which pushed the liquid through the skin without using a needle. It hurt like hell, but within seconds the effects took hold. Decker felt himself relaxing. He could still focus, but he could breathe again.

Piotrowicz looked at the monitor, and looked satisfied.

"My job here is done. You start feeling weird or like it's wearing off, come see me." He put his pack back together and slid it across his shoulders. "I get to carry all the good shit."

Decker nodded and looked at the ship again, taking it in with a clearer, calmer head. Calmer—but not calm. He could still feel that radiating sense of hatred. So far it seemed to be stationary, and the three men who'd been sent off were heading right for it.

1 6

WETWORKS

The side of the ship was dusty and smelled as old as it looked, moldy and bitter. Still, DiTillio was smiling as he climbed up the side and looked at the tunnel ahead. Every moment brought him that much closer to making a shitload of money.

Of course, it also took him further away from the main group. A little over a hundred yards was all that separated them, but it might as well have been a mile. And the shape of the cavern was messing with sound, sometimes muffling it, other times sending out echoes. They were out of direct line of sight, too. Stacks of supplies blocked the view, leaving him guessing where the rest of the team was.

If they needed backup, they'd have to rely on the headsets.

Joyce was right next to him and looking around with wide eyes. His long face was pulled into a smile that showed his uneven teeth.

"What are you grinning about?" DiTillio poked fun at his teammate. He wasn't used to the other merc being so enthusiastic.

"Always wanted to see something like this, mate," Joyce replied. "My whole life."

"What? Aliens?"

"Well, yeah. 'Course. Don't you know how incredible this is?"

"Incredible enough to make us a shitload of money, if we play it right," DiTillio said, and he peered around. "That Decker guy said there's something dangerous over here. I wonder what it is. I hope it's one of the bug things. I want to check those out."

"Well, yeah," Joyce replied. "I mean, I'm glad we're armed. But I just can't believe we're really here. Looking at proof of other beings. Looking at something no other human has ever seen. Almost no one, that is," he added, correcting himself. Then he slapped the surface of the ship. "Touching something most humans have never touched, and never will."

DiTillio allowed himself a grin. The man was right. This was an incredible moment, the sort he could tell his grandkids about some day.

The surface of the vast ship was curved, and they'd been climbing with relative ease, but the going got tougher as they neared the silicon tunnel. The good news was that someone had attempted to string lights over the surface, and the wires worked relatively well as extra purchase. They looked old, though— none of the bulbs worked, a bunch of them were broken, and the insulation was in tatters. Only the dryness of the cavern had prevented them from rusting away.

He wondered if they would find one of the aliens Weyland-Yutani had sent them to retrieve. He'd always planned to study xenobiology, but a stint in the Colonial Marines had made him decide he preferred a life out on the Rim. It was easier, the pay was good, and there were plenty of distractions.

His fingers caught hold of the ship's hull and he pulled himself a little higher. Back on Earth he'd have been working up a hard sweat. Here the lower gravity was making it more like a light workout.

The pulse rifle was strapped to his back, and he had his pistol within easy reach. Fifty caliber shells would take care of any serious issues that might come along.

As old as the ship was, the tunnel moving away from it was much, much newer. The surface looked almost wet, even under the layer of dirt, and there was a hole in the side—that was their goal. He made sure to aim his camera at it, and take in as much as he could. Even if they couldn't pick up the image back at the temporary hub, the camera would still be recording.

He wanted to make a copy to send back to his sister—the one who'd been smart enough to finish college and was working for Weyland-Yutani as a forensic xenobiologist. She made disgustingly good money. Still, he got laid a lot more often.

It was all a matter of perspective.

"You seeing this?" The voice came from his left, where Rodriguez was climbing.

"The fuck is that?" Joyce's voice was almost lost in the cavernous area. He was a soft-spoken man.

The entrance of the tunnel seemed to move. Something dark and wet looking shifted twenty feet above them. It sent a shiver down his spine.

"Looks like a loose piece," DiTillio said. "Something's making it shift. Might be the thing isn't as solid as it looks." He tried to sound more certain than he felt.

"No, it's not loose," Rodriguez said, his voice a little higher. "It's moving. I mean, I think something's actually coming toward us." He held up his reaper, and stared hard at the shadows above them.

"Calm down, Billy," DiTillio said. "I don't think we need to worry about being attacked by a wall."

"Fair enough," Rodriguez said. "But I think we need to—oh, *shit!*"

The loose piece moved faster, dropping toward them, clinging to the side of the ship. It had that same wet look, new and clean, and even had the same sort of patterns along its hide, but this thing had arms and legs and a tail and...

Fuck, those are teeth!

Rodriguez didn't wait to consider whether or not it was friendly. He opened fire. The first round from the reaper struck the broken hull and ricocheted away, the report echoing as the thing dropped toward them.

He never had a second chance.

The thing landed on him, arms and legs and tail and other things all in motion—and before Rodriguez could do anything, say anything, he and the dark mass were both falling, bouncing back down the side of the ship and slamming into a rock formation. Rodriguez broke on impact.

The thing got up and looked like it was ready to spring. Its hide was black, so it was hard to tell.

Broken didn't mean down, though. Rodriguez raised his weapon and took aim even as the dark shape attacked, claws ripping at flesh. He let out a feeble scream and tried to fight as the thing tore at him.

"What the fuck! What the fuck is that thing?" Joyce was panicking, which wasn't exactly helping matters. DiTillio tried to aim at the shape that was dragging Rodriguez closer to the side of the ship's hull. He was having a damned hard time getting a good shot without risking hitting his downed teammate.

And there was the fact that the thing was, well, a *thing*. Joyce had already said it. This was an alien life-form, and they'd never encountered one before. None of them had. It had certain human characteristics—the same basic shape, but beyond the number of arms and legs there wasn't much more to go on. He saw enough to know that this was a Xenomorph, and that the footage in the files hadn't done the monster justice.

"Calm down, Joyce," he gritted, and his voice shook. "You're not helping."

"There are more of them, man," Joyce screeched. "There's more than one!"

DiTillio looked up in time to see the truth of Joyce's words. More shapes spilled from the hole above them, and dropped onto the ruined hull of the ship. They moved fast, scrambling and managing to hold onto the vessel even as they descended.

Joyce let out a throaty cry, but it was cut off almost immediately as one of the glistening black shapes grabbed him from above.

DiTillio had exactly long enough to wish he'd followed

procedure and called for backup. Then two more of the dark shapes were on him. They were vaguely humanoid, but they had sharp claws and they had teeth.

So damned many teeth.

1 7

NECROPOLIS

Sometimes the little things, the ones most easily overlooked, hid all of the best secrets.

They'd broken through a small section of tunnel where air was moving softly. Then they'd returned to their encampment and waited in the mess tent until the probes did their due diligence, and gave the all clear.

So Doctor Nigel Silas stepped outside of the mess tent and strode to the opening they'd blown into the stone wall. Then he stared at the discovery spread out before him, with a smile that couldn't go any wider.

A metropolis, really. It looked to be centuries old.

The city was vast, built on hills and spreading down into areas where, once, there had been valleys, most likely cut by rivers. It was stunning, even with everything in ruin. Scarred and pitted surfaces, buildings that had collapsed nearly to the ground, yet still they were wonders.

The probes were still working diligently, recording every minute detail. He could see them flitting about in the distance. Their lights flickered in and out of sight, lighting the tops of buildings that appeared to have been amazing structures once upon a time, and still held echoes of that long gone magnificence.

Like the ship, the buildings had not been built. They had been grown, formed in a process he couldn't begin to understand, but desperately wished he could study for the next hundred years.

No matter what they did here, none of the team he was working with would live long enough to finish what they had started. They didn't even consider it. All that mattered for now was beginning the excavation.

They had found the remains of a couple of the creatures that had lived here, almost unrecognizable in their antiquity. They were bipedal, with some vaguely canine attributes, and larger than the average human being. How many had populated the city? Judging from the number of buildings they had found thus far, perhaps more than a million.

They hadn't yet delved deep enough to uncover any of the technologies that had run the place. Once they did, who knew how much they would discover? And for each item they found, who knew how long it would take to figure out how it worked? This one city could keep an army of scientists occupied for decades.

The find of a lifetime. He smiled as he thought about that.

Colleen came from the tent behind him and sputtered out a small laugh.

"You're like a big kid," she said. "You know that?"

"How else could I be? Look at this place, Colleen. It's amazing." She smiled and put one of her arms around his waist.

"I know." She paused a bit and enjoyed the view with him, standing in silence, and then said, "Where are we looking today?"

Silas pointed to the road leading down to the closest valley.

"The survey information from the probes is showing what looks like a military complex in that direction," he said. "Well, military or at least industrial. We should look there first. It's likely to offer up a lot of technologies on every level."

She nodded her head. "So let's get this show on the road."

18

UPPING THE ANTE

Decker stayed off to the side, watching and waiting.

They'd been about to enter the wreck when Willis got a call over his comm-link. Whatever the report had been, everything had ground to a halt, and he and Manning were off to one side, conferring. The rest of the mercs were waiting for instructions, and Adams sat nearby. She was knocking back a bottle of water, relishing it like it was the best beer she'd ever tasted.

That seemed to be her approach to everything. Somehow, he found it difficult to be so upbeat.

"Why do you think readouts and probes aren't working, but comm-links still do?" Decker asked.

"Comm-links are a lot simpler, I guess—maybe that has something to do with it." She shrugged. "How the hell should I know? I'm just a grunt."

Manning and Willis moved closer to the group, still deep in conversation, and both of them seemed excited about something. Then Manning split off and called the group together.

"Mister Willis here got a call from Doctor Silas. He's the brain leading the team that's examining the other side of this thing." He gestured at the alien ship. "According to him, it looks like there might be a lot more where this came from." That got everyone's attention. A few of the mercs started to speak, but Manning cut them off with a single gesture. "They've been digging behind this ship, and think they've found what looks like the remains of a city."

Everyone started to talk at once, and Manning let it go. He knew what this meant for them—the possibility of rewards beyond imagining. After a moment, Bridges raised his voice above the rest. Bridges was as close to old school military as they had, with short hair, a thin mustache and well-polished boots.

"A city?" he said. "Are there any signs of life? Maybe the bugs we're looking for?" He was grinning. Like as not the man was already calculating how he would spend his bonus.

It was Willis who answered.

"Understand that they haven't gotten very far yet," he said. "There's no sign of life, but judging from the configuration of what they *have* found, it looks likely that the ship was taking off—not landing. That means a spaceport, and we may be looking at a trove of discoveries the likes of which no one has ever encountered."

He was damned near jumping up and down with excitement, and no wonder. A ship was one thing, but an entire people capable of star travel? An entire race who *grew* their ships? Anyone who had a piece of the salvage was going to be unbelievably wealthy.

The buzz started up again. After a few minutes, Manning reached the limits of his patience.

"Listen up!" he bellowed. "Whatever they've found, we need to focus on the mission. We've got to make certain this dig is secure, and we've got to try and find any living thing that might be crawling through these tunnels. Mister Willis has called for reinforcements, but they won't arrive for a couple of weeks.

"So we're going to be working out a rotating schedule, and covering as much ground as we can. Nothing and no one leaves this site without my knowledge and approval. Do I make myself clear?"

"Got it, boss," Piotrowicz said. "No one comes in, no one leaves. But what about the miners?"

"As far as they know, nothing's changed—it's business as usual down here," Manning said. "They'll be following exactly the same protocols as we will. No one comes in. No one leaves."

"Are you sure the people up there can be trusted?" Piotrowicz asked.

"Their jobs are as much on the line as ours," Willis said. "They'll accept all of the security measures we put into place—those are the rules, no exceptions." His words were met with murmurs of approval all around.

Out of the corner of his eye, Decker saw one of the three techs stand up and move toward Manning. Though they'd all been listening, they'd stayed at their posts. The tech said something that couldn't be heard over the chatter, and the two of them moved back toward the monitor.

Suddenly Manning—or maybe it was both of them—gave off a spike of emotion. Manning said something into his comm-link, then shook his head.

The spike became more intense. Decker frowned.

"Hell, no," Adams said nearby. "I'm buying a mansion and settling myself on Monaco. I like the idea of a planet with nothing but beachfront property."

"You'll burn to a crisp!" the skinny kid said. Garth. "You're so white, your skin scorches when you walk under a strong light."

"Look who's talking," Adams replied. "Besides, I'll hire me a few studs to lotionize me every morning, and twice at night."

Decker shook off the random conversations. Weyland-Yutani owned his ass to the tune of more money than anyone would see from this little expedition. But there was something else that was bugging him—if he could just think through the drugs Piotrowicz had stuck in his arm...

Ah.

Yes.

"If there's a city, what happened to all the people?" He directed the question to Willis.

"What's that?" The man was still smiling, ear-to-ear.

"The aliens who built it," Decker said. "What happened to them?"

Willis frowned and tried to look like he had a clue.

"Well, we don't know that yet."

"I mean, if the ship here was trying to leave, and it went down, shouldn't we be finding some sort of remains?" He waved his hand to take in the immediate area. "For that matter, why did they just leave it here, stuck in the ground? Shouldn't they have taken it, I don't know, someplace else?"

Willis lost his smile.

And at the same time, Manning called out to his team.

"Listen up," he said, and there was an edge to his voice. "We have a situation. Rodriguez, Joyce, and DiTillio aren't responding to the comm." He moved back to the group, and his already rough face looked as if it was carved from the rocks around them. "We have three MIAs on our hands."

All of the chatter came to a halt, and immediately the mercenaries started prepping their equipment. This took Decker by surprise. These were the same people who had beaten and kidnapped him back on Earth. Yet when three of their own went missing, everything else took a back seat. Begrudgingly, he admired that.

The simple fact was that they had to depend on each other in bad situations. Just as he'd depended on Luke and his own team when he was pinned under the core sampler.

He stood up quickly, and immediately his head started spinning. Damn, but he needed to recover from whatever drug was in him. He looked around for Piotrowicz, but couldn't find him—there was too much controlled chaos.

As he searched, that sensation hit him again—the certainty of being watched. He scanned the group, and none of them was paying him the least bit of attention. So he focused as best he could.

It seemed to come from several places at once. Something out there was watching him, *stalking* him. There was no doubt, and panic started nibbling at the edges of his mind again, sending streamers of ice through his stomach to drift and tickle and make him miserably uncomfortable.

"Decker!" Manning's voice cut through the fog. "You picking up something, daydreaming, or maybe just hoping no one will notice you doing nothing?"

"Sorry," he replied. "Whatever Piotrowicz gave me, it's messing with me."

"Well, shake it off and get your ass in gear."

Decker grabbed his pack, which held the two weapons he'd been loaned, and moved to join the rest.

"I don't know how your mojo works," Manning said, "and I don't care. What I need is results. If DiTillio's team ran into trouble, I need to know where they are, and whether or not your alien friends are with them."

Decker closed his eyes again, and concentrated. Though there were impressions coming in from all around, the strongest feeling came from above the ship, where he had felt something before.

Where DiTillio, Joyce, and Rodriguez had gone, on his say-so.

Shit.

"Same spot," he said, pointing as he had earlier.

"Good enough for me." Manning started walking. "Four teams. Cho, you and tech stay here, monitor everything you can. Piotrowicz, flank to the left and keep an eye on the tunnels. Hartsfield, right flank. Warm 'em up, but don't be stupid." With the exception of the techs, the whole group moved splitting apart with comfortable familiarity. It was obvious they'd worked with the different people he chose, and they filed after the leaders. Decker fell into step behind Manning, keeping pace with Adams, even though every fiber of his being screamed *not* to head toward that sensation.

But he needed to live up to his end of the bargain if he wanted to get out of this. Besides, he was surrounded by heavily armed mercenaries.

What could go wrong? He regretted the thought immediately.

Willis trotted over, and Manning stopped.

"What's going on?" he asked. "Where do you think you're going?"

Manning stared at him for a moment.

"It's what I just said," he replied. "Three of our men are missing. We're going to find them."

"All of you?" Willis shook his head. "No. At least a few of you need to be here for when the survey team gets back. In the meantime, we can't just leave this area unguarded."

"Are you trying to tell me how to do my job, Mister Willis?" Manning's voice lowered into an unpleasant rumble.

"I'm trying to remind you that the rules have changed." He stopped, and shifted gears. "Listen, I understand that you're missing a few people, but you don't need your entire team for a search-and-rescue. And you'll be ignoring the mission at hand."

"This is the mission at hand. I just broke the team into three separate—"

"The thing we're *paying* you for," Willis added firmly.

Manning just stared, without emotion. The closest mercs edged closer, waiting to see if their boss would take a swing at their resident bureaucrat.

"Right," Manning said, and he spun around. "Piotrowicz, you, Anderson, Lutz, Estrada, and Vogel are going to stay here with Willis. Your job is to secure the area—especially the lift. Nothing comes down, and nothing goes up without you clearing it through me." Piotrowicz smiled and stepped to the side, as the rest broke off to join him. "Give Adams here the medical supplies. Apparently you're not capable of administering a reasonable dose of jack shit, anyhow."

For a second the thin man looked ready to argue. The look he received convinced him that it would be unwise.

Manning turned to the bruiser with the tattoo on his shaved head.

"Connors, take Groff, Hunsucker, Juergens, and Blake. Head to the far side of this damned thing and find out what's back there. All of you keep your eyes open. We already know there might be bugs, and we know that three people are missing. Everybody communicates through Cho and the rest of comm." He spun hard to look at Willis. "Satisfied?"

Willis nodded, looking smugly victorious. If Manning noticed, he didn't give any indication.

Adams shook her head, a weird smile on her face.

Decker stared at her for a second, reading her amusement. "What?"

"Suits," she said. "Nothing's changed, except Manning lets this feeb think he's made a difference. This is the same breakdown we'd have had anyway. Two secondary teams, half of each team staying nearby, the other half moving further out to guard the perimeter. Main team—the one we're with—heads for the last known site of the MIAs. All he did was piss Manning off, so now more people are coming with the main group."

Decker nodded his head. He was used to dealing with the other end of the scenario. Like as not, there would have been times when he'd have been the Willis in the equation.

A moment later they were heading back for the side of the ship and the long black tube of silicon that rose toward the distant ceiling. Twenty mercenaries headed for the last known location of three missing men.

DiTillio woke in darkness, his body dripping sweat. Something hot and wet was pressing down on his arms, his chest, and he could feel *things* crawling over him.

"What the fuck?"

If anyone else was around to hear him, they did not answer.

The wetness on his chest pressed down and spread out and he felt hands smoothing the heaviness over his clothes. He was having trouble breathing, but not enough to make him panic. The lack of mobility was causing that. Whatever the stuff was that was covering him, it was hardening quickly.

The air stank of oil and metal and something acrid. He tried to see anything at all, but there was no light.

So when the shape crawled over his face, he had no notion of what it might be, except that it moved on long, thin legs. He tried to shake his head, and the fingers clamped into his hair, pulled tightly over his face.

"What?" Panic ate at him, and he shook his head harder as something wrapped around his neck. It was hot enough that it felt like it would burn his flesh, and it constricted like a hangman's noose, causing him to choke. Then it loosened a bit.

DiTillio started to speak again, to beg if he had to, but before he could utter a sound something was in his mouth, pressing past his lips, past his teeth and shoving further still.

Panic didn't even begin to cover what he felt. He tried to thrash his head to the side but the grip was too much. Whatever was in his mouth rammed in harder, pushing into his throat. He would have gagged if he could have, but whatever it was took advantage of the motion and shoved deeper still.

His eyes watered in the darkness. He tried once more to scream.

19

UPWARD TOWARD DARKNESS

As they neared the side of the alien vessel, they saw the blood.

It was Decker who found the first weapon. According to Manning, it belonged to Rodriguez. It was a reaper, much like the one he was wearing holstered on his hip. That hardly inspired confidence. Spatters of blood showed on the ground, and a few more trickled down the side of the ship.

Grimly, they began climbing toward the dark tunnel. It was a relatively simple climb for Decker and the rest.

Emotions were spiking all around him, although there was a lot more anger than fear. Decker sorted through and sought to focus on what was ahead, and he kept coming up with the same thing. There was a pervasive sense of menace that neither grew stronger nor weakened as they climbed.

The blood spots were more frequent as they ascended. Manning gripped the hull nearby, and he called in regularly, keeping Cho and Piotrowicz posted. As they approached the tube, Decker looked down, and could barely see the group at the foot of the ramp, tiny in the distance.

Manning was the first to reach the tunnel's entrance. He pulled out a powerful light, which he strapped to the shoulder of his armor. Several of the others below him did the exact same thing. Decker felt naked without one, but the lights seemed strong enough to let him see.

The mercenary's fingers sought a place to grip the interior of the tunnel and found one. He hauled himself up and in. Decker clung there, frozen in place, but Adams was right behind him and tapped his side.

"Let's go," she said. "Chief ain't gonna wait."

Maybe the sedatives were wearing off. Maybe he was just finally adjusting to them. Whatever the case, he nodded and continued upward, his fingertips finding spots to grip with relative ease. When he reached the tube, he grabbed the edge of the opening, and hoisted himself inside.

Even there, the angle of the tunnel forced him to climb. The spun silicon—which had looked so smooth from below—offered plenty of handholds and footholds alike. There was light moisture clinging to the interior, pooling at times, making it slippery. He felt a hint of claustrophobia, but quickly damped it down.

The sense of malice had not changed—it was still coming from all around them, but the intensity hadn't increased.

Adams remained directly behind him, the light mounted to her shoulder showing him the best spots. Ahead of him Manning continued to climb as the tunnel shifted, leveling out a bit. The way became easier, and the air itself turned moist. There was a scent that was uncomfortably familiar for no reason he could discern.

Then it hit him. It was the scent of the nightmares he'd been suffering for months. But was it possible to smell something in a dream? He had no idea.

Time lost meaning as they moved, climbing and shifting along the course of the tunnel, and then the oddly organic structure opened up, allowing them to stand. The other mercenaries moved up behind them.

The area couldn't exactly be called a room. The walls, floor, and ceiling were all made of stuff that seemed like a cross between being a living entity and molded from glass and steel. It was elegant in a way, though there were too many places with shadows that pooled and could hide almost anything. It shone wetly in the illumination thrown by the shoulder lights.

Adams pulled out a motion sensor, and flipped the switch. Nothing. She shook it, slapped it hard on one side, and then stared at it again.

"Damned Weyland-Yutani piece of crap," she said.

A few of the mercenaries removed the lights from their mounts, and the beams moved dizzyingly over the area. The walls were rounded, and moved smoothly into the ceiling and floor alike. The lights revealed three separate tunnels that stemmed off from the main area, all in different directions.

The smell was worse here.

"Where the hell are we?" Adams asked, and her voice was startlingly loud. Decker shook his head.

"We're either above the ship, *inside* of the ship, or we've exited the cave altogether," Manning said. "I don't know, but we were climbing for a while." His voice remained calm.

Adams crouched and ran her hand along the surface. Her eyes were wide as she studied the stuff, but her mouth pulled down in revulsion, and she stood up again.

"This shit's like a spider's web," she said. "It doesn't feel like a web, but it looks like it. Like it's spun or woven. When I was a kid, my teacher had a colony of funnel spiders in a terrarium. It looked a lot like this. I mean, not exactly, but sort of."

"First spider I see gets blown to shit. I hate those things," Sanchez said. He was lean and hard, and looked disconcertingly nervous.

Decker couldn't blame him.

Manning shot Sanchez a glance, and nodded his agreement.

"Found something." Adams pointed her light toward the base of the wall. There was a substantial pool of liquid there, and the white light revealed it to be blood—likely human. It was already congealing. Manning peered at it, and then turned to Decker.

"Which way, hotshot?"

Decker tried to sort out the sensation that almost seemed like background noise. There was no one focal point to grasp.

He's not going to like this, he thought.

"I have no idea," he said.

Manning's calm faded in an instant, and he leaned in closer until his eyes were inches away from Decker's world.

"That's not good enough," he said, his voice low. "You can sense whatever the fucking things are? Great. *Do it.* Feel for them, or smell them out, or *whatever* the hell you're supposed to be doing, and you tell me where my men are. Or I might just decide that you're a liability I don't need."

Decker felt the merc's anger flare, and his own flared up in response.

"Get out of my face," he growled. "I didn't ask for any of this. You and your employers dragged me here. You act like I'm a fucking bloodhound. Well, I'm not. Yeah, there's something here that's fucking evil. I can feel that. But I can't just perform on command, tell you where that something is, what it looks like, or how many of them there are. It just doesn't work like that."

Manning actually got closer. His eyes looked bloody murder, and he spoke with that same calm, despite the rage Decker felt radiating off of him.

"Make. It. Work," he said. "Find a way. Now."

Decker held his gaze, then took a step back. He lowered his head, closed his eyes, and clenched his fists.

And damned if he didn't feel something.

Shit.

"Shit," he said. "Whatever's out there, it's coming this way."

2 0

A MOMENT'S PEACE

The five of them walked the area slowly, checking for signs of the missing trio. The lights above them were dim, and seemed even fainter as they moved further around the edge of the gigantic ship.

Connors kept his people in sight at all times. Hunsucker chewed at a lump of gum like it had done his family wrong. The man almost never spoke, but he snapped and popped that damn gum. He was long and lean and his skin was darkly tanned. He had hair so blond it was almost white, and stood out in stark contrast. He was carrying a plasma rifle, and the high-pitched whine of the generator was almost as annoying as the sound of chewing.

That said, Connors forgave all his sins because the little sociopath knew how to use his weapon.

Groff was a brooding presence. He'd been a career Marine and he had the badges to prove it—one arm was covered entirely by scar tissue. Put it together with the other one, and they looked like a "before-and-after." His hair was close-cropped salt and pepper, while his face looked like it belonged on a younger man. Unlike most of the mercs, he still wore military combat fatigues, and carried his supplies with him almost everywhere he went. Everything about the man made Connors feel a little better about walking in unexplored territory.

Juergens and Blake were by far the most relaxed of the lot.

Off to one side, they murmured to each other as they moved along. Blake had secured his flashlight to his pulse rifle, which was also humming. He swung the high-power beam along the underbelly of the ship as they moved beneath it. It was a tight fit, and Juergens made sure to check the structure for integrity. They had no idea how long it had been there, or whether or not it was sound—for all they knew, time might have weakened it.

Better safe than dead.

It was more than his urge to live long enough to become a rich man. Everything about the scenario made him uneasy. Rodriguez was a hard ass. The man didn't take shit from anyone, and he could handle himself in a firefight. If someone or something had taken Rodriguez out, then that same something was dangerous.

It might be out and looking for another target.

Abruptly Juergens turned his entire body, and aimed back the way they'd come, his light pointing into the shadows.

"Anyone see that?" he said.

"See what?" Connors spun around and looked for anything that didn't belong.

Nothing.

"Focus your beam, Brent. All you're doing is making more shadows to chase."

Juergens didn't reply, but his light steadied and moved slowly over the large surface.

Connors followed suit, aiming at a different area. Then he froze.

"Hold up," he said, raising an arm.

There was a shape, still some distance away, slowly heading toward them. It was dark, and the way it moved was unsettling. There were four limbs—legs, possibly—moving under the thing, but above it protrusions rose from the back and bobbed in counterpoint to each step it took. The head was an elongated affair that seemed to belong on something much larger. Its tail was almost as long as the body, and ended in a vicious looking barb.

"What the fuck?" His voice was louder than he intended. He made sure the safety was off on his rail rifle. Thing made a lot of noise when it was fired, but whatever got hit knew good and damned well that it was time to die.

"I see it too," Juergens said, his voice high.

"Me, too," Blake said, keeping it low. "What is it?"

It looked almost as if it was made of the same dark glassy substance as the rough tunnels that wove above them and along the distant wall, and even from a distance they could see the shape of the thing's innards under that glossy exoskeleton. Before Connors could respond, it charged, hissing like a broken steam pipe.

Groff opened fire, and three rounds from his pulse rifle carved trenches in the dirt. The fourth nailed the approaching thing in the leg and blew that limb apart.

The hissing noise became a high-pitched shriek, and the creature fell forward, hitting the ground and bleeding fiercely through the gaping hole where the leg had been a moment before. The ground smoldered and smoked.

"They might secrete a liquid that's toxic, or caustic, or both." Still squealing, the thing lunged toward Groff. The merc stepped back and fired another stream of rounds. He was fast, and he was good, and the thing took several more hits before it crashed to the ground and shuddered and... *Please God...* died.

Connors got on the comm.

"Manning! We've got something here. I think we killed it but it's hard to tell." His voice shook. He wished it could have been excitement, but it was fear. Everything about the creature was terrifying. The way it moved, the way it looked—even the way it died.

Manning didn't respond. Connors frowned.

Juergens pointed to his helmet, then to Connors.

"Comm's dead. Whatever that thing bleeds, it got your helmet." Connors pulled it off quickly, and looked at the damage. It could only have been a few drops of whatever passed for blood in the nightmare, but that had been enough. The unit was slagged, and a hole had burned partially through the durable shell of the helmet itself. He flipped the helmet over and realized that the caustic fluid was still burning through. Hydrogen fluoride, was that what the damned file said? He wished they could have brought the downloads with them now. He wished he'd read a little more carefully.

If Juergens hadn't pointed out the damage, there was a chance it would have reached his scalp. Before he could say thanks, Groff spoke up.

"Look lively," he growled. "We've got company." He leveled his pulse rifle. Hunsucker's plasma rifle whined a little louder as he took off the safety.

The darkness came to life. That was the only way to put it. The shadows in the distance began moving, *seething*, and as Connors watched, those shadows broke into smaller forms. He tried counting, but they were too fast and there were too many of them.

Hunsucker took careful aim and fired. A flash of light ripped from his weapon, illuminating everything around them. The ball of plasma burned hot enough to catch the air on fire, and all of them squinted as the missile struck its target. The creature was fast, and almost managed to dodge the blast, but almost didn't count when it came to plasma.

It had enough time to hiss before half of its head melted away.

The creature was dead before it hit the ground. Its wound was cauterized. None of that caustic crap spilled this time.

But there were more where that came from. Hunsucker smiled and fired again, the light nearly blinding them all. This time he missed—his target dropped lower, squatting like a long-limbed spider, and scurried forward. The tiny ball of plasma hit the ship and burned, melting into the ancient surface, leaving a smoking crater as evidence of its passing.

And then the thing jumped, moving with unsettling agility, twisting its body to allow it to kick off the underside of the ship and run directly into Hunsucker even as he tried to track it with the tip of his rifle. The barrel pointed at Connors, who hit the ground to avoid it.

The merc tried to bring the weapon around, but the thing on

top of him pinned his arm to the ground with a powerful grip, and the thick claws at the end of the nightmarish fingers drove through flesh and muscle and bone with unsettling ease.

Hunsucker screamed and kicked at it, but the creature didn't seem to care in the least. The weapon in Hunsucker's hand fell free. He kicked again and sent the monster staggering back. The merc rolled back to his feet as quickly as he could. The thing spun hard and fast, and that serrated tail slapped him in the chest hard enough to lift him off his feet and throw him against the ship.

Cries from the other three pulled his attention away. He knew instantly that everything was jacked up beyond reason. *Everything.* The nightmares were coming closer, and there were a lot of them. His skin tightened, and his pulse rocketed.

Groff stood his ground and opened fire, cutting down one, two, three before the rest of them got to his location. He screamed as they swarmed over him like insects.

"Too many! Too many," Connors screamed. "Retreat!"

Hunsucker was down and out, bleeding from his ruined arm, and the thing that had attacked him was pulling him along the ground, dragging him away from the rest of the combatants.

"… the *fuck* are you?" Juergens screamed into his radio. "We're under attack! We need backup!" His voice was frantic. He tried firing at one of the damned things, but was too slow on the draw. The dark shape rammed into him and they both fell to the ground. Inhuman limbs rose and fell and drew back again and again covered with blood.

Juergens stopped fighting.

Three of them took down Blake. He saw them coming and shook his head. Then he raised his hands above his head.

Shit! Connors thought.

"I surrender!" Juergens screamed. "I give up!" Damned if Connors didn't feel like shooting the bastard right then and there. Before he could move, Juergens disappeared under a black, chitinous wave.

Several of the things surrounded him, peering at him and

moving together, circling him, keeping him busy.

"No," he said. "No way." Connors sighted on the closest one and aimed his rail gun at its oversized head. The loud POOM of the round firing roared through the air. One round punched through the vile thing's hide. Before he could celebrate, the next one came in low and fast, and while he was trying to track it the monster's tail slapped his gun arm aside with ease. His arm flared with pain, and then he couldn't feel it at all.

The creature's flesh was hard and hot and coated with a slick moisture that left a trail of slime on his forearm. Connors kicked the thing in the chest and sent it backward. It hissed and he charged forward, determined to get past it in one piece.

The tail again. The tip came around and slashed at his face, tearing his nose and lips apart. Connors stepped back purely by instinct, and another of the things came up behind him. The damned thing grabbed his arms, the sharp claws of its fingers digging for purchase and sinking easily into his flesh.

He thrashed and fought, but it wasn't enough. They were stronger than he would have ever guessed. Blood streamed down his face, and the one he'd kicked reared up in front of him, face-to-face, hissing as it peeled back its lips and revealed silvery teeth coated in a thin blanket of saliva. Nothing he'd ever seen in his worst nightmares had ever scared him more.

There was a skull buried inside that head, and he could see the hollows where eyes should have been leering at him.

He kicked it again, but this time it was prepared. The blow was solid, but the thing didn't fall back. Instead it came forward, and those teeth parted, and then closed down.

Meat and bone crunched and Connors screamed before he passed out.

2 1

EVERYWHERE

The lift took off while they were looking around the area. Piotrowicz damned near wet himself. But there was no one on board—it was probably the miners, using it to get from one of the upper levels to another.

His group had taken the truck back to the lift area, because Willis wanted to make sure the scene was secured.

Soon after they'd arrived, Willis received an update from the group who found the alien city. Apparently they'd come across some mummified remains, but none of them were complete. They were burned, broken or worse. The best they could come up with was something like a long-limbed dog.

"Have you got any pictures?" Piotrowicz asked curiously. "Of the aliens."

"Nigel's group may have taken some, but they're keeping them tightly under wraps," the bureaucrat replied. "No unauthorized personnel see *anything* we find down here. Some of the crew who found the ship snapped some shots, and their cameras were confiscated immediately.

"If you see *anyone*—miners, even your own men—recording what they find, shut it down immediately, and report to me," he added.

Piotrowicz figured he'd have to be more careful when the time came. Other folks might give up their cameras, but he had no intention of doing the same. Even as he and the desk jockey were talking, everything was being recorded... for posterity.

When the time came, he planned to sell to the highest bidder.

"Okay," he said, "so what's up with the black glass?"

"We're really not sure. At first we thought it was made from the local sand—that black stuff on the surface. But it's different on a chemical level. It's as if there's something out there making the stuff."

"Well, Decker said there's some of this stuff up near the surface, poking up out of the ground. How far down did you say we are?"

"Seven thousand feet, give or take." Willis shook his head. "But that's probably unrelated. Most of the stuff near the surface probably broke off and worked its way upward years ago. Maybe through tectonic activity. Or perhaps it was the storms."

The mercenary shook his head. "I don't get you."

"Well, the city and this ship were likely at the surface, back when the crash happened. The storms were bad enough to bury all of that. For all we know, the black tunnels might have been manufactured on the surface, then buried over the centuries."

Piotrowicz shook his head.

"Not a chance," he said. "Listen, I'm not remotely an expert, but even I can see that stuff is a lot newer."

"What do you mean?"

"It doesn't just *look* wet. I found one of the tubes close to the ground, and there was moisture coming out of it."

"That's impossible," Willis said. "There's no source of moisture down here—it's as dry as a desert."

"We can drive over and check right now if you want to." At that moment the lift started to move again, somewhere above.

"We've got to get a handle on this," Willis said, and he reached for the comm on his hip. "I'll stop them."

Before Piotrowicz could respond he heard Juergens screaming in his ear, "We're under attack! We need backup!" The sound was so sudden and so loud that he almost pulled the headset away before the words registered.

Not far away Anderson shot a look in his direction. Vogel was talking with the three stuck over at the communications base. They tried to respond, but nothing seemed to be getting through. Then Manning came on, trying to raise Juergens from wherever he was.

Nothing.

Piotrowicz called to the team to assemble, and grabbed his weapons. He asked the comm techs if they could locate Connors and his team, but their fancy, state-of-the-art screens didn't show a damned thing.

Worthless piles of crap.

Willis waved for his attention, unaware of what was going on.

"It's the team from level three, using the lift to move a few pieces of digging equipment," he said. "So we'll be stuck down here for a while—but the team at the dig site has already put in a request for when they're done."

"Yeah? Well, right now we've gotta move—on the double," Piotrowicz said. "Our guys who were headed for the dig site just radioed. They're under attack. So you might want to call your people back and alert them."

"Under attack? By who?"

"No fucking idea. But if I were you, I'd make the call."

Without waiting for a reply, he ran, gesturing to the rest of his team to join him at the truck. As soon as the four were aboard, the vehicle was moving.

Juergens was a card. He liked playing practical jokes. But he would never consider crying wolf and calling it a joke. Never.

Manning would have skinned him alive.

No, whatever had happened, they'd been cut off. He hoped that was all it was.

"Manning. What do you want me to do here?" He suspected he knew the answer. He also doubted he was going to like it.

"Get over there. Have comm tell you where to go—they may be able to get a decent reading."

"Negative, chief. They already tried." Perkins answered him just the same, her voice tight with tension.

"Interference. Same as with DiTillio. We're getting nada. Something around here is screwing up our signals."

"Fuck!" Manning said it at the same time as Piotrowicz. "Go check it out, Petey. And be careful."

"Damned straight."

The truck moved under the hull of the ship, and they had to duck their heads. Then it got to the point that the vehicle wouldn't fit—they would have to continue on foot.

Piotrowicz climbed down and gestured to his team. They came on fast and hard, all of them carrying, and all of them looking very seriously like they wanted to kick some ass.

Fine by me, he thought. But he kept quiet, listening...

The distance they covered was a few hundred yards. The reduced gravity made it feel like less, but it still took time to get where they were going. They rounded the side of the wreckage and looked everywhere. As the gloom increased, they locked lights onto their weapons, and flashed them into every shadow.

The lights revealed two dead things. Maybe it was three. The pieces didn't quite seem to match up. Lutz crouched close to one of them and used the barrel of his repeating shotgun to move it around to get a better look.

"The fuck is that?" Lutz's voice was calm enough, but he was looking around with a lot more caution than he'd been managing a minute earlier.

"Comm, can you receive visuals?"

"Negative. I mean you can try, but no promises."

Nothing like a solid, committed answer to make the day go better.

"I'm gonna try. We need to let everyone see this." He leaned in closer and took his time viewing the body. "What's this thing made of?"

"Looks almost like a machine." Vogel's voice was soft. "Are we dealing with bio-mechanical organics here? Like the ship?"

"No idea." Piotrowicz stepped back. There were places on the ground that had burned, wherever the spillage from the things had landed. Spots on the side of the wrecked ship showed similar damage, and even as he was checking it out, Estrada walked over carrying Connors' helmet.

"Manning, it looks like we've got five more down," Piotrowicz reported. "We're seeing evidence of the combat, but no bodies. No *human* bodies. There are other things here. I think we've found the bugs we were supposed to come hunting for."

Manning didn't answer.

He repeated his comment, just to be sure.

No one answered.

And then the sound of an engine reached him. It was large and it was loud, and it didn't sound good.

He gestured for the rest of his team to pull in close to the ship, and was glad of it a moment later. The vehicle came barreling around from the far side of the dig site, where none of them had been yet. It wasn't armored, but it was enclosed. There were lights, but only half of them were working, and the entire massive affair was smoking as if it had been caught in a firestorm. The outer hull was pitted and scarred, with several deep gashes and what looked like at least one hole burned into the side. One of the tires was a slagged mess, flapping and thumping instead of running smoothly over the ground.

Estrada said something, but the roar of the engine was too loud.

The wagon tore past them at high speed, and for a brief moment Piotrowicz saw the driver's face. Her eyes were wide and her lips were drawn back in a rictus of fear. And he could see the reason why. There were black-skinned things hanging onto the top, ripping at the metal shell and trying to get inside.

Piotrowicz and Lutz both fired. One of the nightmares sailed off the side of the vehicle as it rumbled past. Another blew apart. Lutz liked his shotgun for a reason. The damned thing did damage.

It was hard to tell if there were more of the things on the wagon as it shot around the hull and disappeared from sight.

A second later they didn't much give a damn anyway, because the one he'd shot was coming for them, shrieking as it charged. Piotrowicz froze. The damned thing was alive—and it was very, very angry.

Anderson tried to lift her weapon, but too late. The thing took a swipe at her and slapped her back against the ship's hull hard enough to stun her. She never even made a noise. Vogel was right next to her, and she pumped four rounds into the thing, screaming like a banshee the entire time.

One round would have done it. Four was overkill, not that she could be blamed. Then the wounds vomited a sickly substance, and the stuff hit Piotrowicz's arm, his chest, his face. The pain was immediate and he cried out as he wiped at his cheek. The fire spread across his nerves, and the next thing he knew Vogel was knocking him to the ground, dragging his helmet off of his head. Lutz pulled at his vest and jacket.

The incinerating pain calmed down after a moment, though it did not go away completely. His clothes smoldered on the ground and Lutz stood back up, looking around, while Vogel dug into her pack, looking for a first aid kit.

Not five feet away, Anderson was getting back to her feet, her vest slashed open by the claws on the dead thing.

Lutz called on his radio, warning comm about what was coming their way.

Madness.

2 2

DATA STREAM

Eddie Pritchett looked contrite when he came into Andrea Rollins's office onboard the *Kiangya*. And with good reason. When she summoned him, she had wanted him to arrive afraid.

"You called for me, ma'am?"

"I did," she replied brusquely. "It's come to my attention that your actions might have jeopardized our mission."

His eyes flew wide.

"I would never do that, ma'am."

Rollins reached into the top drawer and pulled out a thick folder of papers, which she dropped on the desktop. The folder was really mostly for effect. She didn't need to print out the files. She had a better memory than that.

"Your file," she said, peering at him. "You have a long history with your group. Before you worked for Manning you were with the Colonial Marines, where you were trained as a pilot. Before that you worked with your family, who subcontracts for Weyland-Yutani, and has made a very comfortable living in the delivery business. I believe you are expected to join them eventually."

He listened to her words and nodded slowly. He licked his lips, and did his best not to look too scared.

"What's your point?" he said. Then, "Ma'am."

She stared at him until he looked away.

"My point is really very simple," she said, rising from her chair. "The next time you pull *anything*—any sort of stunt involving one of my drop ships, flying to the surface of a planet, or up to the *Kiangya*, for that matter, I will make it my personal goal to end your career, and any career you might hope to have in the future."

"What?" he answered. "What can you… would you… What are you *talking* about?" She couldn't decide if his indignation was real, or if he was merely putting on a show for her. Ultimately, it didn't matter.

"I watched the drop ship's descent when you were taking Manning and the entire crew down. I also listened. I heard your comments about turbulence and storms, and I know there was none."

"Listen, *ma'am*," he said, "I would *never* endanger a crew onboard my ship." He regained his composure and locked eyes with her again.

"I'm sure you wouldn't, Mister Pritchett. At least not intentionally." She stared hard at him as she leaned forward. "Just the same, I have no doubt that your cargo got bounced around. I'm sure that if I talked to them, I'd hear a few stories about how often you've pulled that sort of stunt."

He did his best to look offended. Still, he didn't look her straight in the eye.

"Let me make this clear," she said, sitting back down. "You are flying a vessel owned by Weyland-Yutani, and leased to Mister Manning. The drop ship at your disposal is worth quite a bit more than you make in a decade. It is substantially more valuable than… well, than *you* are."

Rollins waited for a moment, until he turned back, before she continued.

"You have work to do, and so do I. If your next trip down to the surface isn't a textbook example of how to land a drop ship— without incident, if your return trip isn't just as exemplary, you can say goodbye to your pilot's license."

"Say what?" he bellowed just then.

She remained unimpressed.

"Simply do the job you're being paid for, in a professional manner, and I won't need to bother with you any longer. However, if you fail to follow this simple directive, I promise you will not be happy in your future endeavors.

"The majority of the work your family does relies upon jobs which come from my employer. I occupy a spot high enough in the chain of command to enable me to reassign any contracts I wish to reassign.

"Don't make me threaten your family's livelihood, Mister Pritchett."

He actually took two steps toward her, his hands balling into fists. Then he stopped, spreading his fingers, doing his best to act the part of the wounded victim.

She wasn't playing.

"Were you planning on attacking me, Mister Pritchett?" she asked. "Is this an attempt at intimidation?"

"What?" he said. "No. I… I just…" He lost his ability to speak for a moment.

Then he took exactly three steps back.

Rollins looked him up and down, a small sneer of disapproval clear on her face.

"You can go now."

He left quickly, his eyes downcast.

The door had barely closed when the first tight beam of information reached her desktop. The signal came in clearly, reaching from the transmitters on the surface to the ship in geostationary orbit above the Sea of Sorrows.

What came through looked, for all intents and purposes, like so much white noise. Sometimes that was inevitable, especially in areas where interference caused signal reflection and signal breakdown. Technology being what it is, there were still some issues that hadn't been solved.

Andrea Rollins didn't care in the least about white noise or interference. She did, however, pay a great deal of attention to the signal embedded inside of that synthetic static. Weyland-Yutani owned the patents on the devices that created that artificial signal, and on the hardware and software that could break it down into its component parts. It wasn't a technology currently available on the market.

Hers was the only computer on the ship capable of breaking down the coded information.

She was keeping very careful track of all of the data coming in, as it related to each member of the team on the surface. From her desk she could monitor their life signs, when they changed, and how they changed. She made sure to note when they died.

Rollins used the available equipment to carefully map the entire series of tunnels beneath the surface. Had she been so inclined, she could have given the location of each and every member of the team, and precisely where each chamber lay within the vast network of tunnels. She even had data on the location of the alien life-forms—the Xenomorphs. Not all of them, she suspected, but a decent number. The aliens only registered when they moved. The rest of the time the tunnels they'd created worked brilliantly as camouflage. There were so many potential applications that it was staggering.

But she felt no need to share. The situation was well in hand.

Rollins scanned the data and considered all options. There was no doubt in her mind that there would be excessive collateral damage. That was acceptable. It was expected. It was what she wanted.

Fewer witnesses, in the end.

The mercenaries didn't concern her. They were just there to make a dollar, and they would be the ones who brought her the specimens she needed. It was the others—the more respectable and therefore more credible workers—who posed the greater threat. The fewer of them who survived, the better.

In the end, everyone was expendable.

2 3

LABYRINTH

"We're under attack! We need backup!"

When the call came through, Decker watched the mercenaries. They all froze, just inside of a narrow chamber, and their eyes glazed as they listened to the chaos coming over the comm link. A couple of the men started to talk, and Manning waved a hand for silence. When they didn't get the message, he flat-out roared for them to shut up.

Then it hit him—hard.

This wasn't a general feeling—it was *very* specific. More intense than anything Decker had ever experienced from a human being. For a moment he thought it might have come from the men under attack, a reflection of their deaths, but quickly ruled it out.

This was close, and getting *closer*. He backed away from the entrance they'd come through as fast and hard as he could, pushing past the redheaded kid, Garth. The kid looked at him with wide eyes.

It came up out of the entrance, screeching like hell, and aimed itself right at him. But the chamber was confining, and there were people in the way. Something dark and wet grabbed Garth by his leg and pulled him down as it climbed from the tunnel. The kid screamed in shock and pain, and the thing let out a second screech as it crawled up the poor bastard's body, its claws tearing through his flesh.

Garth bled and screamed and all hell broke loose. They'd been climbing—none of them was prepared for an attack. The savagery was horrifying. The skinny guy—Decker never got his name—tried to fight, and was bent and broken for his trouble, bones popping in his body.

The thing didn't crawl out of the hole so much as it unfolded, slithering into the room and growing larger and larger as it came. It let out another hissing screech as it pushed the broken forms aside, and looked around.

Seeking Decker. He knew it. Felt it. And he backpedaled again as the thing turned toward him.

The claustrophobic space was filled with bodies and noise—everyone was screaming and shouting. A three-clawed hand lashed out and slapped across a man's face, gouging bloody tracks across his features. He staggered under the onslaught and the thing charged, crouching and not really bothering with anyone in the way, simply wading through them on its way to Decker.

He was a dead man. His limbs refused to move, his hands hung loosely at his sides, ignoring his demands that they go for the reaper, reach for another weapon, do *anything* at all.

The butt of Adams's rifle smashed into the thing's face and knocked it sideways. Bridges' massive boot pushed it further down as it tried to recover, and the man lowered a lethal looking, two-pronged muzzle against the creature's torso. He pulled the trigger.

Instead of exploding, the thing arched its entire body and shrieked, thrashed, and shuddered. It slammed to the ground and twitched, but otherwise did not move. The stench of ozone filled the air, along with an odor like hot metal.

Bridges looked down at the thing with a murderous expression on his face. He backed away quickly, and by the time he'd taken two paces most of the people in the room were aiming a very large variety of weapons at the thing on the floor.

They took a moment to look the thing over. It wasn't a spider, not at all. Though there was certainly something insectoid to it.

The long limbs were sealed in a glossy exoskeleton that looked all too much like the dark translucent walls of the tunnel where they currently stood. The head was almost as long as its torso, and half-hidden shapes rested within it. If there were eyes, they weren't visible, but there was no missing the mouth on that monster.

Dread centered around Decker's heart. The thing was unconscious and still he knew it hated him for reasons he did not understand.

Manning looked over at Bridges and slapped him on the arm.

"Got yourself a genuine bug," he said. "Good work." He looked to one of the mercenaries at the back. "Check on Garth."

"That is one ugly motherfucker," Bridges said. He sounded pleased with himself.

Someone crouched down over the kid's form, and then rocked back on his heels.

"Garth didn't make it. Neither did Holbrook."

Manning's face was unreadable, and his voice was low.

"Anyone here got some rope?" he asked. "Maybe a nice steel mesh net?"

A wiry looking man turned his back to Manning, indicating his own backpack.

"Help yourself," he said. "But you'll have to do it yourself—you don't pay me enough to tie that thing up."

"Is it alive, Bridges?" Manning asked.

"Shouldn't be. The shocker's set to kill."

Decker looked at the thing, and shook his head.

"It's alive," he said. "I think it's starting to wake up."

"How can you tell?" Adams peered at him, and then down at the thing on the ground.

"Its emotions—if that's what you can call them." He followed her gaze. "It still wants to kill me."

"What did you do to piss these things off, Decker?" Manning was busily pulling a length of very thin rope from the other man's pack.

"I don't know." He took a very small step toward the thing. It moved perhaps an inch, and he backed up again.

Bridges nailed it again, holding the twin contacts against the creature's skin until they could all see the smoke rising from where the metal had touched. Then he looked at Decker.

"Is it dead now?"

"I have no idea. I can't get anything from it. Maybe that's a good sign," he offered.

Manning nodded and quickly started binding the arms.

"Works for me." He worked very efficiently and made sure to cover the arms, the legs, the feet, and the tail.

The creature remained motionless.

"How the hell are you going to tie up that head?" The man who'd offered the bindings was the one who asked. "It's fucking huge—and that's some seriously badass dental work."

"I got nothing, Wilson. And I'm not getting anywhere near those teeth." He looked toward Alan. "You sense any more of those things, Decker?"

"I don't think so." He stopped for a moment, and focused. The hatred had shifted into background noise—painful, but manageable. "I can't be certain, though. We should head back down the tube."

"But what if there are more where that came from?" Adams asked. "It would've taken more than just this one to bring down DiTillio, Rodriguez, *and* Joyce."

Before he could respond, Manning jumped in.

"I think he's right, and at least we know the way, back where we've been." He looked at the thing on the ground. "We have a specimen. It's maybe alive. We get this thing down to the lift, and we get the hell gone from here. Mission accomplished."

With that, he grabbed one of the cords, and began to drag the creature toward the opening.

"One of you lazy excuses give me a hand here. This thing is stupid heavy." Bridges stepped up, and Manning shook his head "Not you—I need you to take care of Garth. Have Duchamp help with Holbrook's body."

Two other mercs jumped in, and found a grip on the alien shape. Half of the group dropped through the entrance of the tunnel, one at a time. The way was slick at times, making it harder to go down than it had been climbing up.

Manning and another of the mercenaries started lowering the thing down, and then carefully began following it. The rest followed, and somewhere in the middle of the train of bodies, Decker started down, hanging near Adams without even being aware of it.

It was difficult to see where they were going, it smelled like sweat and fear, and the beams of the flashlights sent shadows skittering around. At times the crush of bodies was so dense that the lights hardly penetrated at all. He found handholds, not by sight, but by touch.

What a shitty place this would be to die, he thought.

After what seemed like forever, shouts erupted up ahead. Manning bellowed and someone else let out a loud scream.

"Fuck it," Manning said. "Let the bastard fall, and follow it. We'll pick up the pieces when we get down there."

"Bit right through my damned boot!"

"Your toes still there, Denang?"

"Yeah."

"Then call it a win, and keep going."

After that they traveled a bit faster. The darkness, the body heat, the echoing sounds of voices all grated on Decker's nerves. On all of their nerves, he suspected. Adams was just below him. Suddenly she stopped, and she cursed under her breath. He tapped the guy behind him, telling him to do the same.

She turned around, and shone her light up at him, covering it with her hand so that she didn't blind him.

"We have to start climbing," she said, sounding pissed.

"What? What are you talking about?"

"We have to start climbing."

That made no sense. "Back up to where we were? Why?"

"Because those things blocked the way."

"What?"

"The way we came—it's sealed," she said. "Whatever they are, they're at least a little smart. Manning tried to get down there and something was different. Instead of going into a straight descent, there's a curve now. The tunnel's changed."

Decker's mouth felt dry and pasty.

"How?"

"I don't know. I don't care." Adams pointed her finger. "Manning's pretty sure wherever the tunnel leads to now, it's probably a trap, and we're not taking the bait. So start climbing."

He turned, and the guy behind him cursed. But they started climbing, just the same.

2 4

EXAMINATIONS

The van rolled along like a wounded beast, and slowed only as it rounded the edge of the ship.

The three members of the comm team watched them approach and Dae Cho reached to the side of his console and picked up his assault rifle. Perkins and Dwadji stayed where they were, but their expressions said they approved. The weapon was solid and reliable, and came with four grenades and a launcher. He didn't know exactly what was going on, and he didn't much care. If the people on that truck came at him screaming, they would die that way.

Dina Perkins covered her free ear to block out the ruckus, and focus on what Manning was saying. According to him, they'd subdued a bug, but it had revived and bitten someone. They'd been forced to drop it.

Their pathway in was blocked now, and they would have to find a different way out.

No one could get a response from Connors—he and his team were missing in action. Piotrowicz and his team were still among the living, though at least one of them was wounded.

Cho stood up from his seat and swung his rifle over his shoulder, the barrel pointed toward the heavens as he walked toward the newly arrived vehicle, sitting in a cloud of dust. Perkins stayed at her station and Dwadji stayed beside her, trying again to reach Connors.

Willis was already at the door, pulling it open as the people inside tried to spill out. They crammed together so that no one could get anywhere, until the Weyland-Yutani bureaucrat grabbed a handful of shirt and half hauled the first one out. The rest sort of erupted from the vehicle in a frantic mass, like a grim parody of a clown car, seven in all and none of them remotely calm.

A short, heavyset man in his late fifties grabbed Willis by his shoulders and half fell onto him as he looked around.

"Go!" he said breathlessly, looking around in a panic. "We have to go."

"We can't go anywhere, Doctor Silas," Willis responded. "The lift is topside. We're stuck until it gets back here, Nigel."

"Then call it!" Silas said. "There might be more of those things. We've got to—"

Cho walked over and interrupted.

"More of what things?"

Short-and-round looked at Cho as if he was insane.

"Who are you?" he demanded.

"Security," Cho said, before Willis could speak. "Now tell me what you're in a panic about."

"That city," Silas said. "It's got occupants, and they're evil."

"Wait, you mean the city at the dig site?"

"Yes." The man nodded emphatically. "There are things living there, and all they want is to kill us. We have to get away from here!"

"Chill yourself," Cho said. "We're not going anywhere for a while. Like the man said, the lift is being loaded with mining equipment. Then it's supposed to drop to level four and unload all of that stuff. And *then* it can come down here and get us."

The man looked like the devil himself was on their heels. His thin hair was plastered to his head with sweat and he wiped at it frantically.

"You don't understand! These things are insane!"

There was motion off to the right, and Perkins jumped with surprise. Then she saw Piotrowicz and his group coming toward them. Lutz was dragging something on the ground behind him, hauling it by a line secured to what looked like a leg. Whatever it was, it didn't look human enough for Perkins's comfort. Anderson and Estrada were trailing toward the back, their weapons aimed at the thing. Half of Petey's face was covered in gauze, and he looked like he wanted to kill something in the worst way.

Perkins moved to get a better look at the thing. It was broken and dead and creeped the hell out of her. Her skin grew cold as she studied it. As the new arrivals moved closer still, half a dozen of the people from the transport moved in, scientific curiosity slowly winning over their fear.

She was about to warn Cho, but saw him look past the shouting driver. He held up a hand to silence the man.

"Got five people coming right now that killed the things on your truck," he said. He pointed with his chin, and Short-Round turned. The man took in a deep shuddery breath, and exhaled.

"Listen, where there's one of those damned things, there could be more. We don't know how many there are, but the probes show that there's a lot of territory out there where they could be hiding." He paused to breathe again. "They're fast, and they're deadly, and their one purpose seems to be to kill."

Willis interrupted.

"You said the probes were working in the city?"

"What's that got to do with anything, Tom?" Nigel asked.

"If the probes are working, they should tell us what is down there. Including any life signs." Willis spoke very calmly. "Did you leave any of the probes up and moving?"

Silas swallowed a few times, and did his best not to sound like a lunatic. He wasn't really succeeding but he was trying.

"Tom, we launched more than a dozen probes. They're still working, and still taking readings, but all they can do is map the area. It's much larger than we thought it was. Might be that a lot of it is still buried—we can't tell too easily—but there are places back there where the probes were moving freely, so it looks like we have open spaces."

Piotrowicz and his team reached them. The head of the team didn't speak. He simply stood by to take in the information. Perkins walked over to their prize, and stared at it, trying to make something out of the jumble of limbs, claws, and teeth. Up close it was worse than before. As Piotrowicz stopped, the scientists clustered around his prize, wide-eyed and curious.

Willis gestured to Silas.

"We have thirty or so heavily armed security officers down here with us. You were out doing your survey when they arrived yesterday, but they're here to help secure the area and keep us safe. I have every confidence that they'll manage just fine."

Perkins noticed that he didn't mention the eight people who were missing. No need to fuel the panic. Apparently the rest of the team agreed with her. They all kept their traps shut.

Perkins looked at Piotrowicz.

"Are you okay?" The man's stance said he was pissed off. Still, he managed a smile.

"Yeah. I'm good," he said, but the bandages said otherwise. "Some burns, but nothing that can't wait until everything calms down. Vogel already patched me up."

Cho nodded, looked at Silas, and adopted a placating tone.

"We have a medic here," he said. "Are any of your people hurt?" The short man nodded hard.

" ...We can't find..." He took a deep breath again. "There are four members of our expedition who we left behind when we were attacked. We should send someone to find them. And Colleen was attacked by something that tried to choke her. Whatever it was, it didn't want to let go of her face, but it finally fell off on its own and died."

"Then let's have a look at Colleen first." Cho glanced at Piotrowicz, and gestured toward the van. "You up to a quick look?"

Piotrowicz sighed. Wounded or not, carrying his pack or not, he was still the most experienced when it came to basic first aid. He trudged over, and Vogel went with him, unslinging her backpack. They disappeared inside.

Willis spoke up.

"Did you remember the receiver for the probes?"

Nigel looked at him and nodded.

"It's in the van. Hardwired, actually."

Willis headed over without asking, and Cho looked to Perkins, gesturing for her to go along. If the probes were working and recording, they might provide important information—including readouts with clues as to why the hell they weren't working everywhere.

As Willis and Perkins neared the van, Piotrowicz and Vogel came back out. Vogel was holding the freakiest damned thing Perkins had ever seen, and looking like she might just puke her guts out.

The thing was pale, about three feet long, and hung from her hand by a thick, serpentine tail. The tail ran down to a body that boasted two bulbous sacks and long spidery limbs that had curled in on themselves, like a dead insect. It looked like a deformed cross between a crab and a spider.

Cho looked at the thing and blanched.

Vogel dropped it to the ground and Piotrowicz crouched over it, pulling a very large knife from his boot—the better to probe at the corpse.

Perkins stared and stepped back.

Hell's gonna freeze over before I get close to that thing, she thought to herself.

Cho cleared his throat.

"Is that thing very, very dead?"

"Hell, yes." Vogel nodded. "No way I'd've touched it if it wasn't."

"That's the thing that tried to choke your friend?" Cho directed that at Silas.

The man nodded and swallowed nervously.

"Where is Colleen?"

Piotrowicz looked toward him. "She's dead. I'm sorry, but it looks like she might have been shot."

"But we don't have any weapons." Silas's voice was very small, and he blinked back tears. Whatever existed between him and Colleen, he was feeling the pain of her loss.

"She's got a hole in her chest. There's no heartbeat. I didn't see a hole in the window, but I suppose it's possible she got hit when we were firing at those things."

Silas's eyes were watery.

"No, she was alive when we pulled up. She was lying back across a seat. She was unconscious, but I can't see how you could have shot her."

"Was anyone else on your team injured?" Cho asked.

"No. Just. Just Colleen." Silas looked wretched.

Perkins thought she saw something moving, off in the shadows, but when she turned in that direction there was nothing. It still sent a chill through her. While she was looking, though, Willis climbed onto the transport and went in search of the receiver. Perkins sighed, and then followed.

The inside of the van was chaos. Items were tossed around and kicked under seats, equipment had been pushed aside or knocked over, and a lot of it probably was junk as a result.

Halfway down the length of the vehicle, flat on her back across one of the seats, a dead woman stared at the ceiling. The hole in her chest was huge and bloody, with ribs visible through a ruin of cloth, skin, and flesh. Perkins didn't want to look at her, but she did.

The woman's body was still stippled with sweat, the skin wasn't yet sallow, and the flesh wasn't yet sagging—she had to have died within the past few minutes. A trail of blood ran from the wound all the way to the floor. Damned if it didn't look like something had left little footprints in that mess.

Perkins reached over and closed the woman's unseeing blue eyes, even as she mouthed a small prayer.

Willis was busy examining the readouts. She stepped up behind him, careful not to disturb what he was doing.

"What did you find?" Her voice was enough to make the man

start. His eyes rolled toward her, and he clutched at his chest.

"Not much," he said, sounding disappointed. "I mean, the readouts seem to have died." Perkins looked at them and saw what he meant. There was a good amount of information and a decent rendering of the dig site, but either the probes had stopped recording information or—more likely—the interference between here and the probes was blocking any further reception.

"Shit." She shook her head. *Enough.* She didn't want to be around the corpse any longer anyway. She climbed out of the van and headed back for her group.

By the time she got there, the majority of the research team had calmed down a bit more. A couple of them had actually joined Piotrowicz in his examination of the spider-like thing on the ground, and most of the others were looking at the larger life-form where it lay nearby.

"Whatever it is, I would hardly call it an advanced life-form," Silas said. He seemed to have recovered enough for his scientific curiosity to kick back into gear. "There's no evidence of a highly developed brain apparatus. I can't even see how this creature can eat, in any way that makes sense to you or me."

"Yeah, well, I don't give a shit if it can cook a seven-course dinner," Piotrowicz said. "For us, it's a payday." He dug into Vogel's backpack until he came out with a sterile plastic bag. Vogel followed what he was doing, and crossed her arms.

"You put that goddamned thing in my backpack, you get to carry it. I've had enough of it—I don't want it anywhere near me."

"Quit being such a girl, Vogel." Piotrowicz tried to smile, but it looked as if it hurt like hell.

"I am a girl," she replied. "You should know, you've been trying to get in my pants for long enough."

Willis stepped out of the van and put away his comm unit. He looked less than pleased.

"There was a problem with the equipment they were moving in the mine—they tried to move too much at one time," he said. "The lift needs repairs, and it's going to be another two hours at least, before they can get it down here."

That sent a ripple of disappointment through the group, and several began to voice their objections. Before they could do so, Dwadji's voice came through the comm.

"Still no sign of DiTillio, Rodriguez, or Joyce," he said. "Manning and his group are going higher. They're going to see how far the tubes go, and see if they can locate the missing team."

"Tell Manning about the van," Cho said. "Tell him we have... seven more with us."

"Affirmative."

Cho looked to Willis.

"Are there no backup lifts?" he asked. Perkins was pretty sure he knew the answer, and was grasping at straws.

"Not down here," was the reply. "They only made it down a couple of levels, and were still working on clearing the rubble out of the way on the other side of the vessel."

Piotrowicz walked over from where he'd been talking with Silas. He didn't look happy. He was holding up the bagged body of the spider-thing.

"Well, if this thing is indigenous, there're probably more where it came from," he said. "But Doc Silas can't say how many, or where." He looked up at the silicon tube, and frowned.

"Where the hell did this one come from?" Cho asked, turning on Silas. His expression made it seem as if he held the scientist personally responsible.

"The expedition..." Silas began, cringing under the gaze. "We had only just broken through the latest wall. The ones we left behind—" He cut himself off. "The ones who went through the wall, they must have seen something, but they were cut off before they could report." He looked at the creature. "For all we know, the thing was a pet gone feral, or the equivalent of a rat. We just don't know. We weren't expecting to run across something alive."

"As much as they have their heads stuck up their asses, sometimes the Colonial Marines get it right," Cho growled. "Protocols like quarantines come in handy at a time like this."

Silas looked as if he wanted to explain himself, but Cho waved it aside. "We all know why the Colonials weren't informed, doctor. We're all here for the same reason. I just don't like running around blind with not one, but *two* different predators on my heels." He pointed to the dead thing that Lutz had dragged along. "What can you tell us about that thing?"

"It's fast, it's savage, and it bleeds acid strong enough to melt steel and pop galvanized rubber tires. I smeared a couple of them against walls on my way back here, and when they were hurt the blood ruined everything it touched." Silas peered at it with open fear, as if he thought it might jump up and renew its assault. "Also, it has a second set of teeth inside its mouth, mounted on a very long proboscis."

"Nasty—even if you get in a good shot, the sons of bitches can kill you," Cho said. "What do you think, Mister Willis? Are these the things your employers want us to bring back, or is there something *else* out there?"

He looked around.

"Has anyone seen Willis?"

2 5

DARK TIDES

They waited for something to show up, training their weapons on each of the openings that led to the spot where they'd stopped to take a break. Decker listened for any sound, scanned for any feeling that might indicate that something was approaching.

Nothing.

All he got for his efforts was a raging headache.

After a short time, Manning chose a direction for them to go, up and toward what he hoped would be the ship itself. The tubes got larger the closer they came to the source, and with open space they would be better able to defend themselves without shooting one another in a chaotic firefight.

Decker was up front, with Manning. At times the tunnels became so cramped that they had to crouch, or crawl on hands and knees. The captured creature had been retrieved from where they'd dropped it, and the poor bastards in the rear had to drag it. The thing showed no signs of recovering from the third high-voltage jolt.

Maybe it's finally dead, Decker mused. *One down, and who knows how many more to go.*

"These tunnels must be impervious to the bugs' blood," Manning commented. "Maybe it's the same stuff as their hides, or something a lot like it. Silicon still seems like a safe bet." He paused for a moment, then took a branch that rose steeply in what Decker hoped was the right direction.

"Whatever's in their blood, I don't want it splashing on me—especially in here," the merc continued. "It sounds like the stuff messed up Piotrowicz pretty bad. So if we run into any more, use non-explosive rounds."

"Why?" Decker asked. "I mean why non-explosive? Won't they splatter, regardless of what we use?"

"The tunnels are fairly strong," Manning replied. "But if they get blown to hell, we might not survive the fall."

Decker knocked on the side of the tunnel. The result was a dull thud.

"No. I don't think so," he said. "We're surrounded by dirt and rock now. Back when we started, the tunnel shook a little with each step. Now I think you could jump up and down, and never have to worry about it collapsing."

"Good point, genius." Manning looked down until he met Decker's eyes. "All we'd need to worry about is having a few tons of dirt bury our asses. Shouldn't be a problem."

"Gotcha." Decker had to admit it was a good point.

The air was thick now, and stiflingly hot. Any draft they'd had before didn't stand a chance against more than a dozen tightly packed bodies, all taking in oxygen and generating body heat. He didn't think they could actually suffocate, but it wasn't helping his growing sense of claustrophobia.

He paused.

No. Not claustrophobia.

Despite the medications working in his system, his pulse was rising, he was starting to sweat again, and he fought to catch his breath. Every exhalation felt too shallow, and every intake was a sharp gasp.

"Shit," he said. "I think they're close again." He closed his eyes and focused.

The thing behind him was starting to wake up again—it was still alive, and still radiated the primal urge to *kill*. But there were more of them around now.

Adams cursed behind him. She was trying to get her motion sensor to work, but when she hit it this time, it just gave a crackle of white noise, and the small screen showed nothing but digital snow.

It wasn't just Adams. Several of the mercs had tried again, and failed.

"Where?" Manning tried not to sound exasperated. But he didn't try too hard.

"Best I can tell you is they seem to be above us." He pointed ahead, in the direction they were climbing.

Manning looked up, where the tunnel progressed for some distance into blackness. There was hardly any light, since the tightly packed bodies didn't let much through. He reached for the flashlight he had strapped to his helmet, and increased the beam. Then he started moving again.

"Not seeing anything," he said over his shoulder, "but I'll keep looking, and you keep sniffing, or whatever the hell it is that you do."

Decker didn't bother to reply. Behind him, Adams also increased the power to her flashlight, but he wasn't sure how much it helped. The tunnels were black and glossy—glossier now, as the moisture was thicker. He wondered if that meant this was a newer tunnel. Whatever the case, the damp in the air added to the damp crawling sensation on his skin.

"It's close, Manning," he hissed, keeping his voice low. "Really damned close!" The feeling of hatred aimed his way was so intense it burned. And somehow, the fury was directed at him.

But why? he asked himself. *Was it Ripley? What could she have done to them?* From what he had seen of the creatures, it was a miracle she'd survived. *Of course, in the end, she didn't... Had they marked her? Near as he could tell from the files, she'd never even been to the planet.*

The idea seemed absurd.

They were still crawling upward, and they couldn't have

turned, even if they wanted to. Then, perhaps forty feet down the tunnel Decker heard a man call out in surprise in an area he had already passed. What the merc said was incoherent, more a bark of surprise than anything else, and a moment later the bark became a yell… and then a scream.

Adams pushed into him, half sliding her body along his as she turned as best she could. Her elbow jammed into his leg as she drew one of her firearms. There was a jumble of voices and bodies as the rest of the mercenaries did the same, struggling through the cramped space.

What came was a volley that hit his senses with explosive force, and a second after that the screams of pain began. The tide of bodies, pushing hard to get more room, combined with waves of surprise, and then anger. Yet despite the emotional flood, he felt that hatred again.

Manning cursed and turned, bracing his legs against the sides of the tunnel as he looked down and tried to see past Decker and the mercenaries.

"Pull back from it! Pull back!" he bellowed, but no one seemed to hear—or care. Then an unearthly hiss blended with the chaos of voices.

The monster tore through the first of the mercenaries, clawing and biting and pulling itself up the startled soldier's body as it came. The man tried to fight back, which was where the first explosive noises came in. He opened fire, but all he hit was the wall. Rounds hit the hard surface, cracked through it, but despite Manning's fears the tunnel survived the impacts.

Even as the man fired he was dying. The shape tore his chest open as it crawled up him. His screams were amplified by the narrow space, and then they morphed into a gurgle, followed by silence.

The creature was so intent on its prey—Decker himself—that it ignored some of the mercs that blocked its way, effortlessly thrusting them aside. It moved with an impossible speed, invisible in the darkness, until only three people remained between him and the thing that wanted to kill him. Looking down, he could see past the tangle of limbs—pushing, fighting, trying to get a bead on the thing.

And then he saw it, caught in a beam of light.

2 6

TRAPDOOR SPIDERS

It was bigger than the last one, or maybe it only seemed that way because of the narrow environs. Whatever the case, the woman closest to it—Kelso, he thought it was—opened fire. Her weapon chattered and her arms shook from the recoil.

The clawing, screaming thing below her shrieked and hissed and broke apart, pieces of its body flying back, leaving streamers of the thick goo that passed for blood within its chitinous body. It thrust forward one hand, which disappeared under the assault of her weapon. It tried to throw itself back, but there was no room for escape.

It screamed and it died, and from behind it, from below it, the screams from the mercenaries increased. The blood of the thing rained on them, burning whatever it touched—flesh, weapons, armor. The flesh screamed.

"Good work, Kelso," Adams said, and she let out a breath. Decker did the same, unaware that he'd been holding it until then. "Sonuvabitch, how many down?" she added.

As the nightmare fell back, it revealed a wide hole in the top of the tunnel that hadn't been visible before. It had been hidden within the intricate swirls of the black, glassy substance, enabling the creature to take them entirely by surprise. It hadn't come from behind—it had dropped down from above.

Almost before he realized it, he saw the next nightmare crawling down, peering toward him. The sleek black face shifted as it sought what it wanted, and then he felt that eyeless gaze upon him, and he heard the first deep screech of hatred. The thing was moving, clawing its way up the wall, heading straight for him.

The woman who'd killed the last alien—Kelso—let out a cry and started firing. The people beyond were her comrades, but she wanted to live, and the demon below her, coming toward her, would kill her without even noticing. All that mattered was the prey.

New screams were added to the cries of pain. The creature opened its mouth, and revealed a second set of teeth that bulled into the woman's calf and tore meat and bone apart, even as she fired into the oversized skull. It died violently, but the blood that flew from its death splattered the walls, the people below, and the woman who killed it.

Her leg already in ruins, the mercenary howled and tried to back up even further.

Up above, Manning was bellowing for them to retreat, though he wasn't moving himself. Decker wanted to shout back, wanted to demand to know where he was supposed to go, but part of him understood that the words were meant for the soldiers below, the ones who were trapped in the way of the incidental acid bath that was coming their way.

Still burning, still screaming, Kelso pushed herself higher still as the second black shape fell lifelessly into the tunnel. Manning climbed, making room for Decker, Adams, and the merc behind her to follow suit. There was no choice, really. They could stay where they were and let the people under them die, or they could try to make a little more space, and hope it was enough.

It wasn't. The hole was still there, and even as Decker climbed it gave birth to another black nightmare. The shape was fast and it was savage and it came into the tunnel moving at a hard clip without slowing down.

Kelso tried to fire again, but the thing was there too fast, and its limbs nearly blurred as it shredded her armor and the flesh beneath. She screamed through the process but never fired another round. It clawed past her bloodied corpse, letting her fall with the other dead, onto the people below.

And then there was one man between Adams and Decker and the savagery that was coming for him.

Suddenly the world went bright and the monster fell back shrieking, its head a molten ruin. As it fell it bled, and the bottleneck of corpses and struggling mercenaries received another acid bath. Plasma. It had to be.

And then the attacks stopped. The mercenaries below pushed and clawed their way past the broken dead, climbing the bodies of their fellows, desperate to avoid the burning fluids and the crushing weight of four dead bodies. They screamed and groaned in the process, some wounded, others merely panicking and justifiably desperate to escape.

"Where the hell did they come from?" Manning's voice cut through everything else. The man under Adams pointed to the opening and spoke into his comm-link. Decker didn't hear the words. He was too busy looking at the hole, waiting for whatever would come from it next. He tried to tell if there were more of the damned things nearby, but he couldn't separate out the sensory input. The emotions were too loud, perhaps.

That, or there were no more of the things around.

For now.

Adams was half pinned against him in the narrow tunnel, and she looked into his face for a moment before touching his arm. "Come on, we're going down."

"What?"

"Nico says that hole in the top opens into a bigger area—he climbed up there to get out of the way of that last monster. It's empty now. We're going to check it out."

Decker looked down. Nico must have been close behind Adams, and he was dropping back down from above. Beyond him, the mercs were still working their way past the tangle of dead and wounded.

"What the hell are we going to do in there?"

Adams shrugged. "Regroup."

He looked up toward the merc leader, who nodded his agreement.

"The tunnel's only getting narrower up here—if they hit us again, we'll be dead." He pointed to the opening in the ceiling. "Move it! Come on, let's get this going."

Decker followed orders. Sometimes there's no choice. His life seemed to be made of moments like that lately.

Maybe five minutes later Manning called roll.

They were all gathered in a cylindrical open space, and compared to what they had left, it was like a luxury accommodation. They could stand and there was room to move. Of course there was also room for other things to happen and so several of the team moved to guard the different areas where there were openings into the chamber.

Seven of them had been hurt by the creature's claws or the blood spilling across them. Kelso wasn't hurt—she was dead, and so were three more besides, people whose names Decker had never learned. They had to leave the bodies, which were too covered in acid. Somewhere—probably far below—the thing they had captured earlier was once again on its own, having been dropped in the chaos.

No one offered to retrieve it.

"You have any idea how screwed we are?" A merc whose nametag said "Brumby" was peering down into the tunnel they'd vacated. "They're the same color as everything around us. They have the same sort of texture. They decide to hide, we're going to be lucky to see them at all.

"We are *so* screwed," he repeated.

Manning looked at Decker for a long moment and then spoke up.

"And that's why we want to keep our good buddy here alive and well. He's our little early warning device. He may not be perfect, but he's known both times these things were coming." He held out a headset, and Decker took it. "I want you wearing this from now on."

Decker looked around. Everyone else still had a headset. *Where'd this come from?* he wondered. Then he knew. *Kelso.*

Brumby shook his head. "Where are we going from here?"

"Sooner or later we're going to reach the ship, or the mines," Manning answered. "Likely sooner, if I've estimated the distance right. Once we do, we'll get the hell out of these tunnels." He looked over all of the wounded as he spoke, assessing their injuries. It looked to Decker as if most of them were able to walk at least. "We get back to the cavern, we gather the rest of the team, and we get the hell out of here."

"What about the aliens?" Decker's mouth was flapping before he really thought about it.

"What about them?"

"We are supposed to get specimens." There. He'd said it. "That's what we're here for."

Manning stared at him long and hard. He didn't say a word.

Adams spoke up instead.

"Pretty sure we're going to have more chances there, Decker. I don't think you need to sweat it."

But I do, he thought. *I really do. I can't go home without them, not if I want to have a home to go to.* And ultimately that was true. If he wanted his family safe, he needed an alien.

Once they had one, let Weyland-Yutani worry about how to get it home in one piece. Get it through the quarantine, past the Colonial Marines. Pay off everyone they needed to pay off. How they did it...

He didn't give a damn.

Manning spoke up at last.

"We all know why we're here, Mister Decker," he said, and he spat out the name as if it tasted bad. "No one gets paid by the hour on this assignment. We all know what's at stake."

Decker stared hard, nodded, and said no more. For a while

there was relative peace as the mercenaries tended to the wounded and worked on the best possible route to get the hell away from the very things they were hunting.

2 7

NEGOTIATIONS

Willis didn't go far. He just needed a little privacy.

The group hanging around near the hub was a bit too large. Once away from them, he activated the comm-link he'd been given when the *Kiangya* came into orbit.

This was so much bigger than anyone could have hoped. An entire city worth of relics wasn't far away, and that had to be worth more fortunes than most people could ever imagine. And the living alien life-forms. Whatever they were, they put a different spin on *everything*. The Colonial government was decidedly opposed to any first contact scenario that occurred without their involvement. Weyland-Yutani knew that, of course.

And the people on the surface of New Galveston—they knew it, too. That posed quite a problem.

He needed to make sure that things were kept properly quiet. But it was hard, trying to be in charge of a situation when he was trapped beneath the surface, waiting for the lift.

One call in private, and he could get that taken care of.

Maybe.

Rollins answered almost immediately.

He looked around to make sure that no one was close enough to hear him. No one seemed to care, actually. They were justifiably interested in the creatures they were studying.

Nevertheless, he moved to the far side of the van, and looked back toward the dig site.

"Can you hear me?"

"Of course I can hear you, Mister Willis." Rollins's voice was calm, and carried a tone of authority that Willis found very attractive. He had always been drawn to strong women.

"We've acquired two separate active life-forms down here. We also have a much larger archeological find than originally believed."

There was a notable pause.

"How much larger?"

"Perhaps a full city. More than a town. An ancient, extraterrestrial city. Doctor Silas believes the ship we found might have been taking off when it crashed."

"Continue."

"We need to renegotiate, Ms. Rollins." He needed to be firm about that. Willis had plans, and those plans included moving much higher in the chain of command.

There was a long silence again, long enough to make him wonder if he'd overstepped his boundaries.

"I'm afraid I'll need more information than you've provided thus far," she said. To his relief, she didn't sound upset. "All you've told me is that there's a city. Do you have any details?"

"It's being mapped right now," he lied. "Before long, I can get you complete readings."

"Mister Willis, I already have access to those readings."

"You do?"

"You aren't the only person who is assisting me. I have the readings already." He peered back toward the group.

Who could possibly…?

"That said, you can still be of value to this enterprise. We will need data to back-up the information that has been transmitted. And there are certain… arrangements that will need to be made planetside. You make the appropriate arrangements, and I believe we can discuss a change in our business arrangement."

"Understood," he replied, and he smiled.

He looked back at the mercenaries and the expedition and their collected dead things. Whatever she required, he would provide it. There was always a way.

He'd learned that a long time ago.

2 8

They were awake now. Truly awake, not merely moving while they dreamed. In the darkness they uncoiled themselves from the places where they'd rested and gone into dead-sleep.

For some of them the dead-sleep had gone on too long. They had slumbered and withered and reached a true death, their shells cracking, their lifeblood burning away. For others the sleep was a painful thing and awakening was agony on a level they'd have never conceived.

But they endured.

They thrived. They did what was necessary for the hive.

Through their dark tunnels they heard the sounds of prey. Food, yes, but more importantly, hosts. There was still food in the older places. The desiccated remains of the creatures that had died long ago. It wasn't much, but as long as they spent most of their time in sleep, it sufficed.

But the dead could not host the young. It took life to make life.

And now, at last, life had come again. Soft, and weak and mewling life that would be reborn into the hive.

Eggs had hatched, the breeders had done their work, and now the hosts moaned and made their soft sounds as they prepared to birth new children. And all around them the adults waited.

Not all of the adults.

Some had been sent to locate the destroyer. They moved and hissed and their voices chattered in the darkness. The very thought of the destroyer was enough to send shivers of rage through them. So many had been lost, and not even the long sleep could dull the pain. Most of the queens had been destroyed. Queens! Slaughtered! The lives of so many taken, including the sacred queens.

Most of them.

Not all.

Life prevailed.

And as long as life prevailed, they would hunt the destroyer, and keep their queen safe.

One of the hosts let out a feeble moan and jerked within the confines of the birthing webs.

A moment later lifeblood flowed, and the face of a newborn broke through into the world.

They moved to protect it. The young were so vulnerable.

And the queen in her chamber let out a note of approval.

And all was right with the world.

Or it would be, when the destroyer had been dealt with.

Soon.

Soon.

They were patient. They had to be.

Life prevails.

2 9

DIGNITY

Dwadji and Cho were taking a break and eating, so Perkins settled back at the hub and listened to Manning's orders. The boss man was pissed off, but he was holding it in.

He was trying to find his way back to the mines, and she was trying to help, but there wasn't much she could do. The damned readings were all screwed up. His group was out there, but she couldn't read vitals or get a fix on their location. The best she could manage was to bring him up to date on what was happening at the hub.

And after almost three hours of that, Cho came and relieved her.

When she sat down for chow the tension was thick. Lutz and Vogel were keeping an eye on the landscape while everyone else crashed and burned for a time. No one was sleeping, but they were trying to rest—especially Piotrowicz, whose burnt face was causing him a good deal of pain. He'd opted not to take anything for it. Dulled senses seldom helped in a crisis.

Doctor Silas was staring at the alien remains, with deep worry lines creasing his face. She almost asked him what he was thinking when he spoke.

"Has anyone secured... Colleen's body?" he asked, keeping it together surprisingly well. A few of the mercs glanced at one another.

"Afraid not, Doc," Vogel said.

"I see." Silas nodded quietly, turned, and walked silently toward the ruined vehicle. Perkins grabbed a reaper and followed him.

The damage to the van was terminal. Two tires were flat, one completely shredded. Acid from the bugs had left several holes in the vehicle, and while they had stopped smoldering, they were simply too large to be patched. All the vehicle was good for now was spare parts—and not many of those.

Silas climbed into the van ahead of her, and seemed surprised by her presence when she climbed in behind him. He looked toward her for a moment and then managed a weak, apologetic smile.

"Colleen was a good person," he said. "I just want to show her a bit of dignity."

Perkins nodded. "Let me. Okay?" she said, and she slipped past him. "Let me, and when I'm done you can help me move her to a different location."

He nodded his head and his face twisted into grief. He struggled with it, trying not to show his feelings, but it was obvious to Perkins that the dead woman was more than a colleague.

She'd been down that path a few times over the years. Walker had been her "special friend with benefits" before he got himself killed, and D'Angelo had been something even more before he decided he simply couldn't live the lifestyle any longer. Sometimes, late at night when she was trying to sleep, she still hated him a little for that. She understood it, but she hated him just the same.

There were supplies on the vehicle, and among them she found a cloth sheet large enough to allow her to wrap the body. She was about to do so when Silas spoke, causing her to jump.

"Hold on a moment," he said, and he moved closer, peering at the corpse's chest wound. He reached out, hesitated for a moment, then rolled her over and looked at her back, frowning the entire time.

"What is it?" Perkins asked.

He frowned, grief replaced by curiosity… and something

more. There was something else in his expression.

"It wasn't friendly fire," he said. "We thought it had to be, but it wasn't. Whatever... whatever happened to Colleen, it wasn't a gun blast at all."

"How do you know?"

He pointed with a trembling hand.

"Look carefully. That's an exit wound. But there's no entrance wound." His frown deepened. "Whatever it was that killed her, it did so from inside of her body."

He moved closer to the dead woman and his fingers carefully, ever so gently, examined her mouth and her neck. When he tried to move her face, she resisted. Rigor mortis had taken hold.

Nigel Silas cried silently as he continued to examine her body. Perkins stood with him and bit her tongue. She was a mercenary, and she fought wars for money. She refused to allow herself the luxury of crying for a woman she'd never met, or feeling pity for a man she didn't know.

No matter how much she wanted to.

He stepped back and let her finish the task of wrapping Colleen's body, and then helped her lift it from the van. With the lower gravity on New Galveston, it was likely she could have carried it by herself, even though it was a bit on the heavy side. But it wasn't about proving that she could do it herself. It was about letting the poor man say his goodbyes, and letting Colleen keep a few final dignities, even in death.

When they'd laid her down near the bodies of the alien things, Nigel thanked her and took her hands in his. His were soft. Hers were callused. They lived in different worlds.

He went back to the van and retrieved a case, opening it to reveal some tools. And then he moved over to the spidery thing. For the next fifteen or so minutes, Nigel the man disappeared. Doctor Silas the scientist began working on a puzzle.

Having examined the dead creature, he went back to the van. After a few minutes he emerged, carrying a long strip of translucent hide. It was small, it was wet, and it had several features in common with the full-grown alien—enough to point to a clear connection.

Silas looked it over carefully and set it down next to the spider-thing, still without saying a word.

She almost asked what he was thinking, but decided against it. Most likely it was beyond her, anyhow.

What good could it do?

3 0

WOUNDS

Exhaustion began to take its toll.

They traveled along the pathway that Manning thought most likely would lead to the mines, and they made good progress. But they had been hiking nonstop for hours, much of it uphill, and they needed to rest.

So they found a large enough chamber that they would be able to defend themselves from an assault. They placed lanterns around the area, lighting it as best they could, and dozed in shifts. Most of them, at least. Decker tried to sleep, but every time he began to do so, the nightmares came back more vivid than they had been since his original injuries.

Finally he drifted off, and in his dream he and Adams were locked in a passionate embrace. As he moved to kiss her, streams of spiders came spilling from her mouth and nose and ears. They swarmed over his face, biting him everywhere they landed.

He awoke with a jerk, and instinctively swatted at creatures that weren't there. Rolling over, he tried again to doze, but without success. He was simply too…

They're coming.

Decker bolted upright with a loud gasp, and scanned the area where the group had stopped. Easily half of the freelancers stirred, and several of them grabbed for their weapons.

Instantly alert, Manning looked at him.

"Where?"

Decker paused, then pointed. There was no sign of a tunnel where he pointed, but they awoke the few mercs who remained asleep, and cleared the area he'd indicated, training their weapons. Silent Dave pushed a button on whatever sort of cannon he had unstrapped from his back and the thing let out a long, barely audible whine as it warmed up.

"Won't do to leave our asses bare," Manning said. "Izzo, Simonson, and Foster—watch the tunnels, and make sure nothing comes crawling out."

While the trio moved to comply, the rest focused their weapons on the spot Decker had indicated. As prepared as they were, several of the mercs flinched when the surface opened up. What had been a solid wall swiveled open on an invisible hinge, and the first of the things came in fast, looking around as it stepped through.

It wasn't expecting them to be prepared, however, and instantly it encountered the business end of Bridges' shocker. The creature spasmed as the contacts hit it, and it let out a shriek that was painful to hear. But then it fell, half in and half out of the tunnel.

Another one followed, skittering over the body of the first and making a beeline for Decker. It hissed at him, drooling clear fluids from its mouth as it came, and he stepped back reflexively. Frozen by the hatred of the monsters and the emotions of the humans, he couldn't force his arms to raise his weapon. The sounds they made echoed in his head with a haunting familiarity. In his dreams he knew those noises were words and now those words were directed at him, hurled at him like curses.

Muller was the closest, and he raised his reaper. The first two rounds missed, but the third and fourth and fifth hit their target, blowing sizeable holes through the creature's exoskeleton. The merc danced back to avoid the splash of acid blood, cursing under his breath.

Then the dam broke. Monsters poured into the room in a

frenzy. Claws and whipping tails and black chitin and teeth, so damned many teeth. Decker emptied the clip from his pistol and stepped back, seeking to reload but unable to find the extra clip.

"Damndamndamndamn*damn*!" he chanted, as if it would help.

Manning barked orders, and the mercenaries opened fire. Prepared this time, they were systematic in the massacre, carefully firing and decimating the creatures as they spilled into the room. Decker located his clip, slammed it into place, and joined in the fun.

Then one of the mercenaries let out a scream.

Decker spun and saw the black form of another monster—one that had to have come from another direction. It bit into the man's arm, and it was just a matter of seconds before he was down and the thing was jumping forward, heading for the next in line.

More followed.

The lanterns didn't last long in the melee. Whether they were knocked aside or the things were smart enough to target them, the chamber quickly fell into darkness, punctuated only by the dancing flashlight beams coming from a few of the mercenaries.

Manning was bawling out commands, and the members of his crew were doing their best to listen, but there was no opportunity to regroup. The creatures were relentless as they swarmed their prey. Decker shot another target, knocking it away, then grabbed at Adams, pulling on her arm. She flinched and turned toward him in the semidarkness.

"This way!" he shouted, and she seemed to hear. "Come on!" He pulled and she hesitated, then came with him, calling on the comm for Manning and the rest to follow.

And just like that they were making a tactical retreat. There was no choice really. Not for Decker at least. The flood of emotions from all around threatened to overwhelm him, and all too quickly he would be unable to defend himself. The two of them found a tunnel that was farthest from the swarm, and darted into it.

He heard the running footsteps of several other mercenaries behind them, but didn't pause to look around. The way became narrow, forcing them to crouch, and he worried that they would be forced to go back, but then it widened enough that they could stand.

Manning was nearby, cursing nonstop. And Decker knew why—at the same time as he knew there had been no choice.

Nevertheless, they had done the unthinkable. They left the rest behind.

3 1

The destroyer had escaped. But there were hosts, and they were still alive.

Three-fingered hands and six-fingered hands grabbed the bodies and dragged them toward the birthing chamber. Shape did not matter to the hive. Hosts from the distant past looked different from the hosts they dealt with in the now, but the offspring were all of the hive and the queen's glory. When one of the hosts tried to fight back, it was subdued. The hosts had weapons, but they could not see well in the darkness.

That was good to know. It was best to understand the weaknesses of the prey.

There would be time soon for finding and killing the destroyer. They had not forgotten the sins of the past. They would never forget. There would be no mercy.

The hate burned in them, accompanied by the adoration they felt for the breeders, and their worship for the mother. It was to the glory of the mother that they dragged their latest prizes, and set them before the eggs.

The eggs opened, and the breeders came forth. The hosts screamed with fear as the breeders joined with them, and offered them the life altering seed of the mother. And then the breeders died, as breeders do, that the hosts might be reborn in the glory of the mother.

3 2

PANDEMONIUM

"We need to go back to the city ruins," Silas said. "I think we have a bigger problem than we realize."

"How do you mean?" Cho asked.

"I don't think they're dead," Silas said. "Your men, and my associates. Not yet at least." He waved his hand toward the bodies. "I think they've been taken, the same way poor Colleen was taken."

Cho just stared.

"I don't mean to be cold, doctor, but isn't *that* Colleen?" He pointed to the body that Perkins had helped carry from the van. "How can she *not* be dead?"

Silas looked at the shrouded form and did a few rapid-fire blinks to fight back tears. He managed to hold his own.

"Yes, that's her," he replied. "But I mean I think they might be used the same way she was used." The man's throat worked for a few seconds while he struggled with the words he was trying to say. "I think they put something inside her, to incubate. It broke out of her when it had completed the process, and was ready to emerge."

Cho stared long and hard, and then said something under his breath that Perkins didn't hear. When he spoke up again, his voice was clearer.

"You make it sound as if we're dealing with a bunch of bugs," he said. He paused for a moment, as if a thought had struck him, then waved it away. "I don't have time for this shit. I need to see what's going on with the lift." He headed back for the hub.

Perkins stared after him only for a moment. She understood where he was coming from. All of the scientific information in the world meant less at that moment than the lives of the missing.

Vogel shrugged. "You need to go back to the site? Or only part of the way?"

"Part of the way would suffice, I think," Doctor Silas said. "The ship. It seems to cause the interference. If we can get past that, I can probably link into the readings from the probes. If they're still working, they've likely mapped enough to let us know what we're dealing with." Doctor Silas looked distracted, peering off into the distance. From what she could tell, he seemed that way most of the time.

"Then let's do this." Vogel rose up and headed for the flatbed.

"We need equipment." Silas stood, turning toward the van.

"I'll pull your sensor array, key it to our monitors, and load it onto the flatbed." Perkins sighed. "Let me read the frequency off your remote. Maybe we can make something happen."

She climbed back into the van and felt a chill that she tried to ignore. She didn't believe in ghosts. She did, however, believe in getting the hell out as quickly as she could. She checked the bottom panel of the sensor array for the probes, to see if the frequency was written there. It wasn't.

Of course not, she thought, still ignoring the crawling sensation that ran up and down her back. *Why should* anything *be easy?*

After about five minutes she climbed back out, carrying the entire sensor array. It weighed more than she wanted to think about, but she managed it. While an extremely impatient Vogel waited, she locked the array onto the dashboard of the truck and rigged a power supply.

While she was doing that, Vogel walked over to Cho.

"We're gonna drive the professor over to the other side of the ship," she said, "to see if we can pick up a signal from his probes. Shouldn't take long."

"Like hell you are," Cho responded. "The last thing we need is—"

"No!" Willis said. "That's *exactly* what we need, and I'm going with you. That information could be invaluable." He paused, and added, "The rewards we could reap might be more than you can imagine, Mister Cho."

The tech thought about it for a moment, looking as if he didn't trust what Willis was saying. Then he shrugged, and waved Vogel away.

"Take off, then," he said. "And get the hell back here as fast as you can manage."

They piled onto the truck, started it up, and headed toward the back of the spacecraft. Perkins had the wheel. Willis looked all around as if there might be more of the dark monsters waiting around every corner.

To be fair, there might.

On the flatbed, Silas watched his array, and Vogel kept her weapons ready.

We've gotta do this fast and easy, Perkins thought. *Only as far as we need to go, to get a signal.* She didn't like the idea of going near the place where Piotrowicz got his acid bath. *Upload the data, and get the hell out.*

It took them about ten minutes to reach the other side of the wrecked ship. Vogel was sweating by the time they stopped. She couldn't blame her. She'd actually fought them. Perkins hadn't even seen the things while they were alive, and they scared the shit out of her. She turned the truck, ready to make a fast getaway.

"We can go now," Silas said, breaking the silence.

"What?" Perkins's hand shot toward her gun before she realized what he had said.

"We can go now. We got what we came for." When he heard

that, Willis looked ready to jump out of his skin.

She hit the ignition, and they lurched forward. Silas studied the display as they bounced along, Willis peering over his shoulder, looking as if he wanted to scream. Then they pulled up near the hub, the scientist set the display aside, and hopped from the truck and walked away without saying a word.

"No need to thank us there," Vogel said to the retreating scientist. "We're glad to have helped."

Willis picked up the display and studied it, a look of elation spreading over his face. Perkins craned her neck, trying to look.

"It's not complete, but the probes have been working the entire time," he said. There was an image that looked like the interior of the spacecraft. He tapped a command, and a cavern came into view. There were ruins—structures of every shape and size— stretching back as far as the image could go. "An alien city," he said. "This will keep the research and development people busy for decades."

"Has there ever been a find this big before?" she asked. He looked at her and shook his head.

"I don't know of any," he replied. "And we need to avoid getting ahead of ourselves. It might be that there's nothing down there." He paused and stared at the screen. "But I don't think that's the case. I think there's a lot down there. A lot." He sounded far away, and she suspected he was already planning how he would spend his portion of the earnings.

Despite herself, she smiled.

She left Willis with his monitor and climbed out. As she approached the main group again, there was a ruckus. The look Cho fired her way was one part exasperation and one part plea for assistance.

Silas was in the center of the mix, along with a couple of the others from his group—a heavyset man named Fowler, and a woman who was jabbing a finger into Cho's chest. Perkins picked up the pace, hoping to help the woman avoid getting her finger broken off at the knuckle.

"What's going on over here?" she asked.

They all tried talking at once. Cho bellowed louder than the rest, and for a moment there was quiet.

"Doc Silas thinks we should blow up this entire level," the tech leader said. "Like, right now."

"What?" Perkins looked at the scientist and he stared back, his eyes moist, his lower lip jutting out.

"It's not like th-that," he said, stammering. "Your man, Decker, he was the one who asked the question. Willis told me about it. He said he d-didn't know the answer. I just decided that it needed answering."

"What question?"

"What happened to all the aliens?"

"What?"

"What happened to all of the aliens? I don't mean those things." He waved his hand toward the assortment of dead things, and then waved his other arm toward the wrecked craft and the excavation that lay beyond it. "I mean *them*. The ones who lived here, once upon a time. The race that built the city, and this ship. What happened to all of them?"

Doctor Silas gulped in some air.

"I think I know the answer. I think those *things* happened to them." His finger stabbed in the direction of the dead aliens.

"But I thought the city-builders died off a long time ago." Perkins shook her head. The man's distress was contagious. She contemplated asking Piotrowicz to come over and administer a little something to calm him down.

But Silas smiled and nodded.

"Yes!" he said. "Exactly. And these others, the acid-blooded ones, they should have died, as well. Even if they are responsible for what happened in that city. But they didn't!"

Cho shifted his weight.

"What's the point you're making, doctor," he said. "Whatever these nasties are, they're far from dead, and our orders are to bring one back."

"But we're dealing with an alien species!" Silas answered, and it was his turn to be exasperated. "We don't know what sort of life cycle it has. But if they've been down here since the ship crashed, we must be talking centuries. And they're ready to do to us what they did to an entire *city*."

After that, everyone was silent. Finally Cho got up and waved an impatient hand.

"You handle this, Perkins," he said. "I have to check in with Manning." He stalked off toward the hub.

Chicken shit, Perkins thought, but she didn't say it. "What do you mean, doctor?" she asked. "What makes you think these are the same creatures?"

"There shouldn't be *anything* down here that's alive." He waved his arms to encompass everything around them. "This area was sealed off for a long time. *Centuries*. And no one knew about that city. *No one*. That could have been abandoned for over a thousand years, for all we know.

"There are no water sources down here, less than ten percent humidity, no clean air. There shouldn't be anything bigger than a microbe down here. But when we entered the ship, we found bodies—so old that they were almost beyond recognition. And they all had one thing in common. They had holes in their chests.

"It seemed so impossible, I needed to confirm it, needed to see the data stored in the probes," he continued. "I prayed I was wrong, but it was all there."

"But it's not possible for something to live that long, is it?" Perkins said.

"Whatever we think is possible, something broke out of her body. The same way that something broke out of those old cadavers in the ship." There was real fear in his voice as he pointed at the spider-thing. "It lays eggs in a host. The host enables the egg to mature until it hatches. The thing that comes out grows bigger, until it looks like those things."

The woman with the pointy finger spoke up, but Perkins couldn't understand a word she was saying. Whatever language she was using, it wasn't one she'd heard before.

"To have destroyed an entire city, there had to be hundreds of them." Silas looked at Perkins with wide eyes and practically begged her to understand him. "If that's what happened—and I believe it is—then what happened to the rest of them?"

Perkins was about to respond, when she was cut off by a wail.

3 3

SURPRISES

Piotrowicz winced when Lutz peeled back the bandages on his face. Skin came away and exposed raw nerves, and he wanted to scream. They were out of sight of the others, some distance away. Petey didn't really want to share this particular experience.

Lutz stared at the wound with clinical detachment. He was good at that.

"Bad?" Piotrowicz asked.

"Well, you'll get to keep most of your face. You might want to consider a little plastic surgery when we're done here, though."

"What about the burns? Are they that bad?"

"No. It's just your face—it's ugly as sin." Lutz grinned. "Second degree burns mostly. You've got some blistering, and a little exposed meat, but I think you got lucky on this one." He sprayed chemical scrubbers on Piotrowicz's face that removed any chance of bacterial infection. It stung like hell. Then he painted the burned flesh with a thick salve, and reached for fresh bandages.

While he was questing for the sterile wraps, there was a sudden pain in his hand, as if it had been bitten.

What the hell? He jerked back, and peered at the spot where it had occurred. There he saw a large, black-shelled bug of some sort. The thing hadn't given any warning, and he hadn't even noticed it coming close. It just attacked.

The silvery teeth took most of his hand and wrist in one savage bite.

Lutz let out the tiniest little noise. He looked at the mangled wound where his hand had always been, and gave out a high-pitched wail.

Piotrowicz saw it all happen, but it was so damned fast, and he had his guard down. With people all around, he never thought anything might be able to sneak up on them.

The bug was smaller than the ones they'd fought and killed, and if he had to guess it was younger. That didn't make it any less dangerous. The fucker lashed out at Lutz, that nasty damn tail pounded into the big man's chest and he fell back, a soft sigh coming from the wound as a lung collapsed.

He heard voices nearby, alerted by Lutz's wail, but they still couldn't see him—didn't necessarily know where it had come from.

Piotrowicz reached for his rifle, and his hand found only air. No chance he was taking his eyes off the thing, though. No chance in hell. It jumped and he kept reaching, straining for what should have been right there, *damn it*, and the shining black thing hopped closer and hissed and sprayed wet from its mouth as it reached for him.

He kicked the bastard in the face as hard as he could. The bug snapped backward and hit the ground. He finally risked a look, and the rifle was nowhere to be seen. He felt a cold certainty that he was a dead man.

The thing came at him again, hunkering low to the ground as it scuttled closer. Baby or not, it was a fast learner. The tail lashed back and forth, sometimes rising above its body, and he found himself watching that deadly barb.

"Need a little help here!" he shouted, hoping someone was close enough to come to his aid.

Dwadji's voice came across the comm.

"What's going on, Petey? Where the hell are you?"

"Got a bug here and it's hungry!"

Vogel's voice came from his far left.

"I'm coming," she shouted. "Don't move."

"Don't tell me! Tell this little bastard!"

The alien dropped to all fours and charged, hissing and weaving. That damned tail jabbed for his face and he blocked with his left arm, feeling the ridges on the tail scraping layers of cloth and flesh from his forearm and wrist.

Dwadji was saying something else in his ear, but he couldn't pay enough attention to understand the words. The bug pounced on him, and he managed to catch its arms, but that wasn't enough. Seemed like every limb on the bastard was made for cutting, because the clawed feet walked up his legs and it kicked at his chest, carving trenches into his armor and sending him staggering backward.

The only noise he could make was a gasp. The hind claws kept kicking with enough force to stop him from doing much of anything else, and the unbelievably powerful arms fought to break free from his grip. He was trembling from the effort of holding the damn thing back.

Vogel bellowed at the thing, but it kept attacking, hissing as it tried for his face with that freaky ass secondary mouth. The tail arced up and over its shoulder and came for his skull.

Piotrowicz flinched back and waited to feel the blade at the end of that thing come pounding through his brain. Instead the creature let out a surprised squeal and he felt the hot body of the thing suddenly lifted from him as Vogel smashed it sideways with the butt of her pounder.

The rifle was a grunt's wet dream. It carried ninety rounds in the magazine that fired in single shot, three round, bursts or continuous streams. It sported four slots for artillery and two locations for bayonets. Though it was fairly heavy at eleven pounds, it was also perfectly balanced for use as a hand-to-hand tool. That was where the nickname came from.

Vogel knew how to use a pounder. The bug sailed back from the impact and curled in on itself for a moment as it rolled and skidded to a stop. When it looked back in their direction, Piotrowicz could see the broken shell of its skull. It was bleeding slightly, and the liquid sent up little puffs where it hit the ground.

Vogel flipped the weapon around and fired three rounds that hit chest, face, and the back of its elongated head.

The little bastard hit the ground, and twitched.

Piotrowicz was gasping and shaking as he climbed to his feet and looked down at the thing. It wasn't any more than three feet long. Less than half the size of the things that had been on the van earlier.

"What the fuck is that?" He was jazzed on adrenaline, and barely aware that he was shouting.

Vogel ignored him and shot it twice more, just in case. It stayed exactly as dead as it had been before, but leaked more of its acidic blood all over the ground. Dwadji was screaming into the comm now, asking if Piotrowicz was still alive.

Why don't you just drag your sorry ass over here to see, Piotrowicz thought to himself. "We got it," he said into the comm.

Vogel talked into her headset while Piotrowicz moved over to check on Lutz. The man was alive, but it wasn't looking great. His breathing was labored, and while they had a few medical supplies and he was a decent medic, the majority of their supplies were currently somewhere in the tunnels, far above. He cursed himself for listening to Manning when the man told him to give up his pack.

The rest of their group managed to get to the scene, and Silas moved to examine Lutz. While he wasn't a medical doctor, it turned out that the woman from his group actually was. Her name was Rosemont, and she got to work on keeping Lutz alive—give or take a collapsed lung.

"What the hell happened here?" It was Cho, just arriving, and Piotrowicz filled him in. The tech's jaw tightened, and he walked a short distance away, talking into his comm. Calling for the lift.

But there was no one. Nobody on any of the upper levels responded to his calls.

3 4

REGROUPING

Decker thought he just might start screaming and never stop.

The shaft they were in was narrow, and definitely underground. When they'd finally managed to get away from the ambush and stopped running for all they were worth, Manning called for names and they came up with a total of eight remaining survivors. Only a couple of them—including Decker—had functioning lights, so the darkness wrapped around them. It was one thing to be stuck in the darkness. It was another to think there might not be a light at the end of the tunnel.

Adams kept trying her motion sensors. She wasn't alone. But none of the damned things worked.

The comm was functional, and Cho had reported what was happening back with the rest of the group. It felt as if the hub was an unimaginable distance away.

Not far ahead of him, Manning had taken to tapping the walls with his knife's hilt. At first Decker thought he was just nervous, and wanted to keep a weapon near at hand. But the longer he kept doing it, the less that seemed to make sense. So he asked, and Manning explained as if he were talking to a very stupid relative.

"I want to know it the minute we're not underground any longer," the merc leader said. "We can't do much as long as we're beneath the surface, but once we're out, there's a chance we might blow this damned popsicle stand.

"Now shut the hell up, and let me get back to it."

Since the man was carrying a very large knife, Decker decided to listen to him.

Sometime later—it felt like days, but was probably only an hour or so—the sound of the tapping changed. One moment it was a dull *thud*, and the next it sounded hollow.

Manning stopped, and ran his fingertips over the entire wall of the tunnel, but there was nothing. No hidden door, no seam— nothing that indicated a weakness in the surface. Finally he swore and stepped back.

"Fuck this," he said, and he lifted his plasma rifle. "Close your eyes!" he shouted.

Even with his lids closed, Decker could see the flare of light. The stench of the melting silicon was acrid, and tasted of salt.

"Clear!"

Decker opened his eyes, squinting at the ghost of the glare, and saw the most wonderful sight he could remember in a very long time.

The wall was slagged. The tunnels were strong enough to resist the acid of the aliens' blood, but they weren't able to hold their own against the heat of the plasma discharge. The edges were still white hot, slowly fading to yellow, and beyond the wound in the wall, there were lights. After the pale illumination of the flashlights and lanterns, it seemed almost as bright as a clear day.

After a few moments, Manning tested the edge of the opening he'd made. When he was satisfied, he slipped through, letting the business end of the plasma rifle take the lead. Decker closed his eyes for a moment, trying to tell whether or not there were any of the things out there. It seemed as if they were safe for the moment, and he moved forward, quickly followed by Adams.

In short order they were gathered in a cavernous mine shaft.

There were lights. Lots of them. There was space and that was a blessing. The air was stale and recycled, and it still felt like a cool breeze and tasted sweet on the tongue. Decker took great, deep breaths, and the others around him did the same. A sense of intense relief radiated from the people around him, and mingled with his own.

Adams did several deep knee bends and stretched her body. After only a moment's hesitation Decker joined her and so did several of the others. Manning did not. He kept his eyes in motion, his face nearly expressionless as he scanned the area and assessed their location as best he could.

"Cho," he said into the comm link. "We're out of the damn tunnels and in a mine shaft."

"Any idea what level you're on?"

Manning shook his head. "No, though I think we may be above you. Are you at the console? I want to know if you can get readings off of us yet."

"Hold on." There was silence for a few seconds. "I'm here, but we're still not getting readings."

"Okay. Something's not adding up here, I don't care what's in the soil, or on that ship. Low level radiation wouldn't be causing this much trouble for our systems."

"I get you." Cho's voice was clipped and professional. "I've had Dwadji trying different frequencies, but so far we haven't found one to counter whatever is causing the interference."

"Well, keep at it. I want to know what's causing us all of this grief."

"Gotcha," Cho replied. "Maybe the radiation built up over time, the longer the ship was buried?"

Adams shook her head.

"I gotta cry bullshit on that," she said, and she looked to Decker for confirmation.

He shrugged. "I've seen terraforming disasters, and that level of radiation can cause heavy-duty infiltration, but I have my doubts about the ship. Any level of radiation that could reach more than few hundred feet from the wreckage would have to be much heavier, and likely life-threatening."

Manning listened, and his eyes narrowed.

"Yet Willis guaranteed that it was safe," he said. "And we took him at his word. Something is fucked here. I want to know what."

"We're looking into it, boss," Cho answered. "But it's slow going, and we've had a few shitstorms down here, too."

"Which reminds me. Are your motion sensors working?" When he said that Adams tried hers again, but had no better luck.

"Haven't checked 'em. The way Willis was talking, there didn't seem to be any point."

"Well, check. If they are it helps you know if any more of those things are coming your way."

There was silence for a moment, then Cho spoke again.

"Listen, about that," he said. "Silas, the guy who led the expedition to the ruined city, thinks we might have a major infestation situation on our hands here. If he's right, we may be screwed ten ways from Sunday."

"How so?"

"From what I can understand, he thinks the bugs we've run across might actually be hibernating down in that city." Another pause. "He thinks they might be waking up. We're not talking a couple of these things, if he's right. Silas thinks there could be hundreds of them, or maybe even more.

"He thinks they might have taken out the entire city, back in the day."

Decker looked around, at the other mercenaries. Where they had been letting themselves relax, just a little bit, they were alert again. Weapons at ready, peering in both directions along the mine shaft.

He looked at the hole they'd come through. It was dark in there. *Very* dark. Anything at all could be just a few feet away, and waiting to strike.

Then he looked to his left, and saw nothing but a long expanse of dirt road. To his right was a mirror image. There were no markings, no indications of which way they should go.

Looked inward again, and tried to focus past the background noise.

There… They were nearby. He knew they were close, because he could feel them. The catch was trying to figure out where they were, before they launched another assault.

Hundreds of them? His pulse sped up. He pulled his own plasma rifle from its spot on his back, checked the charge, and reminded himself of exactly where the safety was located.

Somewhere in the distance, something made a noise loud enough to echo down the tunnel. Decker couldn't tell which direction it came from, but he intended to find out.

Hundreds of the things. They only needed one. And then they needed to get the hell away from New Galveston, once and for all. *Eyes on the prize*, he told himself. *And stay alive.*

"Decker!"

He jumped a little at the sound of his name. It was Manning.

"What?" he responded.

"You getting any of your weird feelings?"

He nodded his head, and rolled his eyes involuntarily. He hoped Manning hadn't seen it. But the merc seemed oblivious.

"Which direction?" Adams asked.

"Not sure," he answered. "They're not close now, but I think they're more determined to find me now." It seemed as if their hatred was focusing. He didn't really know how the creatures worked, but it was as if they were homing in on him, like a compass points to the magnetic pole of a planet.

Decker licked his upper lip and tasted salt. He was sweating again. But he was determined not to panic—especially since it might get him killed.

"Okay," Manning said. "So which direction… *feels*… like our best bet to avoid the things?" His control slipped a bit. "Give me something to work with here!"

Decker closed his eyes, and that odd squirming sensation crawled through his scalp again. After a moment, he pointed to the left.

"Then let's go that way first to see if we can figure out where the hell we are." To the rest he said, "Light 'em up. Keep your attention where it needs to be, and don't let anything get near us that isn't wearing a company outfit."

Decker took a deep breath and spoke his mind.

"Listen, don't think I'm crazy here, because I'm not. But maybe we should go *toward* them." A couple of the mercs started to protest, but Manning shut them up, and Decker continued. "If we can find them before they find us, maybe we can get the jump on the fucker."

Manning looked him in the eyes and smiled very briefly.

"Look at you, growing a pair." Decker might have been offended, but he heard the admiration in the man's voice—even *felt* it. Manning was used to thinking he was a coward.

"I'd agree with you, but we don't know enough about the territory," the merc leader continued. "If they're hiding in one of those tunnels, we could spend hours with you looking for them, and never see them. And there's a lot less of us now. We need to keep our eyes open, and get back to the hub."

They started walking, moving with care and watching for anything out of the ordinary. The only good news was that there weren't too many places where the damned things could hide.

Manning got on the comm with Cho again.

"Get me Willis."

A couple of minutes passed, and the bureaucrat came on the line.

"What do you want, Manning?" Something in his voice bothered Decker, but if it affected the merc, he didn't show it. "Where the hell are you?"

"I think we're on a level above you, so there must be a secondary lift—no way are the miners going to wait for days just to hitch a ride." He paused to look around, then continued. "Any idea where we can find it? What should we be looking for?"

Willis tried to give him directions, but Manning cut him off.

"We don't know where *we* are, so directions aren't gonna do squat. What do the miners do, if they need to get out fast?"

Before he could answer, they felt the ground beneath them tremble slightly. Suddenly it began to rock more dramatically, building rapidly until they were knocked off their feet. In the distance, something rumbled loud enough to shake the walls. To protect himself from falling debris, Decker curled into a fetal position on the ground. Fragments of rock pelted them, and dust carried down the long corridor, a roiling cloud that billowed for a moment before it started to settle.

"What the hell was that?" Manning was up and looking back the way they'd come.

"Don't know, chief," Adams said. "But it was a long way off—and it came from the direction we're headed." She checked Decker, then each of the mercs, to make sure no one was hurt.

"Cho!" Manning bellowed into his comm. "What's the situation down there?"

No answer.

"Shit," he said. "Well, we'd better find out what the hell that was."

At Manning's command, they continued the way they were going, shielding their noses and mouths from the dust, which was only just beginning to settle. Decker found himself studying the walls and the ceiling. Whatever had happened could very well have caused structural damage. He wondered if they were in danger of having the entire mine collapsing around them.

As much as that concerned him, there was something even more pressing. He could feel the aliens on the move, that hideous sensation of their malignance creeping through his skull. Whatever had caused the tremor, it seemed to have stirred up the hornet's nest, as well.

His pulse was still too fast and his breaths seemed too small, so he focused himself. Anything else came for him, he intended to handle it as quickly as possible. He checked his plasma rifle again, and reminded himself of an ancient truism.

You're not being paranoid when something really is out to get you.

3 5

BOOM

Perkins stared at the bodies. She needed to get back to the comm. Soon, too, as her break was almost over. *Break.* That was a sad joke.

Just a couple of the creatures had thrown the entire group into chaos, and one of them hadn't even been full-grown. They were all spooked, and no one was following protocol. It was all Cho could do to keep up with Manning and his group, and it sounded as if they had lost a lot of good men.

Now everyone was just coming and going, without rhyme or reason. Hell, she had done it herself.

Cho should've had my ass in a sling, she thought. But he hadn't, and things were getting worse.

Her eyes drifted back to the spider-thing on the ground. What it had done to Colleen was monstrous, and the thing that had killed her from the inside had grown at an unbelievable rate. Only partly grown, it had taken off Lutz's hand, and put him out of commission—if he even lived.

And now, if Silas was right—and she really, really hoped he wasn't—there were hundreds, maybe *thousands* of the things out there. Waking up. Fuck, they had destroyed an entire *city*, killed everyone in it.

She hadn't seen Silas in a while. Willis was missing, too.

Maybe they're off somewhere, cooking something up, she mused. As quickly as she thought it, though, she dismissed the idea. It didn't seem like Silas's speed, not after everything he had been through.

Anderson was walking the tops of a couple of the larger stacks of supplies, doing her best to keep her eyes on the perimeter. Perkins climbed onto one of the shorter stacks and got her attention.

"You seen Willis or Silas?"

Anderson gave a half smile. She was never going to be anyone's idea of a model, but she was attractive enough. They weren't serious, but they'd spent a few nights together over the months they'd worked together.

"Silas was headed for the lift. Willis went off that way." She pointed toward yet another collection of building materials, this one stacked with lighting supplies and, *oh, hallelujah*, portable toilets.

Thinking that he'd had the right idea, Perkins nodded her thanks, and headed for the latrines. Nature was calling.

Halfway there she spotted Willis. He was closing a door in the cavern wall. Not a latrine, but a real door. It looked old— so much so that it blended in with the rock surface, making it almost invisible.

Where the hell does that lead, she wondered. Had she not been heading in that direction, she'd have never seen him.

She started to motion toward him, but before she could do so, the ground bucked under her feet, knocking her to the ground.

The sound was impossible to miss. Thunder hammered down the path leading from the lift, followed by a cloud of dust. A moment later it repeated, and then one more time. Each report was so loud that it sent spears of pain through her skull. Instantly her hearing was gone, replaced by a sharp ringing that pierced her senses.

She scrambled to her feet and headed for the rest of the group. Cho was moving, and so was Piotrowicz, and then they all were, every mercenary and explorer sprinting toward the truck. As they clambered into the cab and onto the flatbed, someone cranked the engine. But while she could feel the vibration, she couldn't hear it. She was vaguely aware of someone trying to talk through the comm, but she couldn't discern any of the words.

The comm would have to wait.

By the time the truck lurched to a stop at the lift site, most of the dust had settled.

Silas stood there, blood flowing in a rivulet down his arm, abrasions on his face and scalp, where the hair was thinnest. He was bleeding from a wound above his ear, but the cut looked superficial. The impact had knocked him to the ground, too. His body was coated with a thick layer of dust. In his hands he held a pulse rifle.

Perkins instinctively reached for her own sidearm. Then she realized his weapon was aimed at the dirt. He looked toward them and said something, but she couldn't hear him.

Cho jumped off of the truck and hit the ground running, heading straight for the scientist, murder in his eyes.

Behind Silas, debris clogged the entirety of the lift shaft. Three of the heavy support posts were shattered. There was no sign that they had been melted, but Perkins did the math. There were four slots on the pulse rifle designed to hold grenades. Even from a distance, she could see that three of the chambers were empty.

Cho reached him first, and grabbed him by the shirt. He drew back to throw a punch, but the scientist just stood there. The tech stopped, his fist still in the air, but then he lowered it.

"What the hell did you do?" Perkins demanded as she skidded up next to them. She could hear herself, but her voice sounded muffled.

Silas looked directly at her and spoke slowly and clearly, his voice loud.

"We can't leave here," he said, as if stating the obvious. "The contamination has to stop. There's a planet full of people above us, and we can't let them all be slaughtered by these things."

She stared at him, but couldn't bring herself to speak. He'd just effectively killed every last one of them.

Then she looked over at the lift, which had fallen down when Silas blew the supports. Mining equipment, raw trimonite ore, and heavy machinery now blocked the only possible exit available to them. She saw something dark, pooling, off to one side, and hoped it was oil. In another place she thought she might have seen an arm, sticking out from under the rubble.

The thought made her shudder.

Tons of raw materials and shattered equipment jammed the entire opening to the shaft above. Even if they could squeeze past, there was no guarantee of how far up the shaft was clogged with debris and ruination. There was no way that the people above them could get to them before they were dead.

"I had to do it!" Silas was screaming now, but even his outraged bellows sounded like they were coming through thick wads of cotton. "You were going to leave here! You might be contaminated!"

Cho drew his pistol. Silas looked right at him as he moved, and Perkins saw the motion out of the corner of her eye. She was still trying to put it all together in her head when Cho fired. The single shot blew Silas's intellect all over the debris that was blocking their exit from the tomb he'd built for them.

"You fucking idiot," he said to the corpse that crumpled at his feet. "You didn't save anyone."

He spat on the body.

She felt her lips press together into a tight line. She should have been outraged. She should have been afraid that Cho might have lost his mind. Maybe he had, come to that. But mostly what she was angry about was that the bastard beat her to it.

If she was going to die down here, she wanted the satisfaction of killing the son of a bitch who had guaranteed her death.

"That prick stole my rifle!" Piotrowicz looked at the wreckage, and the dead doctor and pointed.

Cho stared hard at him for a moment, and then turned away. No one else dared speak—especially not the doctor's former associates.

"We have to find another way out of here." Perkins looked toward the rest of the group. "Any suggestions?"

Rosemont looked back toward the excavation site.

"We could try the tubes." She didn't sound at all thrilled by the idea. "A few people have gone up that way."

Perkins scowled. "The one our team went up is blocked now. Has anyone gone up in those things, and come back down?"

The woman shook her head. "Not really." She was silent for a moment, then offered, "There's also an access tunnel, but it's narrow and it's a very, very long walk up the stairs. I don't even know if it's clear, or if it has those… things in it."

Perkins thought back.

"Would the entrance be off past the latrines?" she asked. The nod she got was all she needed. She nodded in return, and went to find Cho.

She'd just reached him when a crash made her jump. It came from the lift tunnel, and was loud enough to pierce the slowly diminishing deafness. There was nothing to see, but whatever it was, it had to have been heavy.

And then the lights above them flickered, and dimmed a bit.

"What the hell?" Piotrowicz looked around, and his eyes sought the power source for the lights. "Something in there must've hit the cables. I'll take a look and see if I can spot anything." He shook his head as he started to move. "I need to get my damn rifle anyway."

Anderson had given up her place on top of the building materials, and was standing on top of the truck's cabin. It was the best place for an unobstructed view of the surroundings, bleak as they were.

"See anything?" Perkins asked.

"Not yet," she replied. "But I will soon."

"Why do you say that?"

"Ever know anyone who could resist finding out the source of a loud noise? I mean, we came running, didn't we?"

"You think the bugs'll come?"

Anderson's eyes kept scanning the distance, looking from time to time toward the ruined elevator shaft.

"I'd bet on it," she said. "I'd win."

Perkins nodded. Unfortunately, she agreed.

"How do you think this is going to play out?"

"If that dead fuck was right, we're not getting out of this alive. It's seven thousand feet of staircase to get to the top of this mess."

Above them the lights dimmed a second time, leaving the entire area locked into a fading twilight.

Perkins was liking the situation less by the minute.

3 6

SHADOWS

The sun set, and darkness came over the Sea of Sorrows.

No one working on the dig site paid much attention, save to manually activate those few lights that didn't come on automatically. There were always a few, it seemed, regardless of how many redundancies were built into a system.

Luke Rand settled his considerable bulk into a chair in the dining hall. There were others around, but not many. Herschel and Markowitz were near the Hut, waiting while the engineers did what they could to unfuck whatever the hell had happened down there. The lift had crashed down, the teams on most of the levels had come up already, a good number of them shaken but no worse for the wear.

Rand was still working on reducing the toxicity levels in the Sea of Sorrows. The plans to build Laramie Township had been scrapped, but with the discovery of the trimonite, the location remained a priority. More so than before, really. Where there was a profit to be had, Weyland-Yutani liked to be the first on the spot.

Luke looked at his food, picked at it for a while, and decided he wasn't really very hungry.

Seeing Decker had done that to him. He liked Alan. He always had. He was a straight shooter, and that was a rarity. If the man liked you, you knew it. And if he didn't, you knew that, too. He was smart, and he kept an open mind.

So why had he screwed the man over? He couldn't get it out of his head. And to make matters worse, Decker didn't seem to mind. Or maybe he didn't know.

Either way, Luke didn't have much of an appetite. Of course that wasn't exactly a bad thing. He'd put on a few spare pounds, like enough to make an extra person.

The chaos down below made him uncomfortable, too. It seemed too much like Karma, and he didn't like that idea at all. Everyone working on the site knew about the alien ship—that wasn't the sort of thing you could keep under wraps. Not for long. He'd seen it. Not in person, just the pictures that the first couple of teams brought up, but still.

But what about the quarantine rules? Sometimes the damnedest things showed up when you were terraforming a planet. Like on DeLancy. It wasn't pretty, what happened to the people there when a spore frozen in the permafrost had thawed during the terraforming. By the time Rand arrived, he was in full environment gear, helping gather the remains. That was when he decided to get out of the business and retire.

And now he had a chance for that.

All it cost him was Decker's friendship. And a piece of his soul, maybe. It might be that Decker didn't know, but Luke knew. He could barely stand to be around the bastard. He knew what the company had done. He'd received the call from the home office, making damn sure he stuck to the "official" story.

Still, after DeLancy, losing Decker's camaraderie was a small price. He'd pay it ten times over, no problem, if it got him away from this shit once and for all.

He looked at his plate for another minute and gave up. The food all looked like crap and probably tasted just as good.

When he'd cleaned up his mess, he bought a couple of beers—these days he could afford the outrageous price—and left the building, heading for the barracks. A movie or two, and he'd get some sleep.

Off in the semidarkness of the night, he saw something moving across the sand. He squinted to try for a better look. Something was crawling out of the sand, and then it vanished. There were a lot of things wrong with Luke's health—even on a lower gravity planet, the whole weight thing caused issues—but there was nothing wrong with his eyes.

He tucked his beers into his pockets. He wanted his hands free. One hand touched the comm on his hip. The other reached for his shock-stick. Luke was a big guy, and he could certainly handle himself in a fight, but lately there was a lot of talk about security breaches, and he had a lot of money on the line.

He looked out over the sea, checking the mounds and the dunes and the mostly flattened terrain. The sky was getting darker, not because of the sun setting but because of the rain clouds moving in, and he took his time, trying to make sure he wasn't just being paranoid.

Damn. There *was* something out there. Fifty yards out he could see a couple of figures. They were trying not to be seen, but he spotted them.

"Hey, Bentley? You on duty tonight?" His comm crackled in response.

"Yeah. That you, Rand?"

"Got it the first time. Hey, we may have a problem out here. I think I see someone out on the sand."

"Where are they? Near the Hut?"

"No, they're a good ways out. Maybe like a hundred meters past."

"Wouldn't be the rescue team, then," Bentley said. "Might be somebody that found a way out, though."

"Well, you want me to check it?"

"Yeah, it's just me here right now. I can't leave the booth. Would you mind?"

Luke sighed. He'd rather drink a beer. On the other hand, if someone had found a way out from the site, he maybe should check.

"Yeah. I got this." Luke started walking, keeping his eyes on the spot where he'd seen the movements.

"Any news from below?" he asked.

"Yeah, and none of it's good," Bentley responded. "Far as I can tell, they can't get below level three. If there's anyone further down, we haven't heard a peep from them. They're trapped, and most likely dead."

Damn, that doesn't sound good, he thought. *It's hard enough getting a signal down there on a good day.*

"Well, I'll keep you informed," he said to Bentley. "You do the same, yeah? I got friends down there."

"So do I, buddy."

He kept walking, and as he got closer, the shadow-shapes were visible again, and becoming more clearly defined. They were definitely people, but something about them didn't look right. Were they wearing survival masks or something? He couldn't decide.

He covered another dozen yards, and then he stopped dead. The night had deepened further, but not enough to hide what he was seeing. These weren't humans. He didn't know what the hell they were, but humans didn't have tails, or whatever sort of weirdness was sprouting from the backs of those things. And their heads were too damned long.

He reached for his comm.

"Bent?" he muttered, automatically dropping his voice. When there was no response, he spoke louder. "Bentley? I *really* think we got a problem out here."

"What's that? Come again, Rand."

Then the two shapes turned toward the sound of his voice.

"Oh, fuck me." They started to move toward him.

"Say what?"

"Bentley! You gotta get the hell out here!" he said, and he was shouting now. "Bring a weapon. I mean it!" The things were coming faster, and they didn't move right. They moved like dogs or something. They moved so damned *fast*.

He reached for his shock-stick.

Shock-sticks were designed as a non-lethal alternative to firearms and other security measures. They were set to give exactly enough juice to drop a person temporarily.

He managed to shock the first one, and it didn't slow down in the slightest. Then the other one was on him, and he was screaming.

3 7

RED SAND

When he didn't hear back from Rand, Brett Bentley tried reaching him by comm three separate times, even as he armed himself. He started to call for backup, then remembered that damned near everyone on the site was down at the Hut, trying to get to the people in the mine.

This better not be a false alarm, he thought grimly. Like as not the dumb ass has gotten drunk again and then passed out on the sand.

Rand seemed like a nice enough guy, but he'd started drinking more and more since he'd been reassigned. Bentley decided that if he spotted the damned fool out in the sand, sleeping it off, that he'd let him stay out there.

Maybe a good rain shower will sober him up.

He grabbed a hand-held flashlight, and as an added measure lit up the perimeter security lights. Within less than twenty yards he saw fresh footprints, and he followed them about a hundred yards further. He stopped at a dark wet spot on the black sand—at first he couldn't make out what the source of the moisture was.

Maybe he stopped to take a piss, he thought. Then he flashed his light over the area, and saw the red tint that painted some of the black grains. Unless the man was pissing blood, something nasty had happened there.

Looking around, he found the signs of a struggle, then tracks that looked as if something—likely Rand—had been dragged away. Weirdly enough, there weren't any other boot prints—or anything resembling them.

Bentley pulled his pistol. His nerves were singing. Fourteen years he'd worked with the company. In all that time he'd never had to actually draw his weapon. He'd been trained, and he was a capable marksman. What he was not was combat seasoned.

He preferred it stay that way.

Just the same, he had a job to do. He called on the comm, and didn't recognize the voice of the person who responded.

"Talk to me," the voice said.

"I've got a situation out here," Bentley replied. "There's a guy missing—one of the contract employees—and there's blood on the sand. There's sign of an assault. Can you send someone to back me up?"

"Negative," the voice said. "We've got all hands on deck here, and that's still not enough. You'll have to check it out on your own."

"Roger that," Bentley said, adding silently, *Thanks for nothing, asshole.*

He started following the signs of struggle. The sand was dry and soft and held remarkably little detail. He could see a clear ridge where Rand had been dragged along, and there were indistinct marks on either side. So it had to have been two attackers. He followed the trail for about twenty yards.

"Damn it." The trail just sort of faded away. His light played across the soft sand. There was nothing after that. No indication that Rand had broken free, or that his attackers had gone anywhere.

Bentley turned and started back the way he'd come. Without clear cause, he couldn't go further from his post without violating procedure. Before he'd walked ten paces, however, he heard something behind him.

He turned and shone his light into the darkness.

So he had a good, clear look at the teeth of the monster.

3 8

WRECKED

Manning stood right next to Decker as they looked down the shaft at the smoldering ruins of the lift, and several tons of mangled equipment. The merc summed up his feelings by spitting a wad of phlegm down into the wreckage.

Decker looked at the shaft walls and shook his head. The entire thing had been carved from the surrounding stone, and the walls were damned hard. Despite that, he saw long cracks in the stone.

"Holy crap." Adams was looking up. "We're on level *five*." She pointed with the business end of her rifle, toward the markings at the upper edge of where the tunnel met the shaft. "Now all we have to do is find the backup elevators, and maybe we can get out of here."

Cho's voice came through on the comm, and Manning walked away, talking into his headset. The tech had killed the man responsible for the wreckage. It was a scientist from the excavation—he'd been convinced that they had to sacrifice themselves, to stop the creatures from getting loose.

The man had a point, Decker thought, but he kept it to himself. *But I'm not sure* anything *can stop them. Our own chance of surviving, on the other hand…* No. Screw that noise. He had every intention of getting home with his prizes intact. He had a life to get back to, and no intention of surrendering it to Weyland-Yutani, or to whatever weird monsters they might find.

The lights flickered again, and if the power failed them, they were in serious trouble. Then he had a thought.

He looked to Adams, who was scanning the way they'd come, and frowning.

"Hey, Adams?" he said. "Do you guys have anything that'll let you see better in the dark? I mean, as standard issue."

She shook her head. "No such thing as standard issue. We buy our own supplies. So, yeah, some of us have night goggles. They're no good in cramped quarters, like the tunnels—especially with all of us crammed in there together. And they'd've made targeting a bitch. But out in the open, they might just be of some use." She grinned. "I've got 'em in my pack."

"Seriously?"

"Yeah. The goggles work, but they aren't as good as the naked eye unless you're dealing with full darkness. Too much loss of peripheral vision."

"Yeah, I know what you mean." He'd used them on more than one assignment. There were sleeker, less intrusive models on the market, but they cost an arm and a leg. More than a grunt—or a paper pusher like him—could afford.

He didn't bother to ask if she had a spare set.

Something started to make his scalp feel tight, and the background noise ratcheted up a notch… then another. He pulled inward, and reached out with his senses.

"Manning?" His voice was low, and he kept it steady. When the merc didn't respond, he tried again, louder. "*Manning!*"

"What?"

"They're coming!"

Manning crossed the distance in an instant.

"Where are they?" His face took on harder angles. Decker took a minute, and then responded.

"They're coming from several directions," he said. "And they're not going to take long to get here."

"Then let's get our asses in gear, find the damned backup lifts, and get the hell out of here," Adams said, her voice shaking almost imperceptibly.

Manning nodded.

"Let's go. Keep your weapons ready, and check your armor. We'll follow the most traveled pathways." He took point again, carrying his rifle at the ready. This time Decker was in the middle of the group, with three in front of him and four to the rear.

Walking became increasingly difficult for Decker. *Everything* became harder to accomplish. As they approached the hole Manning had burned in the side of the tunnel, the sense of the creatures was so intense that it dragged on him physically.

Shit, he thought with sudden clarity. All he could get out was, "They're here!"

The first ones came through the hole, while other shapes charged from ahead of them, and some came from behind—most likely from the elevator shaft itself. He couldn't hope to count them. He didn't want to. All he could do was take aim and hope he didn't blow his own leg off when he fired.

The freelancers were in motion before he was. They were trained for combat. He was trained for filing reports. That thought had him half giggling even as he tried to find a target. But the mercenaries were in the way.

Four of the dark forms came in fast, barely even making a sound except for the skitter of their nails on the hard-packed soil and rocks. Adams opened fire while they were still a dozen yards away, and let out a grunt each time she pulled the trigger. Four little sounds from her, four loud booms from her weapon, and two of the creatures exploded.

The other two were better at ducking.

One of them leaped through the air, bounced off the wall and plowed into a dark-haired man who was already firing at another shape coming his way. The mercenary just had long enough to realize how screwed he was, before the shape rode him to the ground, clawing and biting the entire time. No one could help him. If they shot the damned thing, the blood would just burn the poor bastard.

He clubbed the thing in the face with his pistol, and tried to push it aside, but it didn't move. The creature's mouth opened and drooled out a slick of moisture even as the secondary mouth drove into the poor bastard's face and ripped at his cheek.

Decker looked away as another of the things leaped at Adams. She tried to track it, but failed. Before she could compensate for its speed, the alien was past the range of her weapon.

Decker didn't think. He just aimed, pulled the trigger, and got blindly lucky. The plasma from his rifle missed Adams and hit the fast moving demon in the upper back, burning through two protrusions that rose like frozen wings from its shoulders. The creature shrieked and bucked, trying to escape the pain.

Then it turned. Even through its agony Decker could feel it focusing on him, noticing him for what he was, for *who* he was, and the feeling of hatred was magnified a dozen times over.

Injured, possibly dying, the damned thing still came for him, clawing at the ground as it changed direction. There wasn't time to fire again, but he tried anyway, and launched a ball of liquid fire into the wall.

The thing had him dead to rights.

Manning caught it across the skull with the butt of his rifle, and drove the screaming nightmare into the ground. The blow was solid, but not enough. The thing was back up in an instant, and once again trying for Decker. He danced backward and ran into another person, but didn't dare look to see who was behind him.

The creature continued lashing out, scrambling to get to him with no concern for anything else. Feeling the creature's thoughts, the primal hatred, the desire to kill him, would have been bad enough, but the mind behind those emotions was so completely foreign that the raw emotions seemed even worse. He felt its single-minded rage, and his own fear rising as a counterpoint.

Manning kicked the thing in the side, and staggered it. Before it could recover a second time he fired, the barrel of his weapon flaring with each pull of the trigger. Four rounds pounded into the creature, and blew it backward with each impact.

It fell, and didn't get back up.

There wasn't time to celebrate as the next pack of the things appeared. The six mercenaries were ready, though, and had enough room to allow them to work in unison. Two opened fire with the explosive rounds that shattered the air and their enemies alike. The backsplash of the acid blood hit armor and flesh, but the splatter was minimized by distance.

Even as the first of the aliens went down, the ones behind them split up and attacked. They were fast and savage, quickly closing the distance and making ranged weapons ineffective. Manning directed his people and they listened, but all the commands in the world didn't change how brutal the attack was. The freelancers were pushed back, and Decker was pushed with them.

The things pushed their advantage without pause.

Adams and Manning and a few of the others quickly took to using their weapons as bludgeons. Manning slammed into one of the things and shoved it backward, grunting with the effort, and as it fell back another merc nailed it with a quick burst from a .44. She let out a yelp as the blood from the thing burned flesh, but instantly recovered and kept fighting.

One of the black-shelled demons jumped over Manning's head while he was pushing back against another. It cleared the distance effortlessly and came down on top of another mercenary, who was knocked flat and likely would have died on the spot, but the thing seemed far more intent on getting to Decker. As quickly as it landed, it jumped again and came for him.

Decker wrestled himself free of the crush of bodies and cursed, swinging his plasma rifle in a tight arc that just managed to save him from getting clawed to shreds.

Instead of carving into him, the creature's claws ripped the weapon from his hands. He didn't have time to think—he charged the creature and knocked it back toward the man it had flattened in its jump.

The mercenary was better prepared the second time, and brought up the double prongs of his shocker, electrocuting the thing with a jolt that should have killed it. He pushed the prongs into the thing's chest and fired voltage through it a second time, and then a third, until it was still. Its glossy black hide was cracked and bleeding.

Decker grabbed back his weapon and tried to catch his breath.

They were everywhere.

"Fall back!" Manning bellowed, and his people did so. Adams pushed Decker along for the ride.

Suddenly a wave of force lifted him and threw him backward. His ears were pounded and a flash blinded him. Manning had dropped a grenade into the middle of the enemy.

He struggled to recover, and looked around. Several of the freelancers were clambering to their feet, shaking off the concussive force and continuing their strategic withdrawal. Manning tossed a small metal ball in a gentle underhand arc, toward still more of the things coming from the direction of the lift. He was a bit further back this time, managed to clear a few more yards before the detonation.

He kept his feet, and so did most of the other fighters, and then they were running—all of them. They moved hard and fast retreating from the scattered black shapes that littered the ground.

He couldn't see how many there were. He didn't dare take the time to find out. The survivors would recover, and they would be joined by more.

So they ran. Oh, they ran.

And the nightmares followed.

Panic was winning, and Decker had to stop it.

He forced himself to gulp in air and to actually look where he was going, because otherwise he would surely die. The things coming from behind made soft, low hisses and high, shrill shrieks, and the hard noises of their bodies in motion offered a sharp counterpoint. He tried glancing back, but all he could see was the mercenaries, several of whom were firing their weapons as they ran.

Adams had told him the rifle in his hands could be switched to automatic. He flipped the weapon over and looked for the control. But before he could do anything with it the terrain changed. The seemingly endless corridor started curving, and he had to pay attention to what was going on ahead of him.

Then they hit a fork.

"Which way, Decker?" He didn't recognize the voice.

Two choices: left or right.

The left fork looked more frequently used and he pointed in that direction, going mostly on instinct. The group went in that direction and he prayed he was right.

While he was praying he came to a stop and adjusted the settings on his plasma rifle. The mercenaries kept running. Heart hammering too hard for him to hear even the sound of his own breath, Decker aimed back the way they'd gone and waited.

The last of the freelancers, Llewellyn, charged past him—were there fewer than he remembered? It surely did seem that way.

The first of the things came skittering around the curve.

Their hatred was very nearly a living thing, another presence moving among the tide of chitinous bodies. They were charging faster than before, and he lowered the barrel of his rifle toward the center of their seething mass. Then he pulled the trigger.

And was blinded.

She had warned him. The air around him seemed to catch fire. One tiny burst of the stuff was enough to melt the flesh of the aliens. By the time he let go of the trigger, he'd unleashed close to a hundred times as much. The heat sent his hair rippling and the glare took away all but the briefest hints of the dark shapes ahead of him. They screamed, not only with their hideous voices, but also with their minds. The hatred washing over him disappeared in a conflagration of plasma and fear.

The walls where they had been were glowing. The stone was running in places and the darker lines—likely the trimonite— shone with a white heat.

"What the fuck is wrong with you?" Manning bellowed, startlingly close. He clamped a hand on Decker's shoulder and began dragging him backward.

Decker couldn't answer—he just allowed himself to be pulled away. His mind was overwhelmed by the brilliant, explosive light, and by the utter *silence* from the horde of things that had been trying to kill him.

Manning yanked the weapon from his hands, spun him around, and pushed him forward.

"Move!"

Decker obeyed, trying to breathe in air that felt too thin and far too hot. He stumbled forward and followed the people ahead of him. Behind him there was only Manning. The aliens were gone.

Just gone.

Up ahead the group slowed as they reached the mesh doors of the secondary lift. Adams looked back at him with wide eyes, and he felt more than he comprehended her shock.

He was feeling a bit shocked himself.

Behind them the heat was, if anything, actually getting worse.

"Ferguson!" Manning's voice cut through his thoughts. "Are the doors working?"

A lean, bloodied man nodded his head.

"Yes, sir!"

"Then get them open, and get us the hell out of here."

The metal bile of the aliens was replaced by the fear and disbelief of the mercenaries. They were in shock, and he didn't know if the bugs were the cause, or his own stupidity. *Probably both.* They entered the lift, and Ferguson closed the doors as the glow of the burning walls behind them lit up the corridor.

"Go!" Manning's voice snapped the order, and a moment later the entire platform they stood on lurched and began ascending.

Manning said nothing, but he stared bloody murder in Decker's direction.

"I stopped them, didn't I?" Decker offered. He hadn't planned on talking but there it was.

"You just dropped a miniature sun's worth of heat down a hallway made of stone and dirt! If we're fucking lucky, the entire thing won't collapse, you dumb bastard!"

He couldn't say he didn't know. He did. He just hadn't been thinking when he did it.

No, that wasn't true. He *was* thinking. He was thinking about getting away from the things that wanted to kill him.

"I shouldn't have given him a plasma rifle," Adams said, and that stung.

Manning turned on her in an instant.

"You think?"

Decker shook his head.

"No. This is on me. She told me not to switch over to automatic. This is all on me." He didn't want her taking the heat for his stupid move.

Manning took a deep, slow breath, and visibly calmed himself.

"Plasma rifles, for the record, tend to heat things up," he said. The lift kept rising, moving with all the speed of a tortoise.

39

COMMUNICATIONS

Rollins sat down at her desk and checked for new messages from the home office. There were none.

Good, she thought. Her superiors only sent responses when she posted a new query. Since she hadn't done so, their silence was the best news.

She began reviewing the various status reports, and Willis called. She didn't respond immediately, letting him stew a bit.

"Talk to me."

"We need your pilot back down here, as quickly as possible," he said, and he sounded out of breath. "I think things are going south in a hurry."

"What do you mean?" She checked the information that had come in, and the only glitch she could see was that one of the probes was no longer functioning. That was puzzling, since they were built for planetary extremes. It would take a lot to knock one out.

"The lift has been disabled," he continued. "There's been some sort of explosion."

"Where are you now?"

"I got myself to an access tunnel. I'm climbing. It's a long haul to the next level, but I'll get there." He seemed confident enough. She opted to let him keep his confidence. It would be short-lived enough, as it was.

"Very good," she said. "When you've reached safety let me know. Until then, good luck."

"Wait! What about the drop ship?"

"I'll be sending it down soon," she replied. "Have you managed to get all of the information I asked you for, Mister Willis?"

"All of the information they gathered on the city is with me right now. I also got pictures of those things."

"You've been very helpful," she said calmly. "Thank you for that. I'll look forward to seeing what you bring me."

"But—"

She killed the communication and called Pritchett into her office. The pilot arrived quickly.

"I need you down there," she said. "I expect we'll be getting what we wanted from this operation, and very soon."

"So they caught your aliens?" he asked.

"There have been complications, but I believe they'll manage. In the meantime, however, they'll need extraction, and it's going to come sooner, rather than later."

Pritchett nodded and left.

Rollins looked at her computer, and began to type.

To: L.Bannister@Weyland-Yutani.com
From: A.Rollins@Weyland-Yutani.com

Subject: New Galveston Acquisitions

Lorne,

It appears likely we will successfully achieve our
goals regarding the biomechanical data we have sought
for some time.

Regarding the dig site, we may only be able to salvage
data. Extracting the trimonite, and any other assets
located on the site, will likely be prohibitively
costly in many ways.

```
Please review the information encrypted in the attached
file. Due to the volume of data, the compression rate
has been increased by a factor of ten. Expect white
noise.

Best,
Andrea
```

She sent the message, stood up, and left her office. She wanted to think and the walls of the room didn't provide a view conducive to stirring her mind's enthusiasm.

Somewhere below her, the company's goals were coming within reach—closer than they had been in a very long time. It was within her reach to save the personnel who were involved, but that might risk the successful conclusion of the mission.

That wasn't an acceptable risk.

4 0

SEARCH AND RESCUE

The Quonset hut was a buzzing hive of activity, with about two-dozen people milling about. No one could figure out what the hell had happened.

The tunnel leading down was wide open, and everyone was very carefully avoiding standing too close to it. It was one hell of a drop if a person got stupid or clumsy. A few of the more adventurous rescue workers had already tried rappeling down the side of the deep pit to see what they could find. Next they were going to try maneuvering one of the rigs closer, and lowering a platform. Assuming they could find someone to work a rig.

The team that should have been doing that was lying broken and very likely dead at the bottom of the shaft. They'd been taking machinery back down to level five when the entire thing had fallen apart.

Lightfoot and Moretti were watching over the smaller, personal rigs of the rescue team, trying to get them low enough to check the next level down. They were there for the explicit purpose of making sure that if a rope got tangled, it got untangled as quickly as possible.

No one expected the ropes to go taut, and then go completely slack, but that was exactly what happened. There were four separate lines dropping down. They weren't connected to each other. Each was independent, and each fed out at its own pace. They had been working fast, but not so fast that it put them at risk.

According to the readout on the first line—the one belonging to Kirby—he had managed a little over five hundred feet when the line snapped tight and spat out a sudden extra thirty feet of high test silk before it came loose. Moretti saw it happen, and let out a little yelp of alarm. By the time he'd turned to Lightfoot to say something, the second line was doing the exact same thing.

Almost immediately, the last two lines repeated the process. Lightfoot hit the autofeeds to pull the lines back up. If any of the rescue team members were hurt, they'd be drawn up at a nice, steady pace and be back to the surface within a couple of minutes, max.

The lines came up quickly and smoothly.

They came up *too* quickly. And in all four cases, the members of the rescue unit didn't come up at all. The lines had been torn apart.

Several people got very busy shining lights down into the shaft and calling out for someone to respond.

But there were no responses. No unexpected noises, no signs that anything had gone wrong, there were simply no responses at all. And that bothered Moretti enough to start him pacing back and forth and chewing on his nails. It bothered Lightfoot enough to make him hunt down four more probes.

It was probably futile, though. All of the probes they had tried sending down had failed to transmit through the interference caused by the Sea of Sorrows. No one knew why—there wasn't any natural phenomenon that would explain it.

Lightfoot retrieved the probes anyway—they had to try. He linked their telemetry to the main console. This close, they were working just fine. So he dropped the probes down the shaft, and the four spherical sensors went to work, correlating information as they moved steadily downward.

Fifty feet down, the readings stopped.

Lightfoot let loose a stream of obscenities, and several others joined him. There had been a brief hope. Now there was nothing.

* * *

Moretti stepped outside of the hut to grab a smoke. He was stressed and he was angry and as much as he hated giving in to his temptations, the alternative was to rant as hard as Lightfoot.

Leaving the door open, he fought against the wind for a moment to light his smoke. Just as it was about to catch, something grabbed him and slammed him against the corrugated steel wall. His attacker was dressed in black armor of some sort, and impossible to see in the gloom. He grunted and started to scream, but a powerful grip caught him by the throat and stopped him with a strangled gurgling sound.

And while he struggled and fought and dropped his cigarette, other shapes came out of the desert and started into the hut, moving without concern for whether or not they were heard or seen.

Fonseca was the first to see them. She took in a deep breath and let out a positively epic shriek. While the people around her were doing their very best to jump out of their skins, at the unexpected sound, the monsters attacked.

There were seven of the things, all a shiny black with long talons, ridged tails, glittering blank faces, and rows of sharp teeth. They moved preternaturally fast, some on two legs, others skittering on four. They moved the wrong way, and made unsettling hissing sounds as they did so.

Few of the personnel were wearing comm-sets, and even fewer were armed. Most of the people participating in the search and rescue were technically off-duty. They were there because they needed to be there.

One of the bizarre creatures grabbed for Lightfoot, and he reacted strictly on reflex. He caught the thing by the wrists as it came for him, grabbing, seeking. He spun at the hip and hurled the nightmare past him and into the deep chasm of the lift tunnel. It screeched and fought for purchase as it dropped into the darkness.

He managed to fight off the second one that came for him, blocking several blows as it kept trying to get past his defenses. Those defenses were not perfect—they didn't take into account that the monster was armored, or that it had barbs along its prehensile tail. Or those damned *teeth*. Quickly he was bleeding from several wounds, even as the people around him were taken down.

Several of them fought, and they did their best, but most of the people were so terrified that they tried to flee instead of trying to defend themselves. Lightfoot was vaguely aware of a stampede for the door as the bug kept attacking, kept pushing him to the limits of his abilities.

And while he was focused on the thing in front of him, the one he'd knocked down the shaft climbed up the side of the deep tunnel and launched itself at him from behind. He'd never even considered that possibility.

One by one the workers, the rescuers, all of them fell. Their shouts and screams diminished, until they stopped altogether. And then they were taken, hauled out of the building and into the light rain that started falling from the night sky. Their unconscious and bleeding forms were dragged across the Sea of Sorrows.

And then the sea reached up and consumed them, until nothing was visible but the blackened sands, flat and unbroken.

4 1

GOOD NEWS

Four new data streams ran from the surface of New Galveston and straight up to the *Kiangya*, where the information was loaded into Andrea Rollins's computer. The news was unexpected, but not unwelcome. Information was power. Rollins knew that better than most.

She studied the new readouts and shook her head. For just a moment a smile played at her lips and then she crushed it.

Time for a new report.

She typed quickly, composing as she went.

To: L.Bannister@Weyland-Yutani.com
From: A.Rollins@Weyland-Yutani.com
Subject: Unexpected results.

Lorne,

It appears that the subject is substantially more
aggressive than we had expected, or even hoped.
Furthermore, data from the surface indicates that the
infestation is far more widespread than was originally
expected. I believe we are looking at a complete
involvement of all test subjects, and the very real
possibility that the team we assembled could actually
be infected before they have achieved their goals.

I have sent down a retrieval ship, in an effort to make their return more feasible. Once we have procured the appropriate samples, we may need to consider taking a different course of action than originally planned, if only to ensure that the property remains exclusive to the company.

I believe the terminology used back before the Expansion was "with extreme prejudice." Unless you respond with a different recommendation, that is the course I will follow. Failure could very well lead to heavy sanctions, and penalties against Weyland-Yutani.

On a related track, the information gathered from the examination of the dig site has been extensive. While we cannot guarantee a complete analysis of the biological-technological fusions, I believe we will be substantially closer to a fruitful merging of biotech and weapons manufacture, based entirely on the samples that have been successfully scanned.

The alien vessel and the buildings found at the dig site indicate similar—if not the same—patterns: organically grown synthetic life. Biotechnological structures, nurtured in a protective environment. The implications are staggering, and I will do everything within my power to ensure that we gain physical samples of the structures, in the hope that we might find sufficient genetic materials to warrant a complete reorganization of the entire biotech division, its goals and objectives.

As before the attached files are strictly encrypted to ensure security. I will retain a full backup, should data be lost in transmission, but I feel it best to let you get started with the examination as soon as possible.

Please advise ASAP should you feel a different course of action is required.

All the best,
Andrea

She sent the message, and then settled back to wait.

And while she waited, she continued to watch the growing wealth of details with a level of clinical detachment that would have done her predecessors proud.

The Biological Technology Division was about to get a very substantial boost, based on the raw data alone. If the team succeeded in procuring live samples, the potential for advancement would be immeasurable, and would justify any sacrifice.

She hoped that Decker made it out alive, though. Whatever it was that linked him to the aliens, it seemed to have potential for further exploitation.

Somewhere far below, the independent multi-functional probes continued their task of reading information.

In front of her, the computer continued the task of defining and recording that information.

4 2

ESCAPE VELOCITY

The lights continued to fade. Perkins looked around in the near darkness, trying to see *anything*, and shivered. There was a fire in the lift, now, but it wasn't enough to help, and the smoke was beginning to be a problem.

"We can't stay here," Cho said. Perkins didn't like the alternatives any better, but she didn't have the energy to argue.

That was okay. Piotrowicz seemed more than willing to handle the task.

"Look, you can climb your ass up into those things if you want, but I think we're better off toughing it out here. Sooner or later, they're going to get someone down to our level."

"Yeah, but all they'll find is our corpses," Cho countered. "I'm not saying it has to be the tubes. I don't much like the idea of going through those things myself, but if Willis found a way out, then we can do the same thing." Cho was keeping his calm, but it was very obviously an effort.

Piotrowicz shook his head.

"It's not defensible."

"And this is?" Cho's voice rose again. Perkins sighed and ground her teeth.

Estrada spoke up.

"Look, I don't want to sit here with my thumb up my ass," he said. "It's getting darker, and I think those fucking things will come for us. We take the stairwell, and we block the access from below, and then we only have one way they can come for us, right?"

Anderson was back to pacing on top of the stacks of construction materials, where she had the best vantage point. Vogel and Dwadji were with her, making sure that they didn't get any more surprises. All three of them had switched over to their night vision goggles. No one was completely sure if they would help in the situation, but no one thought they'd hurt, either.

The problem wasn't just the darkness—it was that no one really knew if the creatures gave off enough ambient body heat to register. To that end each of the three had settings on a different level. One was using ultraviolet—Vogel, she thought—and that was working well enough. But Dwadji tried infrared, and it was seriously problematic. There was a fire in the lift, and if he looked that direction, it was nearly enough to blind him.

The fire had come suddenly, and didn't seem to be from the explosions. There had been a bright flash, like that of a plasma rifle, and burning debris had dropped down, setting fire to the wooden portions of the elevator and the mining equipment. It just compounded their problems, generating enough smoke to cause breathing troubles if somebody didn't do something soon.

Perkins was hot and she was sweating and she was hungry. *And tired.* So damned tired.

Bad as she felt, Lutz was doing worse. He kept fading in and out of consciousness. And when he was awake, he was in pain and bordering on delirious. The wound in his chest was still doing a slow leak and Doctor Rosemont had already intubated it. Even if he improved, she didn't think he'd be able to walk. They'd have to carry him. Actually, the scientific group would have to carry him, because every weapon needed to be available for use, and not a one of them was about to trust any of the explorers with a weapon.

If they tried to move him, especially up a narrow stairway, there was a good chance that Lutz wouldn't survive the strain.

But his odds didn't seem any better if they stayed.

"Listen," Cho said. "The air down here is getting thick. My fucking eyes are burning from the smoke, and I think we need to move. As far as we can tell, there are lifts above us. They just don't reach this level. I know it's a bitch—I get that, and I don't want to risk Lutz either. But if we stay here, we're fucked.

"It's as simple as that."

"We can't stay here," Rosemont echoed. "With the fire, there's a chance the batteries over near the lift will blow up. If those things go, we're going to go with them. If the explosion doesn't get us, the fumes will." She looked to Piotrowicz with an apologetic expression on her round face. "I know you're worried about your friend—I'm worried about him, as well. But if we stay here, we're all going to die. I believe that." She gestured at the other members of the expedition, who looked exhausted and scared. "We'll have to carry him."

Piotrowicz looked at the woman for a long time. Finally he nodded.

"So let's get the hell out of here."

It wasn't long before they'd gathered Lutz and started along the way.

Lower gravity helped. They rigged a stretcher from two posts and a blanket from the van. It looked a little comical, watching someone smaller lifting the heavyset mercenary as they placed it under him.

While they worked, the trio of lookouts kept watch, seldom speaking.

Cho tried to get hold of Manning without success.

There was nothing else to it. They had to move.

They had to go.

So they grabbed everything they could carry, and began to make their way toward the door where Perkins had seen Willis emerge. The three sentries took strategic positions around the group of ten unarmed people. Perkins gave her night vision goggles to Rosemont, so she could guide her people while carrying the injured man.

Vogel called out.

"Here they come!" She pointed with the barrel of her pounder.

The black silicon tunnel, which had allegedly been sealed, vomited out several black shapes. No one saw them but Vogel. Then the other guards caught on and lined up with her.

Still carrying Lutz, Rosemont and her crew ran as best they could, and Perkins and Cho went with them. Piotrowicz, Vogel, Dwadji, and Anderson took their time and aimed for the vile things that skittered down the wall, moving in leaps and bounds, never staying in one place for more than an instant. Perkins slowed for a moment to see what was going on. She didn't want to. What she wanted was just to run. Fear clenched her stomach in a vice.

In the semidarkness, all she could make out was the forms of the aliens—no details. Two of the things got blown away as they descended, and fell to the cavern floor without any sign of life left to them. The others were faster, and got to the ground without being touched. They found cover in the stacks of supplies without anyone tagging them.

The group made it to the door.

Please let it open, Perkins thought. If Willis had—for whatever reason—locked it behind him, they were up shit creek without a paddle. But despite her fears, the thing opened. Cho stepped in first, lit his flashlight, and glanced around quickly. Then he gestured for the rest of the group to join him while he took point. There was no way of knowing what was above them, and it was best to be safe.

"Move it, folks!" Perkins said. "We've got company, and they'll be headed our way." Most likely they didn't need the reminder. She gave it to them anyway.

And then she was through the door and looking back, wishing she had her goggles, watching the others doing their best to fight off the damned things. She couldn't see the bugs.

She could only see her four comrades where they stood on their perches and fired.

She spotted one, just as it came for Piotrowicz. He was standing several feet off the ground and the black shape charged, moving between two of the stacks. She only saw it because that barbed tail whipped fast enough to catch her attention.

She saw it.

Petey did not.

"Piotrowicz!" her voice called out and he turned to look at her.

The thing jumped, clearing the stack with ease. It hit him hard enough to lift him into the air. The monster's front claws landed on his shoulders and pushed him back. She saw the pistol in his hand as it sailed up and away, and even from a distance she thought she heard the sound of his skull cracking as he hit the packed dirt floor.

It seemed to her that she was looking right into his eyes when the beast came down, and bit him in the face. Then she couldn't take it any longer.

Perkins took aim and fired at the thing. She missed, but her charge blew a hole in Petey that was big enough to put her arm through.

"Oh, fuck, *no!*" Her voice cracked as she watched his entire body kick from the impact. She was still staring at him when the monster looked her way and charged. Adrenaline and instinct took over.

She still took the time to aim at the monster and fire.

The damned thing ducked under the blast. That was enough to make her focus. She aimed again, and realized she was too late.

The demon was on her, hissing and clawing, and then her head was slamming against the wall of the access tunnel and there was nothing.

Darkness ate her entire world.

Perkins hated the dark.

43

NESTS

There was a loud grinding noise, and then the entire affair jerked and stuttered and quit. The lift stopped working. They'd been rising at a nice, steady pace.

In that instant, Decker thought they were going to be stuck in the elevator forever. He caught himself breathing too hard and too fast. He needed to get away!

"You're freaking again." Adams was staring at him. "Are they closer?"

He swallowed as best he could, and tried to focus.

"I can't think," he said. "But I don't think it's them." He forced the words out. They didn't want to come. They wanted to stay locked in his throat.

Manning noticed the exchange and hissed out an order, telling Adams to give him a shot. She did so, and in the space of a dozen heartbeats he felt himself calming down. The bands around his chest relaxed, he gasped in a proper breath, and then another, a third.

"They're very close," he said. "They're serious, too. All I get is the sense that I'm the target."

"You mean they weren't serious before?"

"Shut the fuck up, Leibowitz," Manning growled.

"Yeah, they were serious before," Decker said, his resolve

hardening. "But I think there are more of them, and this group seems, I don't know, focused. This isn't a science, you know? It's a gut feeling. There just doesn't seem to be as much white noise coming from them."

Adams sighed loudly next to him. She was exasperated.

Tell me about it, he thought.

Manning called on the comm, but got no answer. No word from Cho. No one answered from any of the levels.

Grunting his own frustration, he turned his attention to the list. Bracing himself, he caught his boot on the railing and reached up until he could open the maintenance hatch above them. Less than a minute of looking around, and he dropped back down.

"It's maybe twelve feet up to the door to the next level. I say we take it." He looked around for a moment. "Any objections?"

There were none.

Manning was the first up, followed by Adams, and then Decker himself. One by one they climbed to the top of the car, and the two mercs pulled a pair of utility gloves from a pocket on their slacks. Like the gloves Decker often used on a work site, they were surprisingly thin, and equally effective, enabling the wearer to retain his sense of touch.

The merc leader used them to hold the cable, occasionally wiping some of the grease from the metal fibers to get a better purchase. In a matter of minutes he was up to the doors and wrestling with the locking mechanism. Adams watched him climb, and Decker watched Adams.

He forced his attention back to the bugs. The medication enabled him to deal with their increasing presence without pissing himself. They were close. They were so damn close he could almost smell them.

Decker glanced around the shaft just to make sure that last part was his imagination, because the bugs seemed adept at hiding in the strangest places. They might even have been the reason for the malfunction.

Seeing what he was doing, Adams pulled her flashlight and

started scanning the area, frowning all the way.

Nothing. Then Manning dropped a line down.

"Make sure you use gloves," he warned. "The line is thin enough to cut flesh."

Decker shook his head. "I don't have any." A moment after that, two grease-coated gloves dropped on his face.

Adams stifled a laugh—though she didn't seem to be trying very hard—and started climbing. He was following a moment later, pulling his body up the line, straining with it. He was very glad of the lower gravity.

He pulled himself through onto the tunnel floor. They waited as the rest climbed, and Decker did his best to sort out the emotional tides swirling around him. Away from the claustrophobic lift, he could pinpoint details better, and there was another sensation—one he couldn't easily define. He tried concentrating on it, separating it out, but without success. It was more like interference than emotions.

"There's something down to the left," he said. "It doesn't feel like the bugs, but it's strong enough to get my attention. And in the midst of all this, that says a lot."

As with the previous level, this corridor was lit well enough, though the lights were less frequent here. Some of them had been broken and others dangled down from the ceiling where the anchors had given out and let go of their prizes.

"You think you can find whatever it is?" Manning asked, retrieving his gloves and shoving them into a pocket of his backpack. His expression had gone back to neutral.

"Yeah, I can." Decker nodded. "Like I said, it's strong. There's something familiar about it, too, but I can't put my finger on why."

"Then don't waste time trying. Lead on." Manning let him take point, but stayed close.

The differences between levels quickly became more evident. Where the fifth level had seemed empty, as if it had been deserted for a very long time, there were far more signs of activity here. Markings on the walls indicated they were on the second level, and some of the signs and notices looked to have been posted recently, over the course of the new activity.

The corridor was as well paved as the previous one, but there were far more chambers off to each side, and they had to check each one before continuing on. Several loaders and trucks were parked haphazardly in designated areas. Manning looked at them with interest, but said nothing.

A very large opening on the right hand side revealed a dark chamber. There were lights, but most of them were damaged or burnt out. The few that remained were dim, and flickered fitfully.

A quick look told them that this was an active mining site. The trimonite vein was very apparent, dark and glistening in the rough-hewn walls. The ceiling was close to twenty feet high in some places, and looked as if it climbed a good deal higher in spots. That must have been where the miners found a particularly rich vein of raw ore.

Decker peered up into the dark recesses, and shrugged.

"Of course," he said. "That's where the feeling is strongest."

"You just never stop being fun, do you?" Manning shook his head and held his rifle a little closer to his chest. "Bridges! I want you up here."

"What the hell did I do?" He was trying to be funny. Manning wasn't in the mood.

"Just think of yourself as the canary in the coal mine," Manning said. When Bridges looked at him without comprehension, he added, "I need someone to use as bait, and you're elected."

Bridges nodded and tapped the shocker against his leg. Decker winced reflexively, expecting the man to howl with pain. A moment later he lifted the weapon, and its light hum could be heard.

Adams stepped up next to him.

"Same routine." She handed Decker a metal baton. "Use the reaper first. You run out of ammo, use this. Hit 'em if they get too close. Otherwise, leave it to me." He wasn't quite foolish enough to ask for the rifle back, but part of him was tempted. Slowly but inexorably, he could tell that the bugs were closing in.

They moved carefully, and Decker advised where to look as the team ran light over the darkened surface of the walls. It wasn't long until they started seeing the same substance used in the construction of the black tunnels. Before long they were sprouting from every available surface.

The weird sensation grew. And then he saw the source.

Along the walls, sprawled in an uneven confusion, shapes stood out against the blackness. None of the forms made much sense until he understood that they weren't just *against* the blackness, but had been consumed by it.

No, not consumed—enclosed within it, woven into the black silicon. Here and there a limb jutted forth, a hand or a fist, a bone or a portion of flesh. Mostly what showed were the faces, some frozen in scowls of pain, others slack and lifeless. There were people here, a *lot* of them. They had been wrapped into the black silicon like flies in a spider's web.

"What the fuck?" He didn't know who spoke, but the emotions spiked for everyone in the group. Horror, anger, fear... all in equal measure.

Most of the trapped forms were unconscious, though some could be seen to be breathing. As the lights flickered over the shapes, Decker had to think that was a blessing. Several of them were dead. They hung slack in their glossy bindings, and universally the dead ones had holes in their stomachs or chests, complete with a thick drool of gore that ran down from the openings. He tried counting them, but the numbers didn't want to stick in his mind. He lost count after fifteen.

There were far too many for all of them to have been mercenaries. There had to be miners and other civilian personnel—he didn't want to know how many.

"Holy cow." Manning looked them up and down. His expression was no longer calm. His teeth were clenched. His gaze stopped on one of the dead ones, and he turned. "Adams? Didn't Cho say something about this?"

"Yeah, it was one of the civilians," she replied. "The scientist with a hole in her chest. Yeah." Adams shone her light over the deep wound and studied it carefully. Decker didn't want to look, but found he couldn't quite look away.

Then he realized something.

The dead weren't the source of the weird feeling, but they were close to it. The unconscious humans weren't the source either. They were unconscious, and anything they gave off was muted by that fact.

"Fuck." He shook his head and stepped back. "It's coming from inside of them." His voice rasped. His whole body went numb. The *presence* of the things flared inside of his head, until his ears were ringing.

"What?" Adams asked.

"The feeling I'm getting," he said. "It's inside the people. Whatever it is, it's inside of their bodies."

Bridges glanced briefly over his shoulder.

"Trust me, there's nothing inside those people." He nodded toward one of the wounds as he said it. Decker couldn't decide if the man was trying to be funny, only that he failed.

"No, not *them*," he hissed. "I mean the ones that are alive. There's something else going on here. There's something *inside* of them." As he said it, the rest murmured oaths, until a gesture from Manning shut them up.

"That's sick!" Adams shook her head. "But it fits with what Cho said. I couldn't picture it before, but now it makes sense."

Manning started to say something, but instead he turned, aimed, and fired in one sure, fast move.

4 4

BREEDING GROUNDS

The result was a squeal of pain from one of the bugs as it got blown in half.

What they'd suspected became fact. The damned things were there. They'd been hiding in the black cascade of silicon, some of them near the trapped victims, and others further away. As Decker watched, the things unfolded themselves from their resting places and very quickly shifted into crouching positions, hissing at the human invasion of their territory.

One looked at him, and its rage increased exponentially. Immediately the sensation spread throughout the room, as all of the creatures recognized him. But unlike before, they did not attack. Instead they hesitated, and... taking positions.

"They're protecting the people." Bridges spoke with a genuine confusion in his voice. "Why would they do that?"

"No." Manning's voice was unsettlingly calm. "They're protecting their young. That's what Cho was saying earlier. They've planted babies inside the people."

Several of the mercenaries behind him let out noises of disbelief. But there it was for all to see. The corpses didn't add their voices to the argument, and neither did the living hosts to the unholy eggs. They could not. They were spared the agony of consciousness.

Through the noise, Decker recognized something. The *things* inside the bodies were keeping their hosts sedate. That's why there was no fear coming from them. They didn't deaden their pain so much as they numbed their emotions. Sedation for the spirit, not for the flesh. The very idea horrified him.

Manning gestured again, and with practiced ease the freelancers stepped into a closer formation. Each one that carried a ranged weapon paired up with another who stood with a bludgeon or some other close-combat device. They took up positions around Decker.

Without warning, the aliens attacked. There was no tensing to act as a forewarning, and they moved with the sudden speed and brutal efficiency of natural predators. And once again, they moved straight for Decker.

"Do this!" Manning opened fire and blew one of the creatures apart as it dropped down to attack. Others did the same, including Adams, who fired on one that was scaling the nearest wall and nearly hanging upside down as it came for them from above. The stench of the alien blood mingled with the rot of the dead and the industrial odors from the mine itself.

Decker tried to look everywhere at once. Despite their focus on him, the creatures seemed to be more careful this time, moving with greater purpose. Some of them seemed to be sacrificing themselves, but even in that there seemed to be a pattern—

Then it hit him.

"They're trying to get us away from their young!"

Manning paused for a moment, and then fired at one of the humans stuck to the web of black. The shot was either very lucky or amazingly accurate because he hit his target in the meat of the shoulder without managing to kill the poor bastard.

The reaction was immediate. The bugs turned their full attention on Manning, and moved to block him from having another clear shot.

"Damned if you aren't right again." Manning fired at the closest bug, and it whipped back and away, narrowly missing becoming another victim. "Now tell me what good that does us."

"You're the fucking tactician," Decker replied. "You tell me!" He could feel them clearly moving toward the area from different directions.

"There's more of the damn things coming from the main corridor," Decker added. "They're going to block us in here."

"Then let's open a path," Manning shouted. "Twelve o'clock, people—give it all you've got."

Manning opened fire, and the rest of his team did the same, concentrating on the ones in front of them, trying to clear a path. When the bugs came too close, Manning shot another of the victims, hanging on the wall. Instantly the creatures shifted toward that spot, as if driven purely by instinct.

Using that method the mercs began to move.

"I don't like this. It stinks of a setup." Bridges spoke and drew his pistol with his free hand. The shocker zapped attackers on his right, and the pistol kicked and boomed from the left. Another bug died.

And then one was on him before he could say anything more. It dropped from above and landed on the big man's shoulders, biting into the back of his neck and ripping its claws down the length of his body. He fell hard, and did not get back up.

The bug climbed off of him and scuttled toward Decker, keeping low to the ground. Adams fired and missed, and then ducked out of the thing's way as it came on. Decker let out a bellow and swung his baton at the glistening black face. The hard metal rod broke the thing's head open, but that wasn't enough. It kept coming, teeth bared and secondary teeth snapping as they dashed for him.

Someone pulled a trigger and the thing blew up, spraying a mist of its blood across Decker's left hand and chest. He wiped the burning viscera from his hand and then frantically pulled at the vest. The pain was enough to cast aside the numbing effects of whatever Adams had injected him with.

No one helped him. They couldn't afford to. Manning pushed

forward and the things cleared out of his way, letting him go. Everyone who could do so followed, one by one stepping over Bridges' corpse as they moved.

From behind them came new sounds, the noises of more of the things coming their way. There was nowhere to move but forward.

Decker pushed past the dead mercenary and the web of living and dead miners. He wasn't the only one close to panic. He could feel it coming from several sources now, and much as he wanted to ignore it, he could not.

The pain in his hand grew worse, and he wiped it again and again on his pants, trying to remove it. But even with the acid wiped away, the enraged nerve endings did not care.

The creatures in front of them kept backing up, and Manning fired on one that wasn't fast enough. Several of the mercenaries were facing behind the group now, keeping their eyes on the way they'd come in case any of the damned things appeared. They would, too. No one doubted it.

One of the miners hanging from the wall bucked and twitched, and a moment later there was blood flowing down his chest. As they watched, something writhed there, and they could see the vague form of one of the creatures, its face pressing against skin and cloth alike.

Adams brushed Decker aside as he stared, and pumped a single round of plasma into the miner's chest. The human host didn't react. The parasitic thing in her chest let loose a weak yowl of pain, and Decker knew in that instant that she'd killed it.

The reaction from the bugs was immediate. They attacked *en masse*, the ones from the corridor coming in fast and prepared to kill every last person. One of the mercenaries called out a warning and threw something at the seething tide of dark chitin. A moment later an explosion tore the things apart. Many of the pursuers were shredded by the impact, but a few came out mostly intact, and continued on.

One by one, the freelancers blew them away.

Up ahead the narrow corridor within the silicon hall opened

into a larger area, and when he reached it, Manning stopped dead.

"Everyone!" he shouted, a new edge to his voice. "Get in here now, and bring the plasma!"

Even before he caught up Decker, too, froze in place. The rest came fast, moving around him. But he couldn't do it—*wouldn't* take another step. He couldn't yet see what had stopped Manning, but he *felt* it. Felt the rage, so much brighter than anything he had felt before, so clearly defined. He did not see it, but he knew it. Knew it from the worst of his nightmares, the dark places he didn't want to remember.

The bugs were bad, but this thing?

This thing would be worse.

A noise came from that chamber, and it was vile. A deep, throaty hiss combined with a high-pitched squeal that screamed *stay away!* The sound dug at his senses and pushed into his brain and it was more than just a noise. There was something past the five senses in that screech.

But then the sound changed, and the new note almost sounded like the growl of a predator.

The thing knew he was close and it wanted him. It wanted him very badly.

Behind him more of the bugs were coming, moving along the ground and crawling over their dead brethren. Slipping along the walls and the ceiling above, lean and hungry. For a brief moment he blocked out the obscenity beyond the next wall. He let his survival instinct drive him toward Manning, and the rest of the mercenaries and their weapons.

Once he was past that final barrier, the pursuers seemed to *stop*, as if unwilling to carry the fight any further. And he saw why.

He saw his every nightmare given form.

4 5

MOTHER-OF-SPIDERS

Vast, ovular masses rose from the ground, wreathed in a low-lying mist that had no right to exist in a mine. He did not know if the shapes created that mist, or if it came from the abomination behind them.

It was so large, so vast, that he almost thought it had to actually be a construct—the cathedral where the demons worshipped. In his nightmares he had dreamed of spiders, but that had been driven by the limits of human experience. The thing had spidery aspects, yes, but was alien beyond comprehension. Massive limbs held the body upright. Vast legs spread above the main body, spreading far and wide, and braced the thing in mid-air.

If the body was the cathedral, then surely the vast head of the beast was the altar. There was a vulgar symmetry to it, a deadly, graceful shape that drew the eyes toward the mouth, where the lips peeled back and bared crystalline teeth that gleamed within that maw.

The great head of the beast turned as he entered the cavernous space and though he again saw nothing like eyes, he felt it looking at him, sensed the probing fingers of the thing's mind. If the rage of the bugs was a crawling heat, then the hatred emanating from this great beast was a swarming mass of fire burning into his mind.

He was aware of motion around him, but he could barely hope to comprehend the things going on at the corners of his eyes. He was too fixated on the thing that shuffled slowly to get a better view of him. It could not go far. The vast body was locked in place by a huge abdomen that writhed and heaved and pumped of its own accord, and vomited another glistening lump to the ground.

Lump. He felt himself edging toward hysterical laughter. Lump. That was rich. That was priceless!

Decker broke away from looking at the monster for a moment, because he had to share the joke.

"That's their mother," he said to Manning, and Adams, and the rest. "She's laying eggs. All around us. Those are fucking *eggs*." And the worst of it? He didn't think she was the only one. He couldn't see the others, but he felt a distant glimmer, an echo of what came from her in different places beneath the Sea of Sorrows. There was more than one of these great nightmares.

Not one of the mercenaries paid him the least bit of attention. They were transfixed by the monster. So he looked away from Adams, away from Manning and the rest, and stared at the eggs themselves. There were *things* moving in them, and some of the oval shapes were jittering as the crests at their tops split open.

Nightmares crept from those eggs.

They were not like the bugs or the great mother of all bugs. They were a different sort of demon entirely. These things did not hate him, did not care about him. They had one agenda that mattered, one desire that was brilliant and cold and horrifying.

"Facehuggers," the files from Weyland-Yutani called them. His mind screamed that they were spiders, the source of his recent arachnophobia. He knew what they wanted. Knew what they did, and that made the sight of them all the worse.

Decker stepped back and his back hit the wall. He tried to push his way through that unmoving surface, and was rebuked for his efforts.

"Oh, fuck me," he muttered.

One of the things scuttled across the ground and jumped,

jumped, and even as it moved, the great monster behind the vast array of eggs let out a roar that shook through human and rock alike. Without fail they all looked—there was no choice really.

Long white legs like impossible fingers spread from the arachnoid body and a vast, thick tail whipped with deadly accuracy. Decker tried to reach Adams in time, but he failed. He lunged even as the thing wrapped its limbs around her face and that tail bullwhipped around her neck as tight as a noose.

Adams dropped her rifle, reaching for the thing on her face. Clawing at it.

Even as she did, another of the damned things jumped for Manning. He fired and the body exploded, washing across the ground and his lower legs as its remains pattered down.

The mercenary started to burn. He reached for the knife on his belt and pulled it free, rapidly cutting at his pants, sawing through the tough fabric. But Decker hardly noticed.

Adams!

Decker looked at the woman on the ground, fighting to free herself from the thing wrapped around her face. Odd bladders on the sides of the creature quivered and flapped and Adams bucked, her fingers failing to get any sort of purchase worth noticing.

He felt the horror she felt, lancing into his senses. A great, suffocating repulsion flowed from her, an utter inability to breathe, carried along the tide of her fear and violation.

The great mother of all nightmares let loose another roar.

The mercenaries didn't come to Adams's aid. Nor did they help Manning. Instead they opened fire on the enormous thing that screamed for their deaths. Explosive rounds and streams of bullets blasted into the shape, cracking through the thick hide and shattering chitinous armor. The mother-spider-beast reared back, almost shocked by the audacity of the tiny creatures that dared attack her. He was hit by the monster's surprise. She was meant to be worshipped. She was meant to be a queen and a goddess and mother to all.

Decker could feel that from her mind, if it could be called that.

The bloated demon shrieked and roared, and behind them the bugs reacted. There was no hesitation. There was no delay. She commanded and they obeyed, utterly willing to throw themselves between her and the enemies. They charged toward Decker and the freelancers and he did the only thing he could think of. He grabbed the plasma rifle from the ground in front of Adams and fired at the first of the things that got too close.

A tiny sun burned the air and missed the intended target. Instead the light cut through the surface of one of the eggs and lit the interior as the crab-thing inside it caught fire and boiled within its shell.

The queen lunged forward and snapped her face toward Decker. She glared at him and the heat of her hatred opened wide.

Images plowed through him, sent, he knew, by the thing that loomed above him. Ellen Ripley's face flashed in his mind, distorted by the Xenomorph's utterly inhuman senses. It saw but not with eyes as he understood them. It tasted and felt and heard, but none of those words were quite enough to show the differences.

In his dreams he had tried to interpret the minds of the Xenomorphs. Here, this close to the queen of the hellish things, the images were unfiltered, raw and painful.

He saw, and as much as he could, he understood. They were connected in ways that humans had often sought, yet failed to achieve. They were a colony, a hive. They shared thoughts on levels that people could not, and he was a part of that now. They had touched his psyche and marked him through his bloodline.

Ellen Ripley was marked in their minds. She was the Destroyer and because of their relationship, Decker too was the Destroyer.

He shut his thoughts down to the alien thing, terrified that somehow it might manage to learn of his children.

The great demoness screeched, her breath washing over his face. Decker aimed and fired, and missed.

All around him the mercenaries did a better job. Most of

them took on the things that were closing in on them, but a couple—Manning among them, despite the burns now visible on his bared skin—attacked the largest of the creatures that were surging forward.

Decker fired again and again, and he found his mojo. Streaks of light ripped from the front of the rifle and buried themselves in targets. Three of the eggs exploded. He changed targets rapidly as the mother screeched and snapped at him. But he did not fire at her. He could not make himself look at her because seeing her made her too real, and his mind already wanted to go running away.

So he looked past her head and to her body, at the swollen collection of eggs she carried within her. And that was where he concentrated his fire.

Knowing his intent, her rage boiled over. The great beast broke free and lunged toward him pulling herself across the floor of the chamber, moving over her eggs in an effort to stop him.

Manning and the remaining four mercenaries kept firing, hitting her with round after round of destruction. Her body broke. Her face shattered. The great crest above her mouth split in two places and bled more acids that burned the soil, yet did nothing to the eggs it touched.

She roared and lurched forward again, reaching for Decker. He did not step back, however, and he prepared himself for death. He needn't have bothered. The great shape writhed and crashed to the ground. Even so, Manning didn't let up. He unloaded every shell he had into the still form, and then reloaded with the efficiency afforded only to longtime shooters.

For one long moment the bugs remained motionless, as their mother-queen collapsed. And then they went mad.

Decker did the only thing he could. He aimed and he fired. All around him the mercenaries did the same, as the tide of monsters swept forward. They attacked. They fought. And one by one they were dying. There was nowhere to go, no way to escape from them.

There was only the fight, as the horrors from his dreams came forth to drown them all.

4 6

Their rage could burn no brighter, but their sorrow was bottomless.

The enemy had killed the queen and he had to be stopped but instinct and hatred do not always mix. The feeling rose hotter and brighter and much as they wanted revenge, there were the breeders to consider. Without breeders the colony would die, and that could not happen.

Several of them fought instinct and defended against the invaders, attacking the enemy and the ones that sought to protect him. As if to prove their instincts right those that tried to attack were killed. Their deaths did not matter. The only death that mattered was the death of the queen. The only survival that mattered was that of the colony.

The breeders had to be saved and so they worked quickly, lifting the eggs, pulling them from the ground and moving with the heavy burdens, seeking another spot away from the flames of the enemy.

The queen was dead.

The colony would live.

4 7

FALLING

Pritchett called several times for permission to land, and had no luck.

Barring combat scenarios, he wasn't used to landing without permission. He didn't like not getting confirmation, because that sort of shit led to paperwork. Nevertheless, he knew where to go. He dropped from the sky and very carefully settled on the hard surface of the landing pad. The black sands had covered most of the markings, and they were revealed again as thrusters stabilized the ship and then slowed the descent to a crawl before he felt the great bulk come to a stop.

He made sure to do everything by the book, from checking the atmosphere and weather conditions to powering down into standby mode. No chance in hell was he giving Rollins an excuse to be pissed at him.

The engine went into sleep mode, and the lights dimmed appropriately.

No one came to greet him when he touched down. It was creepy. The damned place was too big not to have someone on duty, and by now they should have repaired whatever was wrong with their communications.

Looking out the window he could see the rain coming down, and guessed that might be a part of it, but it wasn't like they were dealing with a hurricane. Still, no one showed up. So he settled himself in his seat. For now he got to play the waiting game while the people around him continued with their mission.

He tried using several different frequencies to catch up with the others, but nothing came back. When that failed, much as he hated the notion, Pritchett called on his boss.

"Safely landed down here," he told Rollins over the comm. "It's just a matter of waiting now." At first there was silence, making him wonder if she had heard him. Then she responded.

"Keep yourself prepared, Mister Pritchett," she said. "The situation has heated up substantially."

What the hell does that mean? He didn't ask how she knew what was happening on the surface, and *below* the surface. He really didn't want to know. He just wanted this done.

He wasn't the sort to give in to superstitious ideas, but he had a very bad feeling about the whole situation.

After a few minutes his eye caught something. There was movement out on the sands. That was something at least. He didn't feel so completely abandoned any more.

Not that he was planning on going out there or letting anyone in who didn't knock first. In his experience, you couldn't be too careful.

4 8

LOVE

Perkins's jaw felt like it was ready to fall off. Her lips were swollen and tender. Her neck hurt.

Everything hurt, really.

Somewhere in the distance she heard shouting and weapons fire. There was the kind of screeching the bugs made, but louder.

The darkness wasn't complete—that was the first thing she noticed. She opened her eyes slowly, and felt the ache in the side of her head where she'd gotten her helmet ripped free by the thing that attacked her. She tried reaching for her head, and realized her hands were bound.

So she studied the darkness.

The black stuff from the tunnels was all around her. She could feel it touching her neck, her face. She could wiggle a few fingers on her left hand, and they touched something warm, but her right hand was useless and the attempt to make her fingers move resulted only in a new surge of agony.

The monster had bitten her hand. She remembered how fast it was, and the sudden explosion of pain that ran from her wrist to the tip of her middle finger. She was pretty sure all of her fingers were still there, but *damn* they hurt.

The warmth against her left hand moved a bit and she turned her head as best she could.

Piotrowicz's voice spoke out. He had an unpleasant, wet sound to his speech.

"Wondered if you would wake up."

"Petey? What the hell's going on?"

He laughed. It was a soft chuffing noise that broke into a small coughing fit.

"You probably can't see it, but the spider-things are all over the place. You had one on your face a while ago. So did I. Cho's got one covering his face right now."

"What?" It hurt to talk. She licked her tender lips and tasted something other than blood. She wasn't sure she wanted to know what it was, but the taste was bitter, almost metallic.

"We're done," he said. "We're already dead, Perkins. We just have to wait a while for the rest of it."

"What are you talking about?" Her voice broke. She felt the sting of tears and tried to force them back.

"That civvie from earlier, Colleen something-or-other. She had one of these things attack her. It put something inside. I felt it. I felt that goddamned thing in my mouth, in my throat." His voice was hoarse and he let out a long, shuddery breath. "I think I can feel it moving inside me. We're going to die. It's going to be bad."

"Fuck, Petey."

"I know." She felt the warmth move against her fingers. "Can you reach that?"

"Reach what?" She felt fabric. The cloth was wet and held the sort of heat she always thought of when she touched a kid with a fever. Her nephew Joe always got fevers. The kid was sickly as all get out. Then she felt a metal line slide across her fingertip. "Wait. I think I have something." She wriggled her fingers and strained hard, and felt the thin metal press between her fingers. "I've got it, I think."

"Good. That's good." Piotrowicz coughed. "I was wondering how smart those things are, you know? I mean, they're good hunters. They work together. I've seen whole units didn't work that well together, back in the Colonials. And you remember Phillips, right? Man couldn't even spell teamwork."

"Yeah. I remember him." She hadn't much liked Phillips. He was a bitter man with a bad attitude. Also, he had the worst damned breath.

"Well, I think they're animal smart, not people smart. Know why?"

She didn't really want to play twenty questions, but, really, there wasn't much else to do.

"Tell me."

Before he could answer, another man's voice interrupted. She didn't recognize it—he wasn't one of the mercs.

"Can anyone hear me?" He coughed, a nasty, wet cough. "Something's wrong with me. Really wrong. I can't see, and my chest burns."

He stopped speaking for a moment and Perkins could hear him panting in the distance. When the man started up again, he was praying. After only a few moments of trying to make his way through what she thought was the Lord's Prayer, he started screaming. It was bad. His tone rose in octaves and decibels alike, and then faded away into whimpers.

Piotrowicz spoke again.

"He won't be around long. I think it's coming out of him. I was thinking they aren't very smart, because they left my belt on. I've been working for a while now, trying to get to my belt. Turns out I should have just waited for you."

She almost laughed.

"Petey, I don't care if it's the end of the fucking universe, I'm not taking off your pants."

And in response he did laugh. It was weak, but it was heartfelt, and the only reason he stopped was because the screamer started up again, wailing his pain out into the darkness around them.

From somewhere nearby she heard the sound of one of those things moving. They made a soft clicking noise when their parts rubbed together. Like plastic or glass.

When he could speak again Piotrowicz did so with a note of humor in his voice.

"I really love you, Perkins. But honestly, I always kind of thought of you like a big sister." He paused for a moment. "Doesn't mean I wouldn't have, you know, if the circumstances were different. But no. I mean, they didn't take my belt. And they didn't take the grenade I was trying to reach. The one you've got your fingers on now."

Not far away the screamer spiraled down into sobs.

"Oh." It was all she could think to say.

"I think if I move my hip and you pull at the same time, we can probably get the pin out. After that I just have to wiggle around a bit to depress the striker."

"Are you serious?"

Piotrowicz didn't answer. He let the screamer answer for him. When he stopped, they were silent for a time.

"Okay, Petey."

"Good. I think we can end this a lot faster for all of us."

"Is the charge big enough?"

"Perkins, honey? Have you ever known anyone to accuse me of using anything less than excessive force?"

The screamer started up again and then stopped with a strangled gurgling sound, accompanied by a tearing that sounded like more than cloth.

"Let's do this," she said. "Petey?"

"Yeah?"

"Tell me you love me, one more time." She pulled hard at the pin. Her fingers strained and the wire hoop tried to slip free, but she caught it in time and after five of the longest seconds of her life, she managed to slip it free from the safety.

"I love you, Perkins."

The heat of his body pressed hard against her fingers, and she dropped the pin.

4 9

DIFFERENCES

Somewhere in the distance there was a sound, almost like a detonation, but muffled by the immensity of the rock walls.

Then there was silence.

Decker looked around and saw the dead bugs, the dead mother of all monsters, the dead mercenaries, and wondered exactly how it was that he was still alive.

Mostly that was Manning. The mercenary was still standing, and only a few feet away. He had looked considerably better in the past, but he was alive. There were four of them still standing, and all of them were bloodied.

"Adams," Decker said. His body was shaking from over-exertion and adrenaline, but he moved anyway. Adams lay where she had fallen, that vile thing wrapped around her face. She was alive. He could see her breathing. Like the people they'd seen stuck to the walls, she gave off a different emotional resonance. Being around her actually made his own mind calm down.

"One of those things is on Elway, too," Manning said.

He looked. Elway was an older guy, not exactly prone to speaking up. Hell, the man had never said a single word that Decker could recall.

"They're different."

"What?"

"The things on their faces. They're different." They were, too. The one on Elway was smaller. The one on Adams was larger, and seemed more elaborate. It had webbing between the front and rear legs.

"Whatever," Manning said. He looked around at the dead and the wounded. Then he reached for his knife, and looked at the thing on Elway.

"No," Muller said. "Acid blood. You'll burn his face off."

Manning looked at the thing on his mercenary, and finally nodded.

"We need to get out of this place," he said. "We need to get to the surface."

Decker stared long and hard at Adams.

"So let's go," he said. His hands caught her at the shoulder and at the knee, and he hefted her weight across his shoulders. She seemed to weigh almost nothing, but he knew that wouldn't last. They had a long way to go, and well before they reached their destination she was going to be a very heavy burden.

Manning grabbed Elway and hoisted him over one shoulder, slinging him like a duffle bag. In exchange he dropped most of his supplies, keeping only his rifle, and the belt of knives and assorted tools around his waist.

"Take the lead," the merc leader said.

Decker tried not to think about the people they were leaving behind. He didn't know them. They weren't his friends or his family. Objectively, they were his captors. It still didn't feel right. But there was no other choice.

They moved quickly, heading back the way they'd come. As they passed the bodies stuck to the walls, Decker looked away. Manning did not. He studied each face as they went past. He couldn't guarantee it, but Decker thought the man was memorizing them.

Muller—at least Decker thought that was the man's name— glanced over to where Manning looked and spoke softly.

"Want them left alive?"

Manning kept looking, but shook his head. There were no words.

Muller trailed behind the others. A few moments later Decker heard a series of detonations behind him. He didn't know what Muller had used, and he didn't care.

Eventually the man caught up.

"Where are they?" he asked as he fell into step with them. "Are they all gone, Decker?"

"No." He felt for them. "Not nearly."

"How many of those bastards are there?"

"Lots. Too many. More than I ever could have imagined. But right now they seem to be worrying about something else." He closed his eyes, focused. "They'll come for me again."

"Why?" Manning asked. Decker was surprised by his curiosity.

"I think hatred is the only thing they know. And they hate me. Maybe for what this Ellen Ripley woman did to them. Maybe just because I smell funny to them. I don't know for sure. I just know they want me dead."

"Well, I'm not so fond of you, either," Manning said. "But I like them less. Let's get the hell out of here."

The elevator was down and none of them wanted to climb that entire length of cable. It took them almost twenty minutes to find an access stairway. The damned thing wasn't hidden, but it was unmarked, and nearly lost in shadows.

The door was jammed, but Manning fixed that quickly enough. When they were through, he studied the hinges on the door for a moment and then rammed his knife into the spot between door and jamb. A simple wedge, but it would take a lot of effort to force the door open. For extra measure he looked to the last member of the group.

"Dave, glue that bastard shut."

The man Decker thought of as Llewellyn nodded and dug into his backpack. The goo he laid against the metal made door and frame both sizzle for a few moments, and then run together.

"Shit. How many feet down are we?" Muller's voice was justifiably exasperated.

"About one less with every stair, sunshine." Manning's voice wasn't as encouraging as his words. Just the same Muller took the hint and started upward.

One less foot with every step. Maybe not quite accurate, but it was true enough for Decker. He walked, doing his best not to complain each time Adams's weight shifted on his shoulders. Manning was walking ahead of him, and he made it look like carrying Elway was easy. He hated the bastard just a little more for that.

5 0

THE LONG AND
WINDING ROAD

Willis was suffering from a serious case of the flop sweats.

His legs were shaking and his arms flopped uselessly at his sides, except when he tried to use them to pull him up another set of stairs.

Eyes on the prize. That was what his grandfather always said. *Keep your eyes on the prize and you'll get what you need out of the world.*

What did he need? Currently he needed to get to the top of the endless fucking array of stairs. Who the hell ever thought to drop an access tunnel down the full depth of the mines, without power?

He supposed he should be grateful, but he didn't really give a damn.

Willis first had climbed to the eighth level, planning to take a lift from there. Not the main lift, but one of the secondary or tertiary support lifts. It seemed like a good idea at first. It should have worked, too. But the door wouldn't open. He tried putting his shoulder into it, but all that gave him was a bruised shoulder.

He realized that he should have expected it. He'd taken the better part of a couple of hours to pry open the door on the bottom level. The shaft was part of the original complex, and even the stairs were falling apart in places. He had to be careful not to fall and break his neck.

The sixth level was as far as he made it before he had to give up taking the "easy way." None of the doors were going to open, and he could only pray that the one at the top was going to work.

He tried calling Rollins, and didn't get through. That didn't make sense, since she had given him a comm that was supposed to penetrate any barrier. Yet all he got was silence.

He'd stopped twice already to succumb to dry heaves because as much as he hated to admit it, a life behind the desk had left him in absolutely craptacular shape. His waist was broader than his shoulders and he counted higher than one when he counted his chins. It was easy to lie about that stuff when he was looking in the mirror every day, especially when he managed to find the occasional partner for his bed, but here and now, walking up a flight of stairs that was taller than a lot of skyscrapers, he was having a little more trouble arguing with the facts.

Eyes on the prize. When this was done he would be rich. Not well off, not comfortable, but disgustingly rich. He was a company man, and he liked working for Weyland-Yutani. But after this bloody insanity of a mission, he'd be taking early retirement.

He did, however, promise himself a good long session at a body remodeling facility. Modern science would fix what a bad diet and a desk job had done to him. He'd have the money to guarantee it.

All he had to do was get to the top of the stairs.

He almost wept when he reached the door for the second level. Someone had fused the door shut, for what insane reason he couldn't guess. Maybe to keep the monsters away. He didn't like that idea at all.

He took a moment to rest, to catch his breath, and to try to call Rollins with a progress report. Elation ran through him when she answered after only a few moments.

"I was beginning to worry about you, Mister Willis," she said. "I haven't heard from you in a few hours."

"I've been walking up a lot of stairs," he said. "I *tried* to contact you, but the damned comm wouldn't work." He didn't speak the words. He wheezed them. "I'm almost to the top. Do you have a ship on the way down?"

"No. It's already waiting for you and the rest of the team."

"There may not be a rest of the team."

"Several of them seem to be alive and well. We'll know soon enough."

"Where are they? Do you know?"

"Not exactly. They haven't access to the same communications devices that you do. They've been experiencing... technical difficulties." He nodded his head as if she could see him.

"Listen, it's bad down here. I haven't encountered many of them, but with everything that's going on, I think sterilization might become a necessity."

"We're already considering that option, Mister Willis."

He jerked his head up in surprise. He shouldn't have been shocked, really. He understood how the company worked well enough. Of course, that just made the data he was carrying all the more valuable. Rollins might have some of the scans, but he had the ones from the dig site, and there was no way she could have gotten the same level of detail that he had.

No way in hell. He kept telling himself that. With a grunt, he stood back up on watery legs and started up the stairs. *One more level.* How bad could it be?

"Mister Willis?" Rollins's voice actually startled him. He'd thought she had cut the link.

"Yes," he said. "I'm still here."

"You should be aware that this operation has been very costly to the company."

"Oh, yes." He paused to try catching his breath again. "I imagine it has. But the benefits, Ms. Rollins. They should be dazzling, shouldn't they? The biomechanical aspects from the ship alone should be worth whatever we've spent. If the information can be properly gleaned from the samples..."

"Do you still have the samples from the ship, Mister Willis?"

"Of course. They're in my office. In the safe."

"Wonderful. Please make sure you remember to retrieve them before you get to the drop ship."

"Oh." He stopped walking and caught his breath for a moment. "Do you know I would have forgotten them. Thank you for the reminder."

"Of course. Have a safe trip, Mister Willis. I look forward to meeting you in person."

This time he heard the barely audible click that indicated that the connection had been severed.

His breath was more a whimper than a sigh. He started moving. One step. One step. One step. Pause.

Just a little further.

5 1

A SIDE TRIP

"Mister Pritchett?" Rollins's voice came through clear as glass.

"Yeah. I'm here." He bolted upright in his seat. He'd been drifting. There was nothing to do but listen to the rain.

"Mister Pritchett, do you have access to a video pad?"

It took half a second to locate the screen from which he'd been reading.

"Yep. Right here."

"Good. I'm sending you a compressed file. On that file you will find a schematic of the offices. They're located in the largest building, in front of the barracks. Once you have those, I need you to locate the office of Tom Willis. He's busy right now, and I need you to collect some samples you'll find in the safe in his office."

"In the safe? Won't that be locked?"

"Come now, Mister Pritchett. I'm fully aware of your background. Even if I weren't, I'm also providing you with the combination. I've taken the liberty of overriding the retinal and DNA securities. This is company business, after all."

"You got it." Crock of crap was what it was. She didn't care about having the right to do anything. And he'd have bet his last paycheck that she'd acquired the combination without Willis's approval. The good news was that he didn't care. She wanted something in that safe, and he wanted his bonus.

"Mister Pritchett?"

"Yeah?"

"Arm yourself. There's a possibility that the life-forms we're looking to procure might be around in higher numbers than originally believed. If you should encounter one, I would suggest shooting first and worrying about the creature's intent later."

"You're the boss."

He took the time to arm himself. He also took the time to double check his armor.

He left the ship in standby mode, and locked it down before he left. No one was going anywhere without him.

5 2

The queen was dead.

Decker shook his head, trying to push the thoughts and images away. Still they came, unbidden and unwanted. The voices hissed and clicked in their alien thoughts and his mind interpreted them even as he tried to flee.

The enemy was still alive and the queen was dead. Their fury immeasurable. If they could have, they would have pursued the enemy, but they could not.

No! I'm not your enemy! Leave me alone! If they heard his attempts to speak back, to communicate, they did not react in any way he could understand.

The newborns were hatching, and they had to be protected. The enemy had proven to be as dangerous as their genetic memories had insisted, and for that reason the newborns had to be hidden away.

There would be no mercy from them. Mercy was as alien to them as their inhuman senses were to him.

* * *

They had already lost so much.

They moved among the nests and looked at the hosts. Some were conscious and some were not, that hardly mattered. Some were already giving birth, and others were close.

Then there were seven nests remaining. The past had taught them to be careful. They learned. They adapted. They survived.

The earliest of the new nests were no longer necessary. The hosts had served their purpose and their bodies were merely food now.

A new queen was already growing, carefully guarded and kept away from the enemy. She was taken down to the lowest levels of the hive to the great chambers where they had slept for so long, and remained untouched by the world around them as it changed.

The fear bloomed in his stomach and Decker shoved the thoughts aside. If he thought about the sheer numbers of the things he would truly go insane.

Two nests were gone, destroyed. The enemy still lived. The vile thing climbed away from the hive, and that was good. They would find him, and they would kill him.

They were careful with the new queen. She was so young, so fragile. She would grow strong, of course, but as with all things, time was a requirement.

Once she was secure, the ones who had seen to her safe escort turned their attention back to the enemy. It was close to the surface now, they could feel it crawling through the tunnels the hosts had cut into the ground.

They would follow.

The queen was dead. The queen was born anew. The queen would be protected, no matter what the cost.

5 3

PAYBACK

Karma was a bitch.

Luke Rand woke up not long after the monsters came and beat him into the ground. He'd tried to fight them, and they broke him. Three ribs and his jaw. He couldn't close his mouth, and every breath hurt like a fire being set just above his stomach.

He was underground, in near-complete darkness. And when he didn't think it could get any worse, they proved to him that he had no idea how bad things could get.

The area to which they dragged him was hot and damp, and covered in the glossy black deposits they'd been seeing all around the Sea of Sorrows ever since they'd arrived. He never guessed what they were. Never would have guessed, even if they'd given him a lifetime to figure it out.

The things held him down and when he tried to fight they effortlessly broke his right arm in three places. That pretty much ended his attempts. Still, that wasn't enough for the things. Two of them leaned over him and vomited gray-black goo over his body. The stuff started hardening as soon as it touched the air, and they spread it with their claws and slathered him with it until he was encased in a silicon straight jacket.

Even if he'd had it in him to fight any more, the glassy webbing quickly became too solid for his battered body to fight against.

There were other people around him, some of them were conscious and some of them weren't. He envied the ones who weren't.

Then the crab thing skittered over, and climbed up to his head. He tried to scream, painful as it was, but quickly his cries were muffled as it wrapped itself around his face. It was rape. That was the only way he could think of it and he felt tears of humiliation at the very idea. His jaw was already broken, but the thing didn't care. He tried twisting away, but he was glued down and the damned thing just didn't stop.

After a while everything just flowed into a dull ache, and then the pain went away altogether. He thought he should wonder why, but it didn't seem necessary.

Every bad thing he'd done in his life came back to him in that dark place. Stole a dollar when he was five. Stole a lot more than that when he was in school. He'd done some good things, like fighting for Aneki when the other kids tried to pick on him for being stuck in a wheelchair. But he'd also done his fair share of picking on the weaker ones.

There were people he'd done wrong, but he never thought it was enough to end up like this.

Those things were watching. He saw them moving now and again, and some of them were curled up in the blackness, lost in patterns that almost looked like parts of the walls of the cave. He had to look for them to see them at all, but he had time while he was stuck in one place, and thinking of all the bad things he'd done in his life.

He felt like shit about Decker. The man knew him for what he was, but he still stuck with him.

He felt like shit about a lot of things.

He didn't think he could feel any worse.

The pain came back in his broken ribs. It hammered his insides and moved around his heart and, oh, damn, but the pain was a living thing. It tore at his chest and then into his sides. His broken ribs were enough to make him howl past his broken jaw and bloodied lips.

The pain got worse, and worse again. So much worse.

In the end he couldn't think of a thing he'd ever done to deserve that much pain.

In the end it didn't matter.

Karma was a bitch, and didn't care what he thought.

5 4

BURDENS

The communiqué from the home office was short and to the point. It was also exactly what she had expected.

Andrea Rollins rose from her desk seat and stretched. She had things to do.

She called the bridge.

"Captain Cherbourg?"

"Yes, Ms. Rollins?"

"You should prepare the ship for departure. We won't be here much longer."

"Yes, ma'am."

"And Captain?"

"Yes, Ms. Rollins?"

"Be prepared to deliver your payload."

Cherbourg hesitated for a moment before responding, but only for a moment.

"Yes, ma'am."

Decker set Adams on the ground as gently as he could, and then sat for a moment.

True to his worries, she seemed at least ten times her original weight—at least if he listened to the protests from his shoulders. By comparison, Elway seemed to have only gained a few pounds.

He still hated Manning just a bit more for that.

"We get to the first level, are we going to try for another elevator or are we going to keep walking?" Muller asked. The question was a good one.

Manning looked down at the ground and shook his head.

"If this was a standard operation, we could take a truck back to the surface—there generally are ramps. But it's not. They were still rebuilding this thing, and I don't think they have an access road leading all the way up. So far these stairs have been clear of trouble and I like that, but it's not a guarantee." He paused to look around. "I am also very, very sick of confined spaces.

"When we get to level one, we don't have a schematic. We don't know the lay of the land. We don't know our way out of this place." He stopped talking, and seemed to be weighing the options.

Muller held up a hand and gestured for silence, one finger to his lips. Then he pointed to the stairs.

There was a sound from below.

Manning cleared his throat.

"So I think we have to consider which way is best, but I'm voting for exploring the first level. It'll give us more room to defend ourselves, if we need to."

As he spoke, he made several quick gestures. Muller nodded his head and moved, sliding to the edge of the stairwell and then carefully taking aim with his pistol. He tensed, and then Decker saw the tension leak out of the man's thick neck and shoulders, a little at a time.

"I think we're safe here." He stayed exactly where he was, and slowly lowered his pistol toward the floor.

A moment later they all heard the wheezing voice.

"Oh, thank God."

Manning recognized the voice.

"Willis?"

The bureaucrat was soaked through. His clothes were wet and clung to his bulk, his hair was pasted to his skull, and his face was a deep and unhealthy shade of red.

"Oh, thank you, God." He was climbing on his hands and knees, having apparently given up on the concept of walking.

Manning looked at Adams where she lay on the ground. His eyes flickered to Decker. The backpack she'd been carrying was gone. The backpack with the medical supplies.

"Anyone got a little water for this man?"

Silent Dave came to the rescue and tossed over a small bottle of liquid, rammed full of electrolytes and sugar. They were standard rations for most outposts. Willis's hands were shaking too hard for him to even hold the container. Once he'd calmed down, Manning opened it and handed it over.

"Sip it slowly."

He needn't have bothered. The man could barely even manage to sip. Still, after a few moments he had drunk half the bottle, and was breathing a bit easier.

"So, we're screwed. We need to get to the surface." Manning stared closely at Willis, who returned his look with a frown. "What's the fastest way?"

"There're elevators," he replied slowly. "The main lift is ruined, but one of the others, maybe."

"And you know where they are?"

"Yes. Of course."

"Then why the hell did you take the stairs?"

"Do you think I would have gone through hell like this, if I could get through one of the doors?" Willis answered testily. That seemed to mollify Manning.

"Well, finish catching your breath," the merc said. "We can't be here any more, and if what you say is true, the first level is our best bet."

"Ms. Rollins said she'd send down a drop ship." The words were almost mumbled. As soon as they were freed from his lips, Willis blinked as if slapped, and clammed up.

Decker felt the sudden shift in the man's emotions.

Manning didn't need to feel it. He leaned forward until he was close enough to kiss the man, and he spoke softly.

"Later, when this is over with," he said, "you and I will discuss how long you've been chatting it up with Rollins. For right now, though, get the fuck up. We're going to *move*."

"Wait. What happened to the others on your team?" Willis spoke as he slowly crawled his way up to a standing position.

Manning bared his teeth. No one in their right mind would have called it a smile.

"I didn't have any way to contact Rollins, you see, so things went badly." He cast his eyes toward the ground for a moment, and then back to Willis. "What happened to the rest of my people—the ones who were down on level nine with you?"

Willis looked away.

"I don't know," he said. Then his voice went up an octave. "I panicked, okay? I went for the stairs as soon as the fire started." He was lying. The man was a smarmy prick, and he was a lousy liar. At least from Decker's unique point of view.

Then that crawling sensation slipped weakly across the engineer's mind.

"I think they're coming again," he warned them. "But if they are, they aren't close."

The others made ready to continue to journey upward. Decker carefully slung Adams back over his shoulders, glad they weren't going all the way to the surface, while Manning hauled Elway onto his shoulder and checked the clip on his pistol.

"Can you tell where they're coming from?" he asked.

"No. It's not that clear." Decker shook his head. "Not yet, anyhow. And like you said before, I don't know the layout of the place. If I did, it might help me pinpoint them a little better."

Manning's hand caught Willis's shoulder in a fierce grip, and he bared his teeth again.

"Good news, then. We have our own tour guide."

Willis didn't look happy at the prospect, but he became more energetic as the energy boost ran into his system. Not energetic. Alert. He had probably been in a state of shock. Whatever it was, it enabled him to walk upright as they cleared the last flight of stairs, and reached level one. All that remained above them was the ground floor.

The door to level one opened easily.

This time Muller took the lead, looking left and right and then beckoning the rest of them into the corridor. The area was wrecked. Whatever had happened, it hadn't happened easily. There were broken lights and signs of a struggle, and a few pieces of people left behind.

Willis's eyes bulged in their sockets, but he remained silent.

Manning remedied that.

"Which way?" he demanded.

"There are elevators here—" Willis pointed. "—and elevators down that way." They moved toward the first set of doors, and discovered the same elevators that the group had tried riding up before. So he turned and led them in the opposite direction. After a hundred feet or so, they found a passageway that didn't exist on the lower levels.

"Where the hell does that go?" Manning asked.

"A new mining operation. It's got a lot of junk in the way, but it's got its own lift, and we used it to clear a lot of dirt and stone out of the way. The office and the compound are both in that direction, as well—up above."

"How far *down* does the lift go?"

"This is it," Willis replied. "This is as low as it goes. We found the main mining operation not long after we started here."

Manning shot Decker a glance, and Decker nodded. It was damned convenient that they found the original site that easily.

Damned convenient.

"Let's move," the merc said. And they were off.

Muller stayed in the lead, and they moved quickly. Decker did his best to focus on the minds of the bugs, and to ignore the cold detachment that emanated from the parasites clinging to Adams and Elway.

He wanted desperately to put Adams down, but wouldn't do

that. *Couldn't* do that. She was good people. And he suspected she would have found a way to drag his sorry ass anywhere he needed to be taken. He made a silent promise to her that she'd get out of this alive. He intended to keep that promise, too. One way or another.

Despite the earlier signs of damage and struggle, there was little to see as they moved forward. No more bodies, no signs of a struggle of any kind. Indeed, to Decker's eye, it didn't seem as if the shaft had been used in quite a while. That seemed weird for what Willis had called a "new" operation.

"No one's dug here for some time now," Decker commented. "Why did they abandon it?"

"We didn't find enough trimonite to make it worth our while," Willis said. "It was too far out of the way to use for storage, so we just stopped bothering with it."

Ten minutes of walking got them to the elevator.

Manning looked to Decker.

"Anything?"

"No. Nothing." He pushed past the background noise. "Nothing close by, at least."

So Manning pushed the elevator call button, and double-checked his pistol again. Following his example, Decker checked the clip and the safety on the reaper.

Willis looked at the weapons with a mild hunger.

When the elevator chimed they waited for the doors to slide open and Decker found himself taking aim in that general direction. Anything coming out was going to get an unpleasant reception.

There were no occupants. Muller and Willis went first and the rest piled in quickly. The interior was battered, and large enough to let both Decker and Manning set their burdens down again. Decker rolled his shoulders and felt the muscles creak their gratitude.

He kept looking down the length of the rough corridor, half expecting to see more of the bugs coming their way. He didn't feel them, but he expected them just the same.

Manning seemed to feel the same.

"Damned things are like cockroaches," he muttered. "They keep popping out of nowhere."

Dave spoke up.

"Let 'em. I got three full clips and a serious need to shoot something." The rifle he waved had a big barrel, and looked like it had been designed to hunt small spaceships.

"That's what I like about you, Dave," Manning said. "Your optimism." The doors shut and the lift rose smoothly. The ride stayed smooth and then it jerked to a halt on the top level.

The doors opened into a hallway that was abandoned.

Muller checked anyway. Then he gave the all clear.

"Let's get the hell out of here, gentlemen," Manning said. "We need to find a defensible area and call the shuttle down."

Willis looked up and smiled weakly. "I think the shuttle is already here."

Manning frowned. "It is?"

"I could be wrong, but I believe that was the plan. It should be here already."

Manning nodded his head but kept that skeptical frown.

"If you're right, all the better."

Decker squatted and looked over Adams's still form. Then he very carefully lifted her and stood back up again.

"Let's go."

Willis cleared his throat. "I need to go to my office. I have files I need to retrieve." He pointed down the hallway. "Take two lefts and you'll be at the main doors. The landing pad is across from the barracks."

Manning lifted Elway.

"Don't be long. If it's you or my people, it's going to be my people. Understood?"

"Of course." Willis was still a little shaky, but he headed off toward his offices.

And they were off again, Muller and Dave taking the front and the rear while Alan and Manning carried their burdens. After all they'd been through, the silence seemed deafening, but Decker felt it. The growing sensation that the damned things were coming for him again.

"They're getting closer."

"Where?" Muller looked back at him.

"I don't know. I just know they're getting closer. Damn I hate this." His pulse was hammering, despite the odd calming sensation that emanated from Adams and Elway.

"Let's just move," Manning said. "We need to get to the damn shuttle, and *now*." He was doing his best to look everywhere at once. The strain from carrying Elway was showing itself now, and adding to Decker's discomfort. If Manning looked stressed, it was a bad sign in his book.

They made the two lefts with stops to check for the bugs. Nothing. Nothing at all, but instead of relaxing Decker, it made him stress even more. He knew they were coming, yet there was no sign of them.

"Where are all the people?" Muller mumbled—to himself, most likely, but Decker heard. He didn't answer, but he was wondering the same thing. There were no signs of a disturbance. The violence from below hadn't occurred here. There was no debris, and there were no bodies.

They reached a door, and there was the sound of falling water on the other side. They eased it open, and for the first time they saw the outside. It was dark out, and the rains were heavier than Decker had seen before.

The exterior lights were on, casting brilliant beams through the darkness and leaving the entire area in a dim twilight highlighted by the shining trails of illuminated raindrops. The air was clean, and smelled like a slice of heaven after the burning stench of the alien tunnels. The chill was enough to invigorate.

But it wouldn't last, Decker knew. The bugs were coming. No time to enjoy even the little things, because they were somewhere close by, and he needed to spot them before the damned things got close enough to kill them.

"Where are they, Decker?" Dave said. The man was getting positively chatty.

He looked around and saw the landing platform where the shuttle waited for them.

Of course.

"They're that way."

Manning didn't bother waiting. He started walking and expected the rest to keep pace. They did—even Decker, who had no desire to head toward the things that wanted to tear him to shreds.

The closer they got the more he felt his muscles tensing. They were out there. They had to be.

But damned if he could see them.

5 5

SAMPLES

The safe was exactly where he'd been told it would be, tucked into the floor at the base of a small desk that had delusions of being something better.

When Pritchett opened it, he found a small container with a biohazard symbol on the outside. He opened the seal and saw several small vials of gray and silver tissue samples. That was the stuff. He slid the package into his pants pocket, and took the time to grab a few papers that looked interesting. There was no money, nor any other valuables.

As he stood up the door opened.

The man standing in the doorway looked profoundly shocked by his presence.

That was fair. He felt the same way.

"What are you doing in my office?"

Pritchett looked the man up and down. He was stocky, and filthy dirty. He looked like he'd crawled his way across the entire complex on his belly. What he did not look like was a threat.

"Got orders from above to procure a few samples from your safe." He saw no reason to lie to the man.

Mister Business looked him up and down and scowled.

"Well, you've done your duty, and can hand them over to me."

He actually held out a hand as if expecting Pritchett to surrender the package.

"Yeah. I don't see that happening." He took a step toward the man and placed a hand on his pistol's holster, just in case there was any debate.

"Now you listen here. My name is Tom Willis and I'm in charge of this facility. You need to hand over what you took before things get nasty, mister."

Seriously? He looked the man up and down. "Okay, get this. Your facility is screwed. I'm following orders. I'm also the pilot who's getting you out of here, unless you continue to give me shit. Give me enough trouble and I'll just leave your ass here."

Yeah, that got his attention just fine. The man went white.

"You wouldn't do that."

"Watch me," he replied. "Time to go. I'm just waiting on Manning and his team, and then we're out of here."

"Are there other shuttles coming, for more people?" The officious bravado was fading fast, and the man was looking less like a boss and more like a wage slave. Pritchett liked the change.

"Don't know. Don't care. It's time to go."

"But—"

"Listen, you can stay if you want. I don't care. I'm leaving."

The man looked at his desk, looked over his paperwork and office supplies like they were proof that he should be in charge. Pritchett just walked past him. Let the little bastard stay if he wanted to.

The sonovabitch sucker punched him. Hauled off and drove a fist into the side of Pritchett's head with all he could muster. It was a good punch, but it wasn't great. Pritchett staggered to the side and caught himself as he bounced into the doorjamb.

While the man was grabbing at something from his desk, Pritchett brought his leg around and kicked him in the thigh hard enough to make him scream. Whatever he'd been grabbing at fell from his hand.

Then Pritchett brought his open palm around and nailed his

attacker in the jaw, hard enough to snap his head back.

Willis let out a grunt and tried for him again. Pritchett didn't waste time. There would have been some satisfaction in breaking the bastard's neck, but he was on a deadline. So he just drew the pistol and aimed it at Willis's face.

"No!" And just like that the fight went out of him.

"That's done. Move your ass before I shoot you." He pushed Willis ahead of him and let the man stumble. If he fell all over himself that was just fine.

Willis made four drunken steps into the hallway when he was hit by something big and black. It was fast, too, and it slashed a chunk out of the man's guts in one hard stroke of its fingers. The man fell back, a high keening scream leaking from his lips. He hit the wall, his eyes never once leaving the thing as it came for him a second time.

Pritchett opened fire.

Nothing happened. The safety was still engaged.

He cursed himself as he flipped the switch. The thing changed course and jumped at him, letting loose a few choice noises of its own.

This time when he pulled the trigger the pistol worked just fine. The thing staggered backward as he fired four times, blowing multiple holes into the torso and guts of the beast. It fell backward, kicked, thrashed, and died.

Its guts splashed over Willis, who let out a piercing shriek. His hands shook as his body smoked and burned—he didn't seem to know where to put them or what to do to make the pain go away. It must have been overwhelming. His skin blistered along his face and neck, bubbled over his arms and hands, and he shrieked again, looking toward Pritchett with eyes that seemed to blame him.

Pritchett just gaped, speechless.

Willis screamed again as a hole burned through his lips and half of his nose.

Pritchett reacted by instinct. One shot through Willis's skull— and then he moved for the door.

The ship wasn't that far away, really. He could make it in a couple of minutes, but suddenly it seemed like a lot further than that. The idea that he might run into any more of those things added miles in his mind. He kept his weapon drawn, and scanned his surroundings as he walked.

5 6

PLAIN SIGHT

Decker was happy to discover that Willis had it right. The drop ship was waiting on the landing pad, and the sight of it was like a boost of adrenaline straight to the heart. Suddenly Adams didn't weigh as much, and Decker felt as if he could sprint the short distance.

The mercenaries seemed to feel the same way. They moved faster and they were more alert.

"Where are they?" Manning said, and Decker's euphoria fell into check.

"Right there." He pointed toward the ship, and his voice rose. "They're right in front of us, and getting closer. But I can't see them!"

"You could maybe stop shouting, and telling them where we are, guys," Dave said. "You think maybe that's a good idea?"

Muller nodded and stayed quiet, but kept alert, his pulse rifle at the ready. When he glanced toward the sands, he muttered under his breath.

"No way."

Decker looked. He wished he'd managed not to. There were two of them at first, rising out of the sand. He had no idea where they'd come from until the next one rose.

The damned silicon.

Originally he'd thought they were just deposits, lumps of hardened sand, maybe caused by lightning strikes when the worst of the storms were still ripping the planet apart on a daily basis. Then he'd guessed that they might be debris from the tunnels the aliens were making. But as the sand erupted he realized the truth.

The bugs were craftier than he'd imagined. The silicon lumps he'd found were just the evidence of the trapdoors. Several of them popped up at the same time and the aliens crawled quickly from the tunnels they'd built.

Fully a dozen of the things came out at the same time, skittering across the sand, moving on all fours to better spread their weight and avoid sinking in the soft surface.

And the damn things *saw* him. He felt their anger rise as they did so, and they came faster. Behind them more were rising from their hidden tunnels, and charging toward him, the mercenaries, and their only hope of getting away from the planet.

Muller raised his pistol, aimed, and fired, and one of the bugs exploded. The others kept coming. They were focused on Decker to the exclusion of everything else. They wanted the Destroyer dead.

Decker set Adams down as gently as he could under the circumstances, and took aim with his pistol. Manning dropped Elway without ceremony, letting the man land roughly as he opened fire.

Not-so-silent Dave lifted the wide barrel of his weapon and fired. The noise was loud, a low roar of detonation, and out on the Sea of Sorrows there was a brilliant corresponding flash as several feet of sand and moving alien erupted in a wave of flames.

Dave let out a whooping battle cry and did it again, shifting his target a bit and blowing the shit out of another three yards of everything within range.

Still they came. The aliens moved faster now that they were in the open, and not dodging obstacles. Decker aimed, fired, missed. Aimed, fired and missed. He emptied the clip on the reaper, never certain if he'd hit anything at all.

Manning obliterated one of the things that got too close, and the monster rolled across the ground, leaving a trail of acid blood behind. Decker stared at the thing, suddenly unable to move.

It was dead, but the twitching parts still seemed to reach for him.

Another man came up from behind them and Decker spun, aimed and fired. Had there been any ammunition left in the reaper he'd have killed the stranger, but fate was kinder than that.

It was Pritchett, the pilot. The man slapped the weapon from his hands, pushed him aside and opened fire on the aliens.

Decker grabbed at the plasma rifle slung over his shoulder, but all he managed was to drop the weapon.

Dave fired a total of ten of his explosive rounds, and then switched clips with hands that were almost blindingly fast. The empty clip hit the ground and bounced, and by the time it had finished its short trip the mercenary was once again blowing holes in the desert and the aliens. He was careful to avoid getting too close to the shuttle.

Muller ran out of ammunition on his rifle, let it fall and immediately reached for the plasma rifle Decker had dropped. He grabbed it, his face pulled down in an expression of burning anger.

As Decker had done before, he set the weapon to automatic and unloaded the entire clip of plasma rounds into the approaching horde. Like Dave, he was careful about where he fired, giving the ship a wide berth. The night immediately became day, and the light revealed the monsters as they caught fire and burned, screeching and dying in the sudden conflagration.

Manning kept firing, picking off the shapes that made it through the sudden firestorm and got too close to the shuttle.

As the freelancers decimated the creatures, the panic that tried to eat through Decker's mind calmed, fading with each death. The heat from the plasma fires was almost enough to warm the chill that coursed through him.

Then Manning was reaching for Elway.

As Decker reached for Adams, Pritchett drove a fist into his stomach hard enough to drop him. While he was trying to get back up, the stranger aimed a pistol at his face.

"You lost your fucking mind?" he shouted. "You tried to shoot me!"

Manning reached over and put his hand on the pistol, slowly directing it away from Decker's face.

"Heat of the moment," he said. "Get over it. We need to leave."

"He fucking tried to kill me!"

"I said let it go, Pritchett! Now let. It. Go."

The pilot took a few extra heartbeats to stare blue murder at Decker, and then holstered his weapon.

"Where the fuck is Willis?" Manning barely even bothered to look around. "We need to leave. Now."

"He didn't make it." Pritchett didn't offer anything else.

Manning nodded and started walking.

The rest followed.

"What the fuck *are* those things?" Pritchett looked carefully around and avoided stepping on the burnt remains of the aliens. Then he slid back the protective case on his wrist and tapped a couple of keys on a remote. The lights on the drop ship started up instantly, and the door at the rear opened and descended, offering them access.

"Those are what we came here to find," Manning spat. "Aren't they great?"

Pritchett climbed aboard, and the rest quickly followed. The door began to close with a mechanical whine. Exhaustion tinted Decker's every move. He carried Adams into the seating area and very carefully strapped her into a seat. The thing covering her face shifted just a bit. The legs moved, the tail slid a few millimeters. It took everything left in him not to scream.

That cold feeling still came from the thing. A calm that seemed to promise that everything would be just fine. The sensation slithered into his mind from both of the spider-things, and he shivered. A lie. It had to be a lie. Nothing would ever be all right again. Not in a universe that had vomited these things into existence.

As if to prove him right, another of the bugs came through the door as it was rising back into place, pushing into the area with unsettling speed. Pritchett let out a tiny noise as the monster's claws opened his stomach and sliced through his thigh. The blood flow was immediate and heavy.

By the time he knew he was injured, the pilot was dead.

Dave grabbed the handrail above the aisle and twisted his entire body around. Both of his feet landed in the thing's charging body and sent it backward. While it was recovering, Muller looked around for a weapon, *any* weapon that might let him fight the thing.

It ignored him and went for Decker, silent and fast.

Muller grabbed a pistol and slammed it across the top of the alien's skull. It faltered, but did not fall. There was no room for firing a weapon inside the drop ship—not without risking hitting the wrong target.

Manning scrambled for the front of the ship.

Decker grabbed for anything that he could use against the creature and let out a bellow. Hard claws caught his calf and tore through the fabric of his pants, through the leather of his boot, and into the flesh beneath. He kicked the thing in its featureless face where the hint of a skull lay beneath the smooth back surface, above the gnashing teeth, once, twice, a third time, but it did not care. It just kept coming for him.

Muller hit the damned thing again, then a third time, and it ignored him too, as it pulled Decker closer, crawling over him. Its tail lashed sideways and slapped Muller in the chest hard enough to send him flying.

Dave reached for his pistol. All Decker could think about was how badly that blood was going to burn him, unless of course the monster got him first. He rolled over as best he could with the thing trying to claw its way up his body. Its mouth opened in what looked like a smile of triumph and the teeth parted, revealing a second mouth that drooled and steamed.

Just as those hellish mouths tried to take off Decker's face, Dave grabbed at the thing's tail and hauled it backward. Muller hit it again, this time with a full pack worth of gear. The force was enough to send it sprawling.

"Move!" Manning bellowed, and the mercenaries rolled out of the way, scrambling over seats and diving as far from the thing as they could. Decker pulled into a fetal position, ignoring the flaring pain in his calf as best he could.

A stream of silvery foam washed over the creature, splattering the floor around it and coating its body. It had the consistency of shaving cream, but even from a few feet away Decker could see how it stuck.

Manning kept a stream of the thick foam flowing as the creature fought to get back to its feet. Muller flung his pack as hard as he could and nailed the thing in the chest as it tried to rise. The pack was coated in an instant, and stuck where it hit.

The stream of foam stopped, the canister sputtering empty.

The bug screeched and flailed and tried to throw the pack away. And then it slowed down. More and more, the foam was hardening, sticking to the creature as it tried to get away.

Still the monster tried to reach Decker. It lunged and peeled itself partially from the floor, and pushed and came for him again, the hatred unending, a hellish hammering rage that would never stop until he was dead.

Or it was dead.

Maybe not even then.

Manning walked closer to the thing, dropping the bulky metal canister. It hit the deck with a loud clang and rolled a bit. Manning placed the two prongs of the shock-stick against an exposed part of the creature's head and hit it with enough volts to kill a man. It screamed and shuddered. It lunged and fell—or tried to. It never made it to the deck. Manning laid on the charge a second time and a third. And then stepped back.

"There's a cage in the hold. Let's move fast, before this damn thing wakes up."

Muller and Dave went to work with unsettling efficiency while Decker panted and stared.

"You're going to leave it alive?" His voice cracked as he spoke. Manning's eyes scanned his face. He was once again like stone, his features unreadable. When he spoke it was with unsettling calm.

"The contract says alive pays better," he replied. "So we bring it back alive."

"You've got to be kidding me."

"No. This is a job, same as any other."

Emotion welled up inside of Decker, heating him with raw, primal anger.

"Manning, you've got to kill these things! All of them!" He was standing before he thought about it. His calf pulsed with pain but that didn't matter. He needed to make the man understand. The spider-things on Adams and Elway, the bug that Muller and Dave were putting into a heavy steel case, they had to die.

They had to die now.

Manning shook his head.

"Not happening. Not today."

Decker looked around, as if searching for something that would convince the man of how serious he was. The thing wanted him dead. It wouldn't stop. Couldn't Manning see that? Couldn't he *feel* it?

Decker's heart was hammering away and he was sweating again. This was never going to stop, not as long as any of the creatures were alive. They'd come after him. They'd come after Bethany and Ella and Josh! When the damned things were done with him, they'd still come after his children!

He looked to Elway and felt nothing, but when he looked at Adams there was a flash of regret. Still, it had to happen. They had to die. Those things would come out of them, and the entire goddamn nightmare would start again. They would find him, no matter where he was.

He knew that now.

"Put it down, Decker!" Manning's voice. He was bellowing. Decker realized then that he had a death grip on something. He looked down and saw the reaper in his fist.

"I can't," he said. "They have to be stopped."

Decker pulled the trigger, Elway and the spider-thing on his face were dead in his sights.

The hammer clicked on an empty chamber. He hadn't reloaded. That realization came to him at exactly the same time as Manning's fist smashed into his head.

"… lost your fucking mind!" He tried to shake away the pain, tried to find the words to explain, but before he could so much as wet his too dry lips, Manning's boot found his stomach.

5 7

DELIVERIES

Flanked by four security personnel, Andrea Rollins waited patiently as the drop ship's doors opened. Two of the mercenaries climbed out, their faces drawn. They looked at her and said nothing. A moment later Manning pushed Alan Decker through the walkway and let him fall. Then he disappeared back into the vessel.

Decker couldn't stand up by himself, as he was bound at the ankles and his wrists were strapped behind his back. She gestured to the two men with her, and they picked him up. He was injured. No real surprise there.

Manning came back a moment later carrying a woman. She was incapacitated and her face was hidden behind a mask of hard flesh and long legs that clutched her skull.

Adams. Her name was Adams. He set her on a gurney.

"How is she?" Rollins asked.

"You need to fix this." Manning's voice was as calm as ever.

"We intend to, Mister Manning. I've already got the chambers set up to monitor both Ms. Adams and Mister Elway. We'll take care of them."

She gestured to the other two men and they immediately entered the ship. They knew what to do. She'd explained very carefully. The two of them carried Elway out as if he were made of glass, and placed him on a gurney.

Manning watched carefully the entire time. Then he pointed to the ship.

"One live specimen. It's in the cage you provided and it's glued in place."

"Excellent work, Mister Manning."

He looked at the ship and then at her.

"Costly work."

"We knew that going in, didn't we?"

"Yeah. We did."

Rollins looked at the remaining mercenaries. Including Manning and the two hosts, there were a total of five out of the original thirty-five. But that was nothing compared to the loss of life among those who had been stationed at the base below.

"Do you need to rest right away?" she asked. "Or can I bother you to linger for a few more minutes?"

"I'll survive," Manning replied.

She smiled. "I just need to take care of a few details, and then we can finish this business."

He sat down and stared hard at the ground in front of him. He could have been a statue, if he hadn't breathed.

Rollins took care of arranging the placement of the alien's cage. It would be locked into cryogenic suspension in a chamber devised for exactly that purpose. There would be no chances taken. Weyland-Yutani had sought these particular creatures for a very long time, and she wasn't going to allow anything to go wrong.

Nor, frankly, did she much like the idea of anything that violent breaking loose.

When she was done she stood before the commander of the mercenaries and spoke softly.

"Walk with me, Mister Manning."

He lurched to his feet, and followed as she started to lead.

When they reached the bridge, Manning looked down at New Galveston and the speck far below them that marked the Sea of Sorrows. The flight crew was active, moving about and preparing to leave orbit. The captain, a dark-haired man with dark skin and an equally dark disposition, nodded a perfunctory greeting.

"How bad is it down there, Mister Manning?"

"You can't let them live. If you do, I can pretty much guarantee they'll own that planet in a year's time, perhaps less. The three cities the company put so much money into building will be ghost towns." He remained stoic as he gave his answer.

"Do you understand now why we warned about heavy losses?"

"Your pet, Decker, tried to kill my people at the end. He was scared that the things planted inside them would get out, I guess." He paused, and added, "I'm not sure he's wrong."

"Well, in his defense that was a possibility. But both of your people are now in hypersleep chambers, and already in stasis."

Manning nodded. He was silent for a long while.

Finally Rollins interrupted his reverie.

"So you recommend neutralizing the area?"

"Nuke it," he said without hesitation. "Wipe that mine and everything in there off the map."

"We'll take care of it."

"When?"

Rollins looked toward the captain of the ship. The man peered back at her and nodded his head. She turned back to Manning.

"Does right now suit you?"

"Yes. Right now is your best bet. Those things are smarter than you think."

Rollins knew better. She knew *exactly* how smart they were. Judging from everything that had transpired below, they were very nearly the perfect soldiers.

"Captain Cherbourg, please handle the matter."

The man nodded and spoke into his comm. What he said was too soft for her to hear, but the result was immediate. Four plasma warheads dropped from orbit and headed for the Sea of Sorrows. There was a time and a place for mercy. That time was not now.

The order to clear the area had gone out two days earlier, along with the statement that a viral strain had been located in the mines. No one on New Galveston questioned the instructions.

The Sea of Sorrows was designated a hot zone, biologically speaking. It hadn't been hard to convince the local doctors of the dangers of a pandemic. Every city on the planet was connected by the tube system. The mine wasn't a part of that system, for which everyone was grateful.

The weapons would annihilate anything in the area to a depth of roughly twenty thousand feet.

"Within the hour the Sea of Sorrows will cease to exist, Mister Manning."

Manning nodded his head. He seemed perfectly fine with the notion.

"I'm just going to stand here and wait, if that's all right with you."

Rollins smiled. "I thought you might like to be here for that. I am sorry for your losses, Mister Manning,"

Manning just looked at her.

"Keep the rest of them alive, Ms. Rollins. And keep your part of the bargain."

"I always do, Mister Manning."

She left him there, staring at the small spot that would soon be removed, a cancer on the skin of an otherwise healthy planet. Some tissues had to be cut out in order to be sure the cancer didn't spread. Manning knew that.

5 8

PLAGUES

Decker tried breaking through the straps holding him in place, but it was a futile effort.

One of the men tending to his leg had been nice enough to inject him with a sedative that had him calm again. There was that at least.

He did his best to *remain* calm when Rollins showed up. She asked a few questions just out of his hearing range. One of the medics responded, nodded, and then they left. She pulled over a chair so she could be at eye level with him.

"You've been naughty, Mister Decker."

He looked hard at her and tried to get a reading, anything to let him know how badly he had screwed himself over. Nothing. He might as well have been staring at a wall.

"It was just too much," he said. "And those things... Those things were after me. *Are* after me. Do you understand that? They want me dead!" His voice was shaking by the time he was done, and he thought he might lose it, but he pushed that back.

She was a cold bitch. She simply nodded her head while staring into his face.

"I know," she said. "I know they are. You should know that the entire area is being cleaned. There won't be any of them left."

"Except the ones you have onboard now."

"That's correct." She stared at him. He looked away first, and he hated her for that. As if he needed another reason.

"You don't know how bad it is," he said. "You don't understand at all. They're insatiable."

"*Life* is insatiable, Mister Decker." She smiled thinly. He didn't like her smile. It made him think of lizards, and her lips reminded him too much of the very creatures they were discussing. "Life fights to exist," she continued. "Haven't you realized that? No matter what the universe wants, life insists on surviving. Not just human life. All of it. We've encountered diseases on a dozen different worlds, and they've been burned away, only to show up in other places. Typhen's Disorder, Arcturian Klerhaige, the Lansdale Plague. Doesn't matter what we do, they come back. And they're not alone.

"Life is persistent. Be grateful for that."

He remained silent. She didn't want to understand, and though he couldn't read a single emotion from her, he knew her type well enough. Nothing he said would change her mind.

Finally he broke the silence.

"So what happens now?"

Rollins patted his restrained hand.

"Despite a few bumps, you kept your part of the bargain, and so will the company. You get your job back. You get your life back. You get a nice bonus as a finder's fee. We get our prizes, and everybody wins."

"No," he replied. "As long as those things are around, everybody loses."

"You'll never see them again."

"How can you know that?"

"Because you're going back to Earth. They are going elsewhere." She smiled again. "We're not *that* crazy, Mister Decker. You don't take something like this and drop it into the most populated place imaginable. You study it very carefully in an isolated, controlled environment."

"What about Adams and Elway?"

She stopped smiling.

"I think that's enough questions. You're safe, Mister Decker. Your family is safe. Consider your debt paid."

"You're making a mistake," he said. "I know you think you're doing the right thing, Miss Rollins, but you're making a horrible mistake."

"You should rest now, Mister Decker. We'll be leaving orbit soon."

She left the room, and for a while Decker slept.

He woke up again when they came for him.

The two "escorts" were armed, but needn't have bothered. He was still restrained, and kept that way until they reached the hypersleep chambers.

Manning was stripped down to his underwear and sitting on the edge of his coffin-like chamber.

"They burned," he said. "I watched. I doubt there's anything left down there. Hard to see past the plasma fires, but I think they're all gone."

Decker listened without a word. Before he could think of anything to say, Manning continued.

"I know what you were thinking. I get it. But you even *think* hard about going after any of mine again, and I'll bury you on seven different worlds."

Decker didn't want to look the man in his eyes, but he made himself. He could have thought of a dozen things to say, but instead he just nodded.

Adams deserved better. That was the thing that kept going through his mind. Maybe they'd manage to save her and Elway, but he didn't think so. Manning was pissed, and Muller and Dave—two men who'd saved his life a couple of times each—were staring at him with murder in their hearts. They were resentful. They felt betrayed.

He couldn't blame them in the least. His actions at the end were purely selfish. Screw money and everything else, he was looking after himself and his kids. The mercenaries would never understand that. They weren't capable of that level of empathy.

One of the men who'd brought him into the chambers took the time to remove the restraints.

The other patted the weapon on his hip. It wasn't a shock stick.

"Lie back, Mister Decker." The man wasn't making a request, and he took the hint. A moment later the lid was descending and Decker took a deep breath, same as he always did, not that it made any difference. The chamber sealed itself, and cold sterile air began cycling over his body.

He closed his eyes and felt the gases change. They weren't taking any chances with him. He would be asleep and secured long before the ship left orbit.

He inhaled. He exhaled. He inhaled.

He slept.

5 9

LETTERS HOME

Rollins re-read her communiqué before sending it.

```
To: L.Bannister@Weyland-Yutani.com
From: A.Rollins@Weyland-Yutani.com

Subject: Success

Lorne,


I'm pleased to report what can only be called a
resounding success.


In addition to successfully capturing one of the adults
alive, we have also procured two separate parasites,
already attached to hosts. Though we can't be
completely certain of the maturation cycles, it looks
as if both have successfully implanted embryos within
the host bodies. Judging from the levels of activity we
recorded just before cryogenic suspension I would guess
that they are only hours from hatching.


If you look carefully at the two separate files I've
attached (See: Host One and Host Two), you will note
that the two parasites exhibit several differences, in
both size and shape. Of special interest, note that
Host Two, the female, has attached to her a parasite
```

that seems to have more than one embryo to administer. The embryo that has already been implanted is substantially larger than the implant in Host One, and is structurally different. Judging from the accounts of what the mercenaries encountered planetside, this could very well be a "queen."

Imagine the possibilities.

Additional files include full information gleaned from all of the probes. There's simply too much information to properly correlate from here, and I imagine we will have much to discuss by the time I arrive at the offices.

Lastly, despite initial fears that they might have been left behind on New Galveston, the samples from the ship at the dig site have been safely secured and stored. I did not have time to ascertain whether there was any cellular activity as originally claimed by Doctor Tanaka, but the woman never seemed the sort to exaggerate or make wild claims. Per our previous discussion the samples have been halved, with parts being placed in stasis, and the rest being secured in a safe environment that doesn't risk further cellular degradation.

I wish I had been able to see the ship. Not just the pictures, but the actual vessel. And the city. But judging from what Manning reported, they were lost to us already. What a pity. All we have are schematics and readings.

Until I get back to the offices, good luck with the research.

All the best,
Andrea

She sent the encrypted messages and secured her computer for the trip. The *Kiangya* had already broken orbit and was heading for home, and she was glad of it.

For a moment she looked at the samples from the alien ship,

and smiled. Infinite possibilities. That was what Weyland-Yutani was all about—at a profit of course, but infinite possibilities were a lovely thing.

She made her way to the hypersleep chambers and looked over the other figures, lying in forced slumber.

So many empty chambers, she noted. *So many assets, lost.*

Around her the ship was silent, and most of the lights had dimmed down into sleep mode, conserving energy. Some people were bothered by darkness and the quiet. Decker was likely one of them. That might never change for him. Rollins wasn't disturbed at all by the secrets the darkness might hold, or the mysteries that silences kept. Those were the very things on which she thrived. They were what made her feel complete.

EPILOGUE

The stars kept their secrets and the great ship moved between them, all inhabitants accounted for and locked in slumber. Most of them slept well.

Decker did not. In his dreams there were things chasing him.

No matter how hard he ran, how carefully he hid himself or what he might find as a weapon, he knew they would eventually locate him. It was as inevitable as the dark between the stars.

And in his frozen sleep, no one could hear his screams.

ACKNOWLEDGEMENTS

Every book has a foundation. *Alien: Sea of Sorrows* could not exist without the original stories and movies, and is linked directly to Tim Lebbon's *Alien: Out of the Shadows* and Christopher Golden's *Alien: River of Pain*. Those alone would make a powerful foundation, but *Sea of Sorrows* truly could not exist without the ideas put forth by Steve Asbell of Twentieth Century Fox and the support and efforts of Josh Izzo and Lauren Winarski and Steve Saffel. Thanks also to the rest of the Titan team, including Nick Landau, Vivian Cheung, Katy Wild, Natalie Laverick, and Julia Lloyd. My gratitude to one and all.

ABOUT THE AUTHOR

James A. Moore is the author of over twenty novels, including the critically acclaimed *Fireworks*, *Under The Overtree*, *Blood Red*, *Deeper*, the Serenity Falls trilogy (featuring his recurring anti-hero, Jonathan Crowley) and his most recent novels *Seven Forges* and the forthcoming sequel *The Blasted Lands*.

He has twice been nominated for the Bram Stoker Award and spent three years as an officer in the Horror Writers Association, first as Secretary and later as Vice President.

The author cut his teeth in the industry writing for Marvel Comics and authoring over twenty role-playing supplements for White Wolf Games, *including Berlin by Night*, *Land of 1,000,000 Dreams* and *The Get of Fenris Tribebook*. He also penned the White Wolf novels *Vampire: House of Secrets* and *Werewolf: Hellstorm*.

Moore's first short story collection, *Slices*, sold out before ever seeing print.

He currently lives in the suburbs of Atlanta, Georgia. Meet him on his blog genrefied.blogspot.com and his website

www.jamesamoorebooks.com.

ALIEN™

RIVER OF PAIN

by Christopher Golden

Concluding the all-new, official trilogy set in the Alien Universe! When Ellen Ripley finally returned to Earth, she learned that the planet LV-426—the planet from *Alien*—has been colonized. This novel will reveal for the first time the fate of the colonists, of the Colonial Marines who accompanied them, and how there came to be one survivor: the girl known as Newt.

NOVEMBER 2014

TITANBOOKS.COM